SEA OF GLASS

PATRICK SHATTUCK

Genius
Book Publishing

Published by:
Genius Book Publishing
PO Box 250380
Milwaukee Wisconsin 53225 USA
GeniusBookPublishing.com

ISBN: 978-1-958727-81-2
250907 Digest

SEA OF GLASS

Before the throne, there was, as it were, a sea of glass, like crystal.
— Revelation 4:6

A blue light pulled Shannon from sleep. At first, the girl blamed dawn, but the sky was still dark. Then she thought it was her lava lamp, but the lamp was dark as the sky. Suddenly, it occurred to her that the light was coming from the glass paperweight on her nightstand. Thinking it must be a dream, Shannon rubbed her eyes and slapped her cheeks. But disbelief passed as she gazed into the glowing orb where a billion blue clouds were spinning around as if driven by an angry tempest. The illusory wind finally subsided, and two figures emerged from the gloom. Putting her face closer to the ball, she saw that the shadowy silhouettes were wrapped in an embrace, and the girl felt an inexplicable sadness in her soul. Then the ball snapped into darkness like a house with a blown fuse, and she experienced the sensation of falling through wet leaves. When Shannon came to her senses, the room was flooded with daylight and as silent as a tomb. She instantly picked up the orb and examined it, but it was cold and dark, and the only sign of life was her reflection in the glass.

1

———

Shannon Delaney was jealous of her sister for several reasons. First of all, Sarah was gorgeous—with big blue eyes, a dazzling smile, and a body that could stop traffic, her fraternal twin lit up the world like a supernova, whereas Shannon's light had the pale vitality of one of Jupiter's moons. Additionally, Sarah was really smart—she'd earned straight A's since kindergarten, got a perfect score on the SATs, and was on her way to Berkeley next fall on a full-ride scholarship, while Shannon, who didn't like herself enough to get good grades, would be unceremoniously headed off to the local community college with an undeclared major.

However, the one thing that had kept Shannon's self-esteem afloat was Frankie McCormick. They met back in fifth grade when both played second-string clarinet in band. At the time, Frankie was a pudgy kid with pimples, but Shannon saw though the adolescent blight and fell in love with his astral eyes that brought her to faraway places beyond the reach of her sister's magnetic pull. Therefore, she desperately

held onto him the way a child holds onto her favorite doll—
they ate lunch at the same table and walked home from
school together. Furthermore, they shared a love of Tolkien,
and the two friends enjoyed talking about the Misty Mountains and Mordor in Frankie's treehouse until it was time for
Shannon to go home.

Then in the summer before ninth grade, Frankie under-
went a glorious transformation. The boy grew six inches and
lost his pudge, and his pimples vanished. The bashfulness that
had once been a source of derision was now seen as sensitivity
by the flocks of giggling girls who adored him. Finally, when
he traded in his clarinet for a bass guitar, the change from
band geek to rock star was complete.

Frankie and Shannon were still friends. They waved in the
halls between classes and texted once in a while. But gone
were the days of long conversations about magic runes and
Ringwraiths. In fact, when they did talk now, it was usually
about Frankie's girlfriends. However, Shannon didn't mind
hearing about dumb blondes like Ali Clark and the other big-
breasted bimbos sporting skin-tight Bon Jovi T-shirts because
she knew Frankie would eventually grow tired of their
stupidity and discard them. Additionally, she supported him
when he needed the courage to break up with a floozy, and
she soothed his obligatory guilt after the deed was done.

And this was how Shannon held onto Frankie in high
school—he'd wander off to the land of submental minxes,
grow tired of its inhabitants, and come back to her. Then
everything changed in her senior year when Baldwin High
School entered the Math Marathon. This was a competition
where teams from local schools raced to solve rigorous equations in a grueling, all-day tournament. Because the winning
team received an all-expenses-paid trip to Hawaii, every smart

kid signed up. So when contestants were announced in the school newspaper, it was no surprise that Sarah had been chosen because she had recently aced the AP Physics Exam. Furthermore, the fact that the Meltzer twins, Mookie and Echo, were picked was predictable because both had been solving Rubik's cubes since they were in diapers. But the final choice was a bit unexpected, and since Shannon didn't read the school paper, she didn't know about until one fateful day in October.

As usual, she was walking home from school, remembering the days when she and Frankie had made this journey together. Then, to her amazement, she saw the boy's red F-150 parked outside her house. Shannon ran the rest of the way home through a delicious daydream where Frankie was finally ready to profess his undying love for her. However, her fantasy turned into a nightmare when she walked through the front door and saw Frankie and Sarah sitting on the living room couch together. It was as if Shannon's world, which had been peacefully spinning, came to a screeching stop and her vibrant heart fell from the sky and shattered on the ground.

After an interminable minute, Frankie and Sarah finally acknowledged her presence by saying, "Hey Shannon," at the same time. Then they playfully punched one another to avoid the jinx.

"Got you first," Frankie said.

"No, I got you first," Sarah replied, and then they began punching each other again.

"What are you guys doing?" Shannon asked mechanically.

"Well," her sister responded, "we're supposed to be studying, but goofball here can't focus."

"Studying for what?" she pressed, but the frisky couple continued to frolic as if she hadn't spoken.

Shannon stood like a statue in the vestibule, her arms and legs frozen, her world without sound. Unexpectedly, a boisterous banging made her turn around, and standing on the front steps were the Meltzer twins. She saw her hand open the front door as the brothers flew past her like leaves blown in by the wind. Then Mookie pulled a pile of books out of his backpack and said, "Who's ready to go to Hawaii?"

"Who's ready to go to Hawaii?" his brother repeated. In fact, Echo repeated everything Mookie said, and that's why they called him Echo.

"I'm ready!" Sarah stood up and took the books from Mookie. "Come with me," she said, and the boys followed her out of the room.

As the twins were passing her, Shannon stopped them. "What are you guys doing?"

"Studying for the Math Marathon," Mookie said.

"Studying for the Math Marathon," Echo repeated.

"Even Frankie?" she asked incredulously.

"Yep," they replied at the same time and walked into the kitchen. Shannon remembered that Frankie had been good at math back in junior high school. However, his affinity for numbers had been eclipsed by other things like music and girls, and he hadn't shown interest in the subject for years. After sifting through several scenarios in her mind, Shannon decided to abandon speculation and ask him what the heck was going on. Upon entering the kitchen, she found Mookie, Echo, and Sarah poring over the pages in front of them while Frankie helplessly gazed at her sister like a lost puppy. Shannon furtively positioned herself behind her twin until Frankie looked up. Then she beckoned him to follow her into the dining room. When the two were alone, she whispered, "What's going on?"

"Oh, just chilling," he replied while staring at the wall with moist eyes as if Sarah were still in front of him.

"Frankie!" Shannon smacked him on the arm. "What are you doing here?"

"Ouch." He rubbed his appendage. "What did you do that for?"

"I want to know why you're here!" she demanded.

"We're studying for the Math Marathon," he replied.

"You?" Shannon asked incredulously. "How did that happen?"

"Well," he looked up at the ceiling to avoid her eyes, "Spider dared me to enter the contest."

Spider Rizzo was a parasitical loser who had latched onto Frankie back in tenth grade, and Shannon hated him.

"Spider?" she said with a mixture of disgust and disbelief. "You're doing this because of Spider?"

"Well, no." Frankie looked at her and laughed. "Spider dared me to, but I never thought they'd pick me."

"And?" Shannon pressed.

"And then they picked me," he said, but Shannon could tell by his evasive reply that there was more.

"But Frankie, this doesn't make any sense. You haven't cared about math in years, and here you are studying with my sister and those two dorks."

"Well," he leaned close to her and whispered, "I want to go to the Maui Music Festival."

"Uh, okay," she replied, "but what does that have to do with—"

In the middle of her sentence, Sarah burst into the room, grabbed Frankie by the arm, and pulled him back into the kitchen. Trembling like a volcano about to erupt, Shannon recalled a Christmas long ago when both girls had gotten

Barbie dolls in their stockings. However, Sarah had left hers outside, and the neighbor's dog had chewed half its face off. The next day, her twin had fabricated a tale about the disfigured doll being Shannon's, and their parents believed Sarah because beauty trumps truth every time. She vividly recalled the moment when her mother rushed into her room, pulled the pretty doll out of her hands, and gave it to Sarah. Then their mother threw the disfigured doll onto her bed, and Shannon remembered feeling a painful kinship with the unwanted, ugly toy staring up at her from her pillows.

Laughter from the kitchen tore Shannon from her rueful memory. After that, she went upstairs to her bedroom with nagging questions in her brain and a painful knot of heartbreak and jealousy in her chest.

Following a conversation with Lucy Lewis in study hall the next day, one of the mysteries tormenting Shannon was solved. Lucy was the editor of the school newspaper, and she knew everything about everybody. Because the grand prize for winning the Math Marathon included an all-expenses-paid trip to Hawaii the same week as the Maui Music Festival, every musician at Baldwin had signed up for the cerebral competition. Consequently, Lucy speculated that Frankie's high score on the math portion of the SATs had secured him a spot in the contest.

Lucy's explanation offered Shannon a morsel of relief because now she saw that Frankie's reasons for entering the competition had nothing to do with her sister, whose beauty had mesmerized all the other boys at Baldwin. Furthermore, she found out that Sarah's boyfriend, Chet, the star running back, had recently chosen Cal over Syracuse so that he could be with Sarah. To Lucy, Chet's decision was the same thing as an engagement ring. But

Shannon didn't hear wedding bells. Because even though Chet was good-looking and charismatic, he was a mental midget whose thoughts ran as deep as a puddle, and Shannon had always suspected that one day her sister would want someone more intelligent.

FRANKIE, Mookie, and Echo became permanent fixtures at Shannon's house, and the trio often stayed for dinner to get in a few more hours of studying. However, to Shannon's delight, the palpable, frenetic attraction that existed between Frankie and Sarah seemed to have subsided. Furthermore, the boy even visited her room one late afternoon. Three soft taps on the door made her heart leap because nobody in her house knocked, and she knew it must be Frankie.

"Come in," she said while quickly checking her hair in the mirror.

"Hey, Shannon." He walked in and looked around with a nostalgic smile. "I haven't been in here in years."

"Have a seat." She pointed to a beanbag chair, but he sat down on the bed next to her.

"Oh my God!" He pointed at the large glass paperweight he gave her back in seventh grade. "You still have that thing?"

"I still have everything you gave me, Frankie." She took the opaque sphere off her nightstand and handed it to him.

"The Palantir." He held it up to the light. "Be careful with this thing. Remember what happened to Pippin," he said, referring to the inquisitive hobbit from *The Lord of the Rings* who collapsed after seeing frightening visions in the indestructible evil orb.

Shannon brushed aside her memory of the blue light that

had roused her from sleep. "Don't worry about it, Frankie. This one always stays dark." Then she took the ball from him.

"Yeah, but don't forget what happened to my Great Aunt Mary," he jested.

"The lady who heard singing in the mailbox?" Shannon asked with a dollop of sarcasm.

"Actually, she saw visions in that." He pointed to the paperweight.

"She was insane, Frankie." Shannon put the paperweight back on the nightstand.

"Yeah but she saw my Uncle Mike's death in that ball before it happened," he said.

"I remember you told me that," Shannon rejoined. "Wasn't he the lush who had like fifteen DUIs before that?"

"Yup. Smashed his '63 Fairlane into a tree. Best car ever made."

"Best car, huh?" she asked.

"Two-sixty V-8. I'm gonna have one someday," he said wistfully.

"So," Shannon steered away from the gloomy subject, "are you guys ready for the Math Marathon?"

A breeze of discomfort crossed his face. "Yeah." He rubbed his thighs. "But I think Sarah's pissed at me."

"How come?" Shannon asked.

"I haven't been studying, and the competition is tomorrow."

"But you're here all the time!" she protested.

"Yeah, but we're supposed to be doing all this stuff on our own, and I haven't been."

Although Frankie's replies seemed straightforward, there was something specious about his tone, as if he was reading from a script, and Shannon could tell there was more.

However, just as she was about to cross-examine him, the imperious horn of a BMW split the air.

"Chet's here." Shannon walked to the window. But rather than looking outside, she furtively glanced at Frankie who followed her—his face was etched in pain, as if there were shards of glass in his underpants, and Shannon felt a surge of panic.

"What's the matter?" she asked in a hoarse whisper.

"Huh?" Frankie pulled himself together. "Oh, I can't stand that guy."

"Chet? How come?" Shannon asked.

"He's an arrogant jock," he replied bitterly.

In all the years Shannon had known Frankie, she had never heard him disparage anyone. Clearly, the snake of jealousy was gnawing at his heart.

"Frankie," she touched him on the arm, "Chet's a moron. Why do you care about him?"

"Oh, I don't," he retorted, "but he and some of his gorillas gave Spider a wedgie in the locker room last week."

"Good!" Shannon laughed. "I'm sure Spider deserved it."

Just then, the BMW emitted three more bossy beeps, and Sarah emerged from the house, ran across the lawn, and hopped into the black sedan, which sped away as soon as her door closed.

Shannon turned to Frankie. "Are you staying for dinner?"

"What?" he snapped.

"I said are you staying for dinner?"

"Oh," he collected himself, "no, I'm gonna go home. Thanks, though."

Just then, Shannon heard the sound of her front door closing, and moments later she saw Mookie and Echo walking down the sidewalk. The comical scene of the two brains walking down the sidewalk with their backpacks stuffed with books lay in sharp contrast to the sad spectacle of Frankie at the window with fractured eyes. Shannon pitied him because she knew that he'd been pulled in by Sarah's scintillating gravity, and now he was hopelessly trapped like an insignificant asteroid in her atmosphere.

After he left, Shannon lamented over all the things Sarah had stolen from her—dolls, friends, her mother's attention, and now Frankie, the one thing she cherished more than anything else. Looking into the bruised sky, she made a fervent wish for something she could call her own.

Later that night, Shannon was awakened by the blue light again. Her eyes instantly went to the paperweight where sapphire clouds were sailing around inside the sphere. When Shannon sat up, the storm subsided and raindrops slid down the glass like tears down a cheek. Then the shadowy figures appeared again beneath a frail light. When the picture finally came into focus, the light was the snow-covered streetlamp outside her house and the spectral lovers were Frankie and Sarah. Shannon could see their glistening eyes and the white flakes in Sarah's braided hair. When the ball went dark, Shannon sat on the edge of her bed for several minutes, wondering if it had been a nightmare. Since the visions in the ball seemed like an emotional collage of her recent suspicions, this made sense. However, she still felt the remnants of the sapphire storm in her fingertips and knew in her heart that it hadn't been a dream.

2

Despite the sub-zero temperatures, Baldwin High was wrapped in a sheet of excitement because it was the first day of the Math Marathon, and the school was hosting the auspicious event. Purple-and-gold banners with math equations printed on them twisted in the icy winds while volunteers, dressed up as parallelograms, showed visitors where to park. Inside, the halls were packed with contestants from different schools waiting to sign in at tables where snooty members of the PTA checked off lists and handed out nametags.

Seniors at Baldwin had been given the opportunity to miss classes that day if they were willing to volunteer at the event. Despite the fact that Sarah and Frankie were competing, Shannon had opted to endure the insipid drudgery of school. However, after last night's visions, she regretted her decision because she felt that the orb was telling the truth, and now she had a burning desire to monitor them. So, before heading to first period, Shannon stopped in the main office, which students had dubbed "Dragon's Lair," because

Miss Parish, the principal, was a cranky old lizard who despised teenagers. However, Shannon manufactured a smile and said in a saccharine voice, "Good morning, Miss Parish."

The woman looked up from her computer with cold, reptilian eyes and snapped, "What is it?"

"Well," Shannon began, "it looks like they could use some help out there." She jabbed her thumb at the crowded hall. "And I wanted to volunteer."

"That's very thoughtful of you, Miss Delaney," the old worm replied with withering sarcasm, "but the deadline to volunteer was last week."

"Oh, I realize that," Shannon rejoined, "but they seem—"

"We needed help *last week*," Miss Parish hissed as the first-period bell rang.

Shannon felt the wind leave her sails and said, "Well, can you at least give me a pass, so I'm not marked tardy?"

The dragon sighed, signed a piece of paper, slid it across the desk, and began pecking at her computer again. Shannon retrieved the document and turned around. As she was leaving, however, she saw a pile of purple volunteer aprons on a chair and snatched one on her way out the door.

MR. REED, Shannon's snooty English teacher, had a list of pet peeves posted on his door. Among them were *coming unprepared, cross-talk, cell phones, bathroom requests,* and written in red at the very top was *tardiness*. Additionally, to further express his disdain for lack of punctuality, he locked his door after the bell rang. Meaning that latecomers had to go to the office and get a pass from the wrathful Miss Parish before being permitted to enter. If a student showed up without a pass, he would close the door in their face and mark them absent. Shannon, well aware of her teacher's rigid rules, slipped on her volunteer apron and held the pass in her hand when she knocked. After a few moments, she heard the cold click of the lock, and Mr. Reed opened the door wearing one of his sleeveless V-neck sweaters that had gone out of style fifty years ago.

"Nice of you to join us, Delaney," he said derisively.

"I just wanted to stop by and give you this." Shannon handed him the pass, which he perused with haughty eyes.

"Hold on." The man walked back to his desk and returned with a clipboard. "How come I don't see your name on this list?"

"That's because Miss Parish just asked me to help out." She pointed to the floor. "They're super-busy down there."

As Mr. Reed was attempting to digest Shannon's explanation, an ill-timed shriek of feedback from the P.A. system lit the air on fire, and the classroom came alive with conversation. Because Mr. Reed detested "chatter," he accepted her dubious story and dismissed her with a wave of his hand. Shannon ran down the empty stairwell with a blush of satisfaction on her cheeks because she had fooled her arrogant teacher with a fraudulent tale.

The audio issues that had caused the strident blast of sound had obviously been resolved, because when Shannon entered the gym, she could hear Mrs. Rodriguez, her tenth-grade math teacher, welcoming guests and explaining protocols. Surveying the room, Shannon saw an area cordoned off by the scoreboard with round tables, and at those tables sat the contestants from different schools. Among them were the "rich kids" from Dalton, the "Jesus freaks" from Valley Christian, the "thugs" from Nottingham, the "hammer heads" from

Solvay Tech, and sporting the purple and gold of Baldwin High sat Sarah, Frankie, and the Meltzer twins. At each table, a volunteer stood holding sealed envelopes containing the math questions that would be given to the contestants at eight-thirty. In the first four rounds, which lasted fifteen minutes each, teams worked on three problems of varying difficulty worth fifteen points per round. However, in the fifth round, which lasted thirty minutes, the pressure mounted because contestants were given more challenging equations, ranging from trigonometry, probability, and statistics that they needed to solve individually. In rounds six, seven, eight, and nine, groups worked together again. Then in round ten, they were given another brain buster that had to be solved separately. After this, there was a sixty-minute intermission, and then they did it all over again.

Contestants tore open the envelopes when the scoreboard buzzed, and with the vision in the orb still fresh in Shannon's mind, she peered at Sarah and Frankie. Though they were huddled together in a tense conference with the Meltzer twins, she could detect no evidence of smoldering affection between them. However, to truly get an honest account of their behavior, Shannon realized that she'd have to get closer, so she examined the room—judges at their tables, visitors on the bleachers, along with various volunteers. But when she saw Maryanne Newman walking around with a bucket of sharpened pencils, she knew what she had to do.

Maryanne had been born with water on the brain, which had left her cognitively impaired, and over the years, kids had taken advantage of her disability. During a game of hide-and-seek back in second grade, Meg Edwards, a mean girl, had convinced Maryanne to climb inside a dumpster. Sadly, when the recess bell rang, the kids ran back into the school and forgot all about her. Because there was a substitute teacher that day with a raisin-sized intellect, Maryanne wasn't missed until she didn't get on the short bus after school. Then a full-scale search ensued—students were interrogated, parents were called, police cars combed the streets as helicopters circled above. Finally, later that evening, a penitent Meg Edwards confessed her transgressions and Maryanne was found. When police shone their flashlights in the dumpster, they found the girl sitting in the trash still patiently waiting for her turn to "go seek." Shannon had never teased Maryanne, and she detested deceit. Nevertheless, the image of Sarah and Frankie embracing in the orb was haunting her, and she *needed* that bucket of pencils to get a closer view of them. When she spied an empty chair by the gymnasium door, a lie blossomed in her mind.

"Hey, Maryanne," Shannon said while approaching her peer with feigned effervescence.

"Hi," the girl replied absently.

"Miss Parish has an important job for you," Shannon lied.

"For me?" Maryanne pointed at herself.

"Yes," Shannon answered. "See that chair over there?"

"By the door?" the girl asked.

"Yes, by the door," Shannon replied. "Miss Parish wants you to be on escort duty."

Maryanne's eyes lit up. "Escort duty! What's that?"

"See all these visitors?" Shannon waved at the crowd as if her hand was a magic wand. "Well, none of them know where the bathrooms are, and you need to escort them."

Maryanne's face looked like a scattered jigsaw puzzle. "Bring them to the bathroom now?" she asked.

"No, not now." Shannon giggled. "Escort them if they need to go."

Maryanne looked around the room, then whispered, "How will I know when they need to go?"

"They'll tell you," Shannon reassured her and led her over to the chair.

"What should I do with these?" The gullible girl held out the pencils.

"I'll take care of those." As Shannon walked away with the bucket, a feeling of smug satisfaction coursed through her veins because now she'd be able to spy on Sarah and Frankie. However, it didn't occur to her that she, a girl who prided herself on being honest, had just told two brazen lies in the span of ten minutes. As she moved toward the contestants' tables, it was as if she were under a spell, like a moth drawn to the intoxicating flame. Then, as if an airy hand had touched her on the shoulder, Shannon suddenly turned around. As she beheld Maryanne waiting by the door with a vacant smile on her face, a stab of guilt almost compelled her to return the pencils until the scoreboard buzzer, announcing round two, shattered her fragile sympathy.

"Hey, Shannon," said Mookie Meltzer as she approached the table.

"Hey, Shannon," Echo repeated.

"Hi, guys," she whispered. "Do you need any pencils?"

Sarah gave her sister a perfunctory nod of acknowledgment and then returned to the problem in front of her. Meanwhile, Frankie beamed up at Shannon with a warm smile that turned her knees to water.

"Here you go," said Mookie, handing her the blunt utensils he had collected for her.

"Here you go," Echo repeated without looking up from the table.

"Thanks, guys." Shannon left a bunch of freshly sharpened number twos on the table and walked away with the dull ones. Yet, as soon as the arrogant kids from Dalton demanded more pencils, she realized that she hadn't thought about this part of her duty. Which created a problem because there weren't any sharpeners in the gym, and she had no idea where to go. Asking Maryanne was out of the question since she didn't want to burden the girl with unnecessary mental stress. So she decided to ask Mrs. Rodriguez, who told her about a sharpener in Miss Parish's office. This clearly wasn't an option because if the old dragon saw Shannon in a volunteer's apron, she'd incinerate her with a mouthful of fire. Then, as she heard the second period bell ring, another problem occurred to her—fibbing her way out of English had worked. But there were three periods left, and if she was going to monitor Sarah and Frankie all day, she'd need an alibi for each class. Nevertheless, the lie she told Mr. Reed had worked, and because he was by far her most skeptical teacher, Shannon felt confident that the rest of her teachers would believe it, too. So, with the bucket of pencils in hand, she went to her second period teacher, Mr. Michaels, a hefty man with thick eyebrows who let her use his sharpener and eagerly swallowed her story like a seal at feeding time.

When Shannon returned to the gym, contestants at several tables were clamoring for more pencils, and after delivering the desired utensils, she realized she'd have to go and sharpen the blunt ones again. Because interrupting Mr. Michaels twice wasn't a prudent plan, she sifted through possible solutions until an idea drifted across her mind—Miss Parish monitored the cafeteria during the first lunch period. Which meant that only her secretary, Mrs. Mahoney, a feeble-minded old lady, would be in the office, and fooling her wouldn't be a problem. Furthermore, there was a supply room there, which contained everything, including the pre-sharpened Ticonderoga number twos that the teachers used and not the cheap half pencils without erasers that they gave the kids.

After making her rounds, Shannon positioned herself on the bleachers and watched Sarah and Frankie. They were in the middle of the third round. Except for a few exchanges of dialog, the two barely looked at one another. When the buzzer rang again, Shannon watched as the group clustered together to take one more look at their answer before turning it in. She thought that Frankie may have blushed when he looked at Sarah. Yet it occurred to her that her sister's beauty could make a mailbox blush, and she banished the thought. Following another quick tour of the room, Shannon positioned herself on the bleachers and got ready to spy again. However, this was the period Miss Parish would be out of her office, and she needed to get a fresh supply of sharpened pencils that would last the rest of the day. So she went to the Dragon's Lair.

As expected, Miss Parish was monitoring first lunch and Mrs. Mahoney was the only one in the office.

"Good morning, Mrs. Mahoney," Shannon said.

"Good morning, dearie." The ancient woman looked up from the computer.

"I'm here to sharpen these." Shannon held up the bucket of pencils.

"Oh, of course. It's right over there, dearie." Mrs. Mahoney pointed to a small electric sharpener by the window.

While putting fresh points on the pencils, Shannon surveyed the supply room, which, fortunately, was behind Mrs. Mahoney. However, to her chagrin, the door was locked.

After muttering a few curse words to herself, she considered abandoning the idea until a new idea flourished in her mind.

"Mrs. Mahoney?" Shannon asked.

"Yes, dearie?" The old woman turned around.

"I forgot to tell you that Mrs. Rodriguez wanted me to get more pencils out of the supply room."

"Oh, okay." The secretary rose slowly from her chair like a sofa being hoisted up by a rusty crane. "Let me see here." She walked over and tried to turn the handle. "What do you know? It's locked."

"It is?" Shannon feigned surprise.

"Yes… hmm." The secretary looked around. "I wonder where that key is."

"Hmm," Shannon repeated the interjection and then said, "maybe in the desk?"

"The desk!" Mrs. Mahoney cried. "Why didn't I think of that?" Then the woman lumbered over, opened the drawer, and pulled out a key with a label that said "supply room" on it. "Here you go, dearie."

Shannon opened the door, turned on the light, and searched for pencils amidst shelves stocked with erasers, markers, tissues, ceiling hooks, hangers, calendars, notepads, Post-it Notes, and there, nestled between the magnets and the paper clips, stood ten boxes of pre-sharpened Ticonderoga number twos. However, as Shannon reached for the loot, she heard something that made her blood run cold.

"Where the hell are my referral slips?!" Miss Parish bellowed upon entering the office.

"Your what?" Mrs. Mahoney asked.

"My referral slips!" the principal snapped. "One of those damn retards started a food fight!"

When Shannon realized that the supply room door was

wide open, panic began to well up inside her. But then a feeling of calm emerged as she watched her hand, as if acting under its own will, slowly reach over and pull it closed. Amidst a muffled conversation between Miss Parish and Mrs. Mahoney, Shannon marveled at her own equanimity—yesterday, she would have panicked, but today she was as cool as a cucumber. Finally, the dialog between the dragon and her minion ceased. So Shannon loaded up her bucket with the ten boxes of number twos, took a deep breath, and opened the door. To her delight, the office was completely empty. Then she turned off the light in the supply room, closed and locked the door, and put the key back in the desk.

Walking down the hall, Shannon was in a state of sublime elation. Her successful duplicity had made her feel euphoric the way a line of cocaine exhilarates the addict. Additionally, she felt as if she had perfect vision while the rest of the world was blind. Upon entering the gym, she made a beeline to her perch on the bleachers, but Maryanne beckoned to her. Approaching the beguiled girl, Shannon felt a faint twinge of remorse, but spying on Sarah and Frankie had become the only thing that mattered.

"How's it going, Maryanne?" she asked with fake enthusiasm.

Maryanne gestured for Shannon to move closer. Then the naïve girl blushed and said, "Nobody needs to go to the bathroom."

"Not yet, but see that over there?" Shannon pointed to a table where members of the PTA were selling coffee and hot cocoa.

"Yeah," Maryanne answered.

"Well, after a few cups of that stuff, they'll all have to piss like racehorses."

Maryanne stared at the table with wide-open eyes. "You mean the coffee will make them have to pee?"

Shannon bent down and whispered, "Yup, and that nasty hot cocoa will make them poop."

Maryanne buried her face in her hands and laughed, as Shannon, convinced that the girl had a new appreciation for her post, made her way over to the bleachers. Round five was underway, and groups were working on individual problems. Therefore, there wasn't any eye contact or any physical interplay to examine. However, given the fact Frankie was probably working on some hellacious trigonometry problem, Shannon was surprised to see that he looked even more calm and composed than the Meltzer twins and Sarah, who were scratching away at their papers and periodically checking the time. In fact, when the scoreboard buzzed, Frankie was the first one to hand his finished problem to a volunteer.

Fortunately, the next four rounds required collaboration, so Shannon would finally be able to monitor them closely. After the next problems were handed out, the group huddled close and looked at the questions together. Because they were on opposite ends of the Meltzer twins, Sarah and Frankie weren't actually touching, but Shannon felt that if they were any cloaked affections, she'd be able to perceive them. However, she had a burning desire to hear what they were saying, so she decided that it was time to make her rounds.

"No, no, no," Sarah was saying as Shannon approached their table. "To find the area of a scalene triangle, you use base and height."

"Well, yes," stammered Mookie Meltzer, "but I was using Heron's formula."

"But you didn't tell us that!" Sarah snapped at him. "Now we have to start all over again."

When Shannon glanced at Frankie, he was holding his face with steepled fingers, and she could tell that he was bored to death. After handing Echo an ample amount of Ticonderoga number twos, she brought pencils to the rest of the tables, resumed her perch on the bleachers, and began spying again. Rounds seven, eight, and nine were carbon copies of round six—a volunteer delivered a problem, Sarah tore open the envelope, barked orders at the group, and they acquiesced to her demands. Furthermore, the interactions between Frankie and her sister remained markedly benign. They engaged in snippets of dialog and swapped glances from time to time, but all exchanges were void of emotion. Shannon began to think that last night's vision had been a dream conjured by jealousy, and she scolded herself for being so petty. However, at the end of round ten, something happened that restored her faith in the prescient power of the orb on her nightstand.

As contestants were finishing their last problems before intermission, Chet came into the gym carrying a bag from Subway. He walked over to Sarah's table, put the bag down, and kissed her on the cheek. Although delivering lunch was a kind gesture that most girls would have cherished, Sarah was clearly mortified by his presence. She turned crimson and threw a heavy look at him that could have knocked over a bus. But this wasn't what made Shannon believe in the power of the ball because she knew her sister hated public displays of affection. Rather, it's what happened after Chet left—the scoreboard buzzed, and the silent gym descended into strident discord. Some contestants raced out for lunch while others scribbled furiously on documents being pulled out of their hands by frustrated volunteers. Amidst the ruckus, Shannon witnessed an astonishing spectacle that took her breath away. At their otherwise abandoned table, Frankie stared at the floor with lifeless arms while Sarah talked to him in hushed tones. Then he slowly rose from his chair and drifted out the door, as her sister buried her face in her hands and wept. Last night's vision suddenly took possession of Shannon. She saw their embrace beneath the streetlamp, the moist light in their eyes, the snowflakes clinging to their clothes, and she knew that Sarah and Frankie were in love. For a split second, Shannon felt pity for her twin. But this feeling was quicky gobbled up by jealousy, and she didn't know how to feel. However, Shannon didn't have time for emotional conundrums because another drama was unfolding. Across the gym, Miss Parish was talking to Maryanne Newman. An electric current of fear coursed through Shannon's veins. She began to sneak away, but the old dragon glared at her with fiery eyes, and she knew she'd been busted.

WITHIN THE CONFINES of her office, Miss Parish unleashed a torrent of scalding reprimands and caustic threats. Apparently, Shannon was guilty of several "suspendable" infractions including "willful disobedience," "defiance," and "theft." Furthermore, her behavior was "inimical" to the welfare of another student. Aside from exploiting and manipulating Maryanne, the naïve girl was supposed to have gone to speech therapy during fifth period. However, because of Shannon's deceit, she had missed the class. After spewing poison from her furfuraceous lips, the principal folded her hands, sat back in her chair, and stared at her.

"I'm sorry, Miss P—" Shannon began.

"You're not sorry," the dragon cut her off. "Not the least bit."

"I am, though," she replied feebly.

Miss Parish paused to let the silence mock Shannon's weak assertion. Then she said, "How about telling the truth, Delaney?"

Shannon thought about the orb and the vision and realized there was no way she could tell the truth. But lying to this cunning lizard was out of the question, so she said, "You wouldn't understand."

"Oh, but I *do* understand," Miss Parish said in a virulent voice dripping with honey.

"You do?" Shannon asked dubiously.

"Why, of course I do," the dragon replied. "You're jealous of your sister."

The accurate assumption tore through Shannon's skin like a fierce winter wind, and she suddenly felt naked, cold, and afraid. Miss Parish, sensing that she had hit her target, smiled, and all her teeth emerged like piano keys yellowed by sunlight.

"But how did you—" Shannon started to say but stopped herself.

"Oh, Miss Delaney." The principal chuckled. "You're as predictable as a paperback novel."

"What do you mean?" Shannon asked.

"I've seen you languishing in your sister's shadow for years." The principal grabbed a file on her desk. "Freshman year, you tried out for the lead in the school play, but Sarah got the part, remember?"

"Yes, Miss Parish." Shannon recalled her sister playing Wendy in *Peter Pan*. "I remember."

"And then in sophomore year, you tried a different tactic,

remember?" Miss Parish put on her glasses and opened the file.

"No," Shannon replied.

"No?" The dragon looked up at her. "Well, then let me refresh your memory. You pulled the fire alarm. The entire school evacuated. Fire trucks came. Remember now?"

Shannon recalled the smoldering Bunsen burner in the chemistry lab and muttered, "But I saw smoke."

"Lies!" Miss Parish shouted. "You saw an opportunity!"

Shannon sat back and stared at her. "What are you talking about?"

"You knew you couldn't compete with your sister, so you tried to steal the attention!"

"That's not true," she mumbled.

"Oh no? Then why did you pull the alarm on the same day Sarah was receiving her National Honor Society Award?"

Shannon had never considered the timing of her act. Now she began to wonder if it actually had been a case of subconscious sabotage but wasn't about to admit it. "It's not my fault you guys have science equipment from the 1950s," she said defiantly.

Miss Parish closed the file and took off her glasses as a hideous smile crept across her face. "If you can't beat 'em, join 'em. Isn't that right, Miss Delaney?"

"I'm not sure I understand what you mean," Shannon said.

"Well, then let me clarify," she hissed. "You've finally accepted the brightness of Sarah's star, and you've decided to become a part of its glow. Am I right?"

Although Shannon felt shaken by Miss Parish's perceptions, she breathed a sigh of relief knowing that the lizard's clairvoyant powers were limited. Yes, the principal had been right about the jealousy gnawing at Shannon's heart, but she didn't know about the vision in the orb, the catalyst for today's subterfuge. Now that she perceived fissures in this woman's mental prowess, she decided to exploit them by releasing the tears that had been gathering behind her eyes since lunch.

"There, there," said Miss Parish, handing her a tissue. "I had a pretty sister, too, you know."

"No, I didn't know," Shannon said, blowing her nose.

"Oh, yes. Betsy. Beautiful, but a real bitch. Know what I mean?"

Shannon thought of Sarah and said, "Yes, I know what you mean."

"Now about today," Miss Parish folded her veined fingers, "I don't see any reason to suspend you."

"Thank you, Miss Parish," Shannon said while wiping away the last few tears off her cheek.

"Don't thank me. I'm not doing it to be nice. And besides," the toxicity returned to her voice, "news of your suspension would spread, and that would take away from Sarah's big day, and we wouldn't want that, now would we?"

"No, we wouldn't want that," Shannon agreed.

Before leaving her office, Miss Parish made Shannon promise to go to her teachers, explain her transgressions, and willingly submit to any punishments they prescribed. Then she ordered her to apologize to Maryanne. Furthermore, she would be expected to replace the ten boxes of pencils that she stole.

The rest of the day moved slowly, and because her last class was right above the gym, Shannon could hear the muffled sounds of the Math Marathon below. Every time the scoreboard buzzed, she'd recall the morning's dramatic events, and questions would blossom in her mind: Where was Frankie? Had he come back? Had Sarah pulled herself together? At one point, she decided to test her own mystical powers by staring at the floor with the fatuous hope that enough concentration could melt the carpet and give her an aerial view of the gym. But after five minutes, all she received for her psychic efforts was a headache.

When the bell rang, Shannon raced downstairs. However, upon entering the gym, she saw janitors breaking down the tables, a cluster of volunteers stacking chairs, and she correctly surmised that the Math Marathon had ended. Fortunately, Mrs. Rodriguez, her sophomore math teacher, was still on the bleachers with a pile of papers in her lap. Shannon approached her and asked, "Who won?"

The teacher looked up with tired eyes and a faint blemish on her cheek. "Valley Christian."

Snow falling past the window reminded Shannon of the ivory flakes clinging to Sarah's braids in the vision, and an exhausted sadness wrapped around her as the stress of the day finally took its toll on her little frame.

Mrs. Rodriguez, misconstruing Shannon's mood, said, "We came in second. That's pretty good, right?"

"Huh?" Shannon asked as if awoken from a dream.

"I said we came in second," the teacher repeated.

"Oh, yeah, we came in second," she said absently and walked out the door.

Shannon called Frankie on her walk home, but it went straight to voicemail. After that, she called Lucy Lewis, the town gossip. Apparently, nobody was talking about Frankie's departure. In fact, his premature exit hadn't been noticed because five minutes into the eleventh round, the Dalton School had been caught cheating—Mrs. Rodriguez noticed one of the contestants looking up answers on an Apple Watch and disqualified the team. However, while the disgraced student had accepted the punishment with stoic composure, his combustible mother did not. When their school's name disappeared from the scoreboard, a woman in a mink coat with chemically altered lips began screaming at Mrs. Rodriguez, who did her best to quell the situation. But to no avail, because the raving mother hit the teacher in the face with a thousand-dollar Louis Vuitton bag. After a stunned silence enveloped the gym, mortified members of the Dalton team bum-rushed the hysterical woman and dragged her outside. Seconds after the door closed, the room erupted in strident chatter.

Within a few minutes, Mrs. Rodriguez and the other teachers miraculously restored order, and the Math Marathon resumed. Lucy didn't know whether Frankie had returned because his existence was immaterial to her. So Shannon called Mookie Meltzer. Evidently, Frankie never came back, and this was the reason they lost because, unfortunately, he had been the team's geometry expert and the last problem on the Cartesian plane had doomed them. After hanging up with Mookie, Shannon approached her house and noticed how lonely it looked with its windows staring into the dim afternoon and cold breezes making ghosts of snow on the steps.

Then she stopped in front of the streetlamp that had appeared in the vision and noted how different it looked during the day. At night it was a spirit that banished the darkness with a halo of light. But when morning came, it was just another femur in a pile of bones. It suddenly occurred to Shannon that she had never witnessed the streetlamp's glorious transformation. She sat down on the steps and waited for it to turn on. As dusk slowly gathered, she remembered how magical winter had been years ago. Building snowmen in the yard, sledding down the driveway, drinking hot cocoa in the kitchen. Yet now the cold was hassle, the snow was an inconvenience, and she wondered how many other beautiful things had died on the road through adolescence.

Just as she was lamenting the lost treasures of childhood, a cold wind slapped her in the face, and she realized she'd have to see the streetlamp's transformation another day because she was freezing her ass off.

Except for a few shadows on the walls, the house was completely empty. Reluctantly, Shannon went to her bedroom. She picked up the orb on her nightstand and examined it by the window. The cold glass in her hands paired with the opaque surface made her doubt, once again, the mystical power of the ball. She'd actually been aware of the passion between Sarah and Frankie for a few weeks. For a moment, she reasoned that the vision in the ball had merely been a nightmare created by anxiety. However, the intensity of the sapphire storm blossomed in her memory, and her rationale collapsed like a house of cards.

Shannon put the orb down and tried calling Frankie again, but he didn't answer. Then she wrapped herself in a blanket, curled up on the bed, and soon the soothing sound of the wind outside pulled her into a peaceful slumber.

3

Shannon's parents had gotten divorced two years ago, and the wounds caused by this rift hadn't healed because her father had been her hero and her best friend. In fact, everybody called the little girl at Paul Delaney's side his "shadow" because they were always together—in the grocery store, at the bowling alley, taking their dog on an evening walk, or buying vintage baseball cards in Mel's Memorabilia on James Street. In fact, Shannon had an impressive collection, including a 1952 Topps Mickey Mantle and a signed Derek Jeter rookie card. However, father and daughter could most often be seen sitting together on the third base line in MacArthur Park with their baseball gloves waiting to catch foul balls. Because the Triple-A Chiefs wore the same uniforms as the New York Yankees, Shannon thought they were the Bronx Bombers when she was a little girl, which added to the mystique of her memories. But she hadn't been to any games in a while because when her father left, her love of baseball, along with her joy, went with him. And although it was Paul Delaney who moved to a different city with his mistress, Shannon blamed her mother for the split because she saw her dad through lovestruck eyes that turned his vices into virtues.

With her father gone, Shannon searched for other sources of affirmation. Freshman year, she tried out for the JV Swim Team but actually made Varsity because of her time in the one-hundred-meter breaststroke. In fact, the coach said she had the "best lungs" on the team because she was able to swim underwater longer than anybody else. However, the accolades didn't mesh with her demolished self-esteem, and she quit the team before their first meet. Furthermore, this was the same year that Frankie's transition to the cool crowd put distance between them. Combined with Sarah's popularity growing every day, she felt abandoned and invisible.

However, young hearts are resilient. If one resource falters, they'll find another, and Shannon stumbled across a wellspring on a gloomy Monday morning back in tenth grade. She had been doodling in her notebook with her mind a million miles away while the teacher was showing a PowerPoint on the Battle of Saratoga. Unexpectedly, the image of a musket appeared on the screen, and for no reason at all, she announced to the class that they had one of these archaic rifles at home. Mr. Mason, a chill dude who wore tie-dye T-shirts and Birkenstocks, started asking her questions, and when Shannon looked up from her drawings, she realized that the entire class was watching her. The attention from her teacher and peers felt like a soft rain falling on her fallow heart, and she didn't want it to stop. Fortunately, Saratoga was only an hour away. Moreover, she had visited the historic site with her dad, so she was able to keep the yarn going with vivid descriptions about the make-believe musket for several minutes. Yet, even after Mr. Mason transitioned to his next slide about Burgoyne's surrender, Shannon still felt the warm residue of recognition, which left her wanting more.

In her sophomore English class, they'd been reading *The Crucible*, and she boasted that she'd visited Salem. Once on a family vacation to Cape Cod, they saw a sign for the infamous town on the Massachusetts Turnpike, but that was as close to the place as she had ever come. But that didn't stop her from relaying vivid descriptions of the Witch House, Old Burying Point, and Gallows Hill. Unfortunately, during the next few weeks, she fabricated too often, and soon the warm smiles that had replenished her starving heart became jaded masks of incredulity. Then the hammer came down on her glass life one day when she was summoned to the guidance office.

"What's going on with you, girl?" Mrs. Walker, a Brooklynite with a big heart, asked when Shannon walked in.

"Not much," Shannon replied. "What's going on with you?"

"Have a seat." Her counselor pointed to a chair, and with classic New York candor, she cut right to the chase. "I hear you've been making up stories."

"What are you talking about?" Shannon asked as she sat down.

"Well, let's see." Mrs. Walker looked down at a file in front of her. "Apparently, you've been to the Burj Khalifa in Dubai and the Eiffel Tower, you've met Derek Jeter and Mariano Rivera, you own the football David Tyree caught in the Super Bowl, and you're related to Spiro Agnew." Mrs. Walker looked up from the file and began to laugh. "Spiro Agnew? Hell, honey, at least say Richard Nixon. Nobody cares about vice presidents."

Back when these lies had left Shannon's mouth, they'd

seemed credible. However, when Mrs. Walker repeated them, they sounded absurd, and when she realized what a fool she'd made of herself, she started to cry.

"Now, now," Mrs. Walker handed her a box of tissues, "it'll be all right."

"But I feel like such a jerk," Shannon sobbed.

"Why?" Mrs. Walker asked. "You're not the first one to tell a few lies. Hell, when my father left us, I made up a million tales. Told my friends about picnics with him in the park and going to the movies, but those stories were my way of keeping him around. Same as you're trying to do now."

Mrs. Walker's words struck Shannon like bolts of lightning because she had thought her parents' divorce had been a secret.

"But how did you know?" she stammered.

"Well, let's see." Mrs. Walker's voice became as gentle as a breeze. "Young girl walking around with bags under her sad eyes, making up stories. Looks like divorce to me."

"Nobody told you?" the teen inquired.

"Nobody had to tell me. But you know what gave it away?" her counselor asked.

When Shannon raised her shoulders to indicate bewilderment, Miss Walker pointed to her head.

"My hair?" Shannon asked.

"No, no," Mrs. Walker said softly. "Your Yankees hat isn't there anymore."

When she realized that she hadn't worn her favorite cap for several weeks, she put her face in her hands and began to sob. As the tears passed through her fingers, random memories of her dad played in her mind. She saw him smiling in the audience when she played Bashful in *Snow White*, running alongside her bike the day they took the training wheels off, and lying inert in the snow the day he fell off the ladder putting Christmas lights on the house. After a while, the rain in her soul turned to sprinkles. Then the clouds slowly crumbled, and frail rays of light gathered around her wounded heart. When she looked up, Mrs. Walker was smiling at her.

"Feel better?" Mrs. Walker asked.

"A little." Shannon wiped her eyes with her sleeve.

"I'm glad," Mrs. Walker replied and began writing out a pass so Shannon could return to class. "Now if I hear you're telling stories about skyscrapers in Saudi Arabia or meeting Babe Ruth, I'm gonna come get you. Okay?"

"Okay." Shannon laughed.

"And remember something, honey," her counselor continued. "The truth will lead you out of the pain, so focus on what's real."

This wouldn't be the last time Shannon visited Mrs. Walker during her tempestuous sophomore year. Back then, she had skipped a few classes, committed numerous dress code violations, plagiarized a paper, and pulled a fire alarm. In fact, when Miss Parish was ready to expel her, it had been Mrs. Walker who believed her story about the smoking Bunsen burner and defended her. After it was discovered that much of the science equipment was outdated and potentially hazardous, the expulsion case was dropped. However, the incident had placed Shannon on the principal's shit list.

MISS PARISH HAD ORDERED Shannon to apologize to her teachers and Maryanne, so she basically *had* to come clean. However, there was one small problem—how could she tell people about the vision that had started it all? Explaining yesterday's lies without the orb would be like explaining photosynthesis without mentioning the sun. But if she told people that she'd seen Frankie and Sarah embracing in a paperweight on her nightstand, they'd lock her up in a loony bin and throw away the key. Since she didn't want to spend the rest of her days tied to a bed, she decided to leave the glass ball out of her confession.

As Shannon walked to school the next morning through the freshly-fallen snow, she planned out her path of atonement. Since Mr. Reed was her first-period teacher, she would start with him. An apple of dread grew in her throat when she pictured his face because he was a haughty, unsympathetic asshole, and she feared his response. She decided to be inconspicuous during class and then apologize to him when it was over. Given the small window of time between periods, his wrathful reprimand would have to be quick.

She blended in with the throng of students entering the room when the bell rang and took her seat behind Porky Peterson, a red-face roly-poly who weighed well over three hundred pounds. Although Porky had body odor and glimpses of his colossal buttcrack frequently frightened her, today Shannon was thankful for his presence because he provided a fortuitous barrier between herself and the persnickety pedagogue. Mr. Reed rattled off her name during roll call without blinking an eye, and twenty minutes into his boring lecture on *The House of the Seven Gables*, she began to feel as if her plan was working. However, when the class began discussing Judge Pyncheon's duplicity, he suddenly looked directly at her.

"Speaking of duplicity," he said in his snobby voice, "it seems Miss Delaney has something she wants to share with the class."

Shannon felt a sudden shock as the inquisitive eyes of her classmates pounded into her skin like nails. However, she tried to collect herself because she realized that this was a key moment in salvaging her reputation.

"Actually," she replied, "I have something I want to tell *you*, but it can wait."

The class shifted its eyes back to Mr. Reed because Shannon had gracefully returned the ball back to his court.

"*Actually*," the teacher mimicked her, "I have a note from Miss Parish saying you will apologize to all wronged parties, and since your little performance stole instructional minutes from your classmates, your reparation includes them."

Normally, Mr. Reed could disguise his venomous tone with a few sprinkles of civility, but today his bitterness burst like a ruptured spleen, and he looked like a jerk. Fortunately, Shannon suddenly remembered something her father had said long ago—*kindness*, he told her, *is stronger than meanness, so be nice to bullies and they'll go away.* Although Mr. Reed didn't look like the brutes who shoved kids into lockers and stole their lunch money, he was a pathetic bully with gray hair and a cardigan sweater. Armed with these truths, Shannon rose from her chair.

"Yesterday, I wanted to see my sister in the Math Marathon, so I told Mr. Reed I was a volunteer, but I wasn't. I'm sorry I lied to everyone." Shannon looked at her classmates, and to her surprise, their eyes were filled with sympathy, not scorn.

"Not so fast, Delaney," Mr. Reed interjected. "You left out the part about your little *theft*." He emphasized the last word with the vain hope of turning the class against her.

So Shannon stood up again and said, "Oh yeah. I stole a volunteer's apron and some pencils, too." But when she looked around, most of the students were already chatting or checking their phones in search of some new amusement. Mr. Reed, frustrated by his failure to humiliate her, gave three students detention for texting during class. Then he assigned a hellacious amount of reading for homework. When the bell rang, Shannon left the room with a rouge of pride on her cheeks because she had defeated Mr. Reed. Furthermore, she knew that apologizing to her second period teacher, Mr. Michaels, wouldn't be difficult because he was a nice person, and unlike most of the faculty at Baldwin, he actually liked kids. However, her positive mood began to crumble when she considered the final stage of her reparations, which was apologizing to Maryanne. The girl was a harmless, kind-hearted soul, and Shannon had taken advantage of her. In fact, Shannon had been no different from the heartless losers who convinced Maryanne to get in the dumpster back in second grade, and she felt terrible about it. Coinciding with her guilt was a feeling of complete bewilderment regarding her actions yesterday. Although it took effort at times, Shannon always tried to be a nice person, but yesterday she had been a selfish bitch, and she wondered where that ugly side of her had come from. It was as if her heart had been a shiny coin that suddenly flipped, revealing a wicked face on the other side. However, she didn't have time to ponder this puzzling shift in her character because she ran into Maryanne while racing up the stairs, causing her to drop her books.

"Oh my God, I'm so sorry!" Shannon cried while bending down to pick up the fallen texts.

"That's okay," she replied blithely. However, when Maryanne recognized Shannon, her eyes frosted over, and she headed down the stairs.

"Wait a minute!" Shannon cried and followed her. "Here."

She handed over the books when Maryanne stopped. "I wanted to say sorry for yesterday."

"Okay, go ahead, then." Her eyes drifted up to the ceiling like balloons as she waited for the offering of remorse.

"You see, I wanted to see my sister in the Math Marathon, and you were closer to her, so I lied to you." As the words left Shannon's mouth, she realized how stupid and completely unnecessary yesterday's subterfuge was because nobody had been monitoring the volunteers and she could have done whatever she wanted. Then it occurred to her that her odyssey with the pencils had been a waste of time as well. When the bell rang and Maryanne began walking away, Shannon knew that she had squandered the moment because she'd been giving a circuitous explanation rather than an apology.

"Wait!" She followed her down the hall again.

But this time Maryanne spun around with tears of anger in her eyes. "Do you want me to miss another class?!"

"No, no, I'm trying to apologize for yesterday," Shannon offered.

Maryanne's lips fluttered as she tried to frame a response. Then she screamed, "Leave me alone!" and walked briskly away.

Shannon's heart dropped like a stone because she hadn't anticipated this response, but she couldn't digest the moment because second period had already begun. With sweaty palms, she booked up the stairs. Fortunately, the morning announcements were blaring on the loudspeaker, and Mr. Michaels, writing an equation on the board with his back turned to the class, hadn't noticed her late entrance. All things considered, her morning hadn't gone that badly. Except for the fact that Maryanne, the nicest kid in the school, hated her guts, she had cleaned up yesterday's mess with surprising dexterity.

Now all she had to was apologize to Mr. Michaels, replace the boxes of pencils, and her mission would be complete.

In the midst of her meditation, Shannon looked out the window as a sliver of sunlight slipped through the brooding winter clouds and softly landed in a tree. Draped like a glittering necklace in the barren branches, this luminous fragment suddenly filled her mind with hopeful thoughts—even if she had acted like a horrible bitch and Maryanne despised her, she knew her peer would eventually find forgiveness in her heart. Additionally, even if Sarah and Frankie were in love, maybe it was a meteoric passion that would gradually fizzle out once they got to know one another's maddening peccadillos. And maybe, just maybe, her interpretation of yesterday had been wrong. Maybe Frankie's swift departure from school and Sarah's subsequent tears had been the culmination of stress caused by too many days and nights of studying for the Math Marathon. Maybe they weren't in love at all.

Shannon confessed her transgressions to Mr. Michaels after class. When he graciously accepted her apology and even added that he was proud of her for coming forward, she felt light and bubbly like a freshly poured glass of champagne. Then she examined yesterday's events through a rational lens and laughed at herself for being so stupid. First of all, the idea of some old ornament with mystical powers was absurd. Moreover, the only thing less reasonable than a magical orb was a romantic union between her brilliant, scrupulous sister and her hairbrained, libidinous friend. To her delight, a few things happened later in the day that gave credence to these optimistic suppositions. During lunch, she saw Sarah and Chet sitting at their usual table in the cafeteria. Yet she was surprised by her sister's manner. Normally, her studious sibling would have her face buried a textbook, but today she gazed at Chet with moist eyes and held his hands across the table as if he was the gravity that kept her planet in place.

Later on in study hall, Lucy Lewis told her that "a few reliable sources" had seen the star running back in Harrison's Jewelry looking at rings. Furthermore, Bull McCabe, a monstrous linebacker on the team, had told Sally Beckett, a cheerleader, that Chet was going to propose to Sarah on Christmas Eve. Leaving school that afternoon, Shannon happened to see Kathy Wallace, a lewd girl with an IQ of twenty who was more commonly known as "the community chest," hopping into Frankie's red F-150. Thus, Shannon faced the bitter walk home with a smile because the order in her universe had been restored.

4

When Shannon and Sarah were young, they decorated their Christmas tree on November 28th, the start of Advent, when Catholics prepared for the return of Christ. However, they were more excited about the return of Santa Claus than the arrival of the half-naked man they'd seen nailed to a tree in church. Aside from the nativity scene in their living room with the kneeling parents, the rich guys in colorful robes, the random animals, and the baby in the straw bed, there was barely any mention of Christ, which was confusing. But they were willing to ignore this conundrum as long as it meant presents.

On Advent Sunday, they'd pick up their domineering grandmother, Tilly, after church and head home to trim the tree. While the elderly matriarch sipped Seven and Sevens by the fire with a tray of smoldering Pall Malls at her elbow, Shannon and Sarah got the decorations out of the Elf Room. This was a crawl space in the attic where they stored all their ornaments and lights. Because it had a little green door, they were sure that this was the place where Santa's diminutive helpers made their toys. In an effort to enhance his daughters' fantasy, Paul Delaney had always put two small presents in there, which he said the elves, in a rush to get back to the North Pole, must have left behind. These gifts always turned out to be ornaments, and the girls would wait until the tree was completely trimmed to hang them on the branches.

However, those magical days now seemed as distant as stars. Since their father moved to Chicago with Carol, the hairdresser turned homewrecker, and Tilly had relocated to Woodlawn Cemetery, the ritual of picking out a tree and decorating it at home had become a burden like shoveling the front walk. In fact, last year, their mom, a nurse who'd just finished a twelve-hour shift, had raced out on Christmas Eve and returned with the only tree she could find, a Douglas Fir on death's door that lost half its needles on the ride home. She had hoped that some trimmings would hide the shrub's moribund appearance, but the ornaments desperately clinging to the sagging branches only heightened its gloom. Sarah and their mom laughed about the sickly shrub, but Shannon saw the tree as a symbol of her family—a dead thing kept alive by decorations and denial.

This year, Shannon decided to take matters into her own hands. On Advent Sunday, she borrowed her mother's 1972 International Harvester Scout II and bought a hearty tree at her dad's favorite nursery on Route 5. After dragging it inside, she was surprised to hear noises upstairs because the house was dark, her mom was at work, and Sarah always spent Sundays watching football at Chet's. She paused to listen again, and when she heard another thump followed by heavy feet, she thought it might be a robber. To her relief, Sarah came down the stairs carrying a box of garland.

"How did you know I got a tree?" Shannon asked.

"I saw you taking it out of Mom's truck," her sibling replied.

"Okay, well, can you help me with this?" She pointed to the prostrate shrub still wrapped in netting on the floor.

"Of course!" Sarah put down the box and helped pull the tree into the living room. Then she said, "Let me grab the stand!" and ran back up the stairs.

While her sibling's footsteps faded away, Shannon stared at the ceiling in a state of mild shock because Sarah hadn't been this pleasant in years. Although she and her sister lived together and went to the same school, they never talked anymore. Rather, they passed each other in the halls like ghosts who happened to haunt the same dwellings. Yet now Sarah was going out of her way to be helpful and kind. When her twin returned with the tree stand, Shannon almost asked about her bright disposition but decided against it in case it was a delicate mood that could be shattered by inquiry.

"Remember this?" Sarah held up a Frosty the Snowman stocking Tilly had made for her.

"On my God!" Shannon started laughing. "You still have that?"

"Of course!" Sarah replied.

On past Christmas Eves, they always received holiday-themed stockings their grandmother had knitted for them. Some years, Rudolph would fly through an embroidered sky. Other years, Santa would emerge from a woolen chimney with a sack of toys. However, they could easily tell which parts of the stockings were made while Tilly was sober and which parts were stitched after a few Seven and Sevens. For instance, one year, a jagged stitch made the Star of Bethlehem look like a bolt of lightning that struck the Little Drummer Boy in the ass. Another time, Tilly forgot to put reindeer in front of Santa's sleigh, and the old elf sailing toward the moon with a crimson face looked like a drunk driver.

As they decorated the tree and laughed about bad presents and weird relatives, Shannon felt a funeral passing through her heart. She realized how close they used to be and how distant they had become. Although she despised Sarah's hypercritical, bossy nature and envied her scintillating beauty and prodigious talents, Shannon loved her sister with a primordial passion that ran deeper than the ridges of nickel at the Earth's inner core.

After hanging the last ornament, they remembered that the tree-lighting ceremony had always been accompanied by a cup of Christmas cheer. They didn't have Tilly's spiked eggnog, so they made hot cocoa instead. After pouring two mugs, they counted to three and plugged in the tree. Now that the house was wrapped in dusk, the suddenly luminous limbs had a magical effect on the room—the solemn walls became florid tapestries, and the lights in the windows looked like prismatic stars shimmering above a sea of glass. Although the transition was sublime, they recognized it right away. It was simply the spirit of Christmas that hadn't visited them in years. Sarah decided that a fire was needed, so she went outside in search of kindling while Shannon swept the ashes out of the hearth. Soon after, Sarah returned with wood, they had a nice blaze going, and for a while both silently gazed into the flames.

"No football games on today?" Shannon finally spoke.

"Yeah, but I'm sick of watching the Jets," her sister replied, referring to New York's ugly stepchild squad that hadn't won a meaningful game in forty years.

"The Jets!" Shannon cried. "Chet likes the Jets?!"

Sarah shook her head in shame because their father had

raised them to be Giants fans. "Yes," she begrudgingly admitted. "He likes the Jets."

"Oh my God!" Shannon covered her face with her hands. "Don't tell me he also likes the Mets."

"Fortunately, he doesn't like baseball," her sister replied.

"Thank goodness," Shannon said, and they both laughed.

Here another silence emerged. For Sarah, the silence was soothing because she felt comfortable with her sister. But Shannon, more high-strung than her composed sibling, had always felt that she was being strangled if two people were in a room who weren't talking.

"So, I hear Chet's going to Cal," she said.

"Yeah, I heard that, too," Sarah replied ironically.

"Isn't that a good thing?" Shannon asked.

"Oh, of course it is," her sister replied, "but plenty of people are mad at me because they think I'm making him go."

"Why would they be mad at you?"

"Because this is Orange country!" Sarah alluded to the hoard of Central New Yorkers who fanatically followed the Syracuse football team.

"Oh, right." Shannon finally caught her sister's meaning.

"They all thought he was going to be the next Joe Morris, and when he dashed their dreams, they blamed me."

"That's messed up," Shannon said.

"Mr. McCrory won't even look at me anymore," Sarah said, referring to their senile custodian who had been cleaning the high school for fifty years.

"That's because he forgot who you are," Shannon quipped, and they both laughed again.

Just then, a pair of headlights swept across the room, a car door closed, and they knew that their mom had been dropped off by Myrtle, a nurse she sometimes carpooled with.

"Come on!" Sarah grabbed her sister's hand. "Let's hide!" Both girls ran behind the scintillating pine.

After a few moments, the front door opened and closed. They were expecting to hear their names called, but all they perceived was a barely audible gasp followed by complete silence. Sensing something might be wrong, Shannon and Sarah decided to come out of hiding. When they emerged from behind the tree, they found their mother crying.

"What's the matter?" they asked simultaneously, and both rushed over to her.

Their mom pointed to the tree with a trembling hand. "I wasn't expecting this." Then she pulled both girls into a hug and burst into sobs. Soon, all three had large teardrops rolling down their cheeks, and though nobody said a word, they all shared the same sorrow—since Paul Delaney left two years ago, their home had become a gloomy dwelling rife with resentment. However, at the core of their rancor was an unspoken sadness that had been growing between them like a malignant tumor every day. However, the simple magic of a Christmas tree had obliterated the cyst, and the family was whole again.

After their tears had been shed, they ordered pizza, made popcorn, and watched *The Sound of Music*. Though they had seen the film on countless occasions, every time the camera found Maria spinning around on the mountain, it was like seeing her for the first time. Furthermore, the movie served as a makeshift karaoke machine because they all sang along with every ballad. Their mom, a former prom queen whose beauty had mostly remained intact after forty-eight years on this planet, had a beautiful voice. Yet her musical talent hadn't been passed down to her daughters, who sounded like drowning cats whenever they harmonized.

However, despite the raucous racket, they sang unabashedly until the von Trapps crossed the Alps on their way to freedom at the end.

This season of Advent was truly a happy time in the Delaney home because Shannon and Sarah were spending time together again like they had when they were children. They knitted a Christmas sweater for their mother, traded clothes, and talked shit about the teachers and students at Baldwin. One night when they were on the subject of all the kids they wouldn't miss after graduation, Shannon worked up the courage to ask Sarah about Frankie's dramatic exit from the Math Marathon. She had mostly dismissed her suspicions about an amorous affection between her sister and her crush, but she had one nagging thread of doubt that she wanted to clip from her thoughts.

"Can I ask you something, Sarah?"

"Of course," her sister replied.

"What happened to Frankie the day of the Math Marathon?" While her question was still hovering in the air, Shannon scanned her sibling's face for any hint of embarrassment or distress but couldn't detect any.

"I'll tell you what happened to Frankie," Sarah replied after a moment of reflection. "He was supposed to study the Cartesian plane, but he didn't, and he bungled a problem on polar coordinates right before lunch."

"Polar what?" Shannon asked with a painfully bewildered expression on her face.

"Polar coordinates," her sister rejoined, "are two-dimensional structures where a point on a plane is defined by a distance from a point and an angle."

"Oh, polar coordinates, right." Shannon pretended to know what her sister meant.

"Anyway," Sarah continued, "he felt bad, but I made it worse."

"How did you make it worse?"

"Well," she started laughing, "when he turned in a blank answer sheet, I threw a tantrum."

Now Sarah's tears and Frankie's departure all made sense, and the suspicion that had been haunting Shannon's mind evaporated like the darkness at dawn.

Later that night while she was reading in bed, Shannon picked up the orb on her nightstand, the catalyst of her sordid subterfuge that got her in trouble with the principal, her teachers, and had damaged her relationship with Maryanne, the sweetest kid at Baldwin High School. While gazing at the dark sphere, she felt an odd mixture of relief and disappointment—she was thankful that the vision had turned out to be nothing more than a silly dream with no bearing on reality, but she also felt the sting of disillusionment. Her world had been an enchanted place with wonders around every corner when she believed in the magic of the orb, and now it was a dreary realm driven by patterns and predictability. Feeling somewhat betrayed by the ball, she put it on a shelf in her closet with the rest of the disenchanted objects from childhood like her mood ring, a silver Christmas bell, and the Buffalo nickel the tooth fairy left on her nightstand ten years ago.

Living in Central New York was like having a bipolar spouse because the weather was ruthlessly unforgiving and extreme—the summer was a panoply of searing heat and stifling humidity while the winter was rife with skin-cracking cold and frigid winds that came from the bowels of hell. However, the one thing that made this situation bearable was the promise of a White Christmas. There was nothing more splendid than waking up to a world covered in snow with piles of presents beneath a tree. This year, however, after a frigid start, December became unseasonably warm as daytime temperatures soared into the sixties, snowmen melted, and languid clouds crowded the sky like piles of dirty laundry. But then on Christmas Eve morning, a cold wind blew across the Great Lakes, the dew on the lawns froze, and the sky turned the color of tea.

When the first white flakes twirled past the window, Shannon and Sarah ran outside screaming with delight and tried to catch them on their tongues. But then the clouds opened up like cushions ruptured during a pillow fight, and soon the lawn, the trees, and the streets were covered in snow. As they were heading inside, a frozen ball hit Shannon in the back while another grazed Sarah's head. Turning around, they saw their mother in her bathrobe packing another projectile with a mischievous smile on her face. The girls retaliated, and soon a battle was underway. In the initial phases of the fray, they tried to cut off their mom's supplies by backing her into a corner with a bombardment. Yet she outflanked them by going around the garage where she found a new source of ammunition. Then they feigned a retreat in the hopes of drawing her out into the open, but their mom sniffed out their plot and continued her deadly assault. Finally, with cold hands and wet socks, they waved a tissue from Sarah's pocket to signify capitulation, and their mom graciously honored their surrender.

Once inside, they all changed into dry clothes and made hot chocolate. Not the instant crap composed of corn syrup, hydrogenated coconut oil, and a bunch of other bizarre ingredients, but *real* hot chocolate made with unsweetened chocolate, sugar, milk, a teaspoon of vanilla extract, and a pinch of salt for good measure. Then they sat at the kitchen table, sipped their beverages, and laughed about past Christmases. There was the time Midnight, their deceased black lab got on the dining room table. The pooch ate the honey-glazed ham along with the scalloped potatoes and sprayed diarrhea all over the house. Another time the tablecloth caught on fire and Shannon threw a pitcher of eggnog on it but hit Tilly, their late grandmother, instead. Then they talked about the time their dad fell off the ladder hanging lights on the house. However, when they noticed the light in their mother's eyes dim at the mention of her ex-husband, they pulled out the recipe box and began making Christmas cookies.

First on the agenda were peanut butter blossoms. Since some of the ingredients were missing, the trio piled into their truck and went to the store. After buying enough baking soda, light brown sugar, and chocolate kisses to feed a small country, they left. On their way home, they saw an inflatable Santa Claus crawling out of a chimney and decided to drive around and look at the decorations. Back in the day, it had been a holiday tradition to traverse the neighborhood with Tilly and look at lights. The old woman had always said that you could tell a lot about a family by the way they decorated their house at Christmas. And she was right. On the corner of Sedgwick Drive and Brattle Road stood the Bartletts' house. The Bartletts were perfect. Mom and Dad had a perfect marriage. The kids had perfect teeth. Their poodles were perfectly groomed, and their house at Christmas reflected their impeccability—electric candles stood dead center in every windowsill, and lights stretched across the eaves with symmetrical precision.

Down the street stood the Robertsons' house. The Robertsons were pretentious. Dad drove an Aston Martin. Mom wore a mink coat to the grocery store. The kids all went to private school, and the Norway Spruce covered in Swarovski ornaments in the bay window of their sprawling English Tudor made onlookers feel like the juvenile pickpockets in *Oliver Twist*.

Next on the tour was the Billings' residence. The Billings were weird. Mom was a drunk, Dad was in prison, and their lone Christmas decoration consisted of a nativity scene in the front lawn ominously missing the baby Jesus.

When her own house came into view, Shannon saw the tree glowing in the window and the bell wreath on the front door. *Not bad*, she thought. *Although the icicle lights that used to hang off the eaves are missing.* However, what was really missing, she knew, was her father.

For the next few hours, the kitchen was a flurry of flour, greased pans, measuring cups, and wax paper as they cranked out batches of peanut butter blossoms, sugar cookies, ginger snaps, and pecan snowballs. At dusk, they made another round of hot chocolate and planned on watching *Scrooge*. But Sarah got a text from Chet reminding her that they had dinner reservations at Phoebe's, the swankiest restaurant in town, so she flew up the stairs in a mad rush to get ready. Shannon suddenly remembered what Lucy Lewis had said about Chet proposing on Christmas Eve, and she stared at her sister's empty chair with a whimsical expression on her face.

"Phoebe's?" Shannon's mother looked at her with a raised eyebrow.

"Guess so," Shannon replied.

"The place with the caviar nachos?" their mother continued.

Shannon shrugged her shoulders to indicate bewilderment, but her charade wasn't working. "Come on," her mother persisted. "You know something."

The teen held her ground. "I really don't have a clue. Why don't you ask Sarah?"

Through the ceiling, they heard feet running down the hall followed by a slammed door.

"How can I ask her?" her mother replied. "She's flying around upstairs like a poltergeist."

Shannon stirred her hot chocolate to avoid her mother's gaze, but when she looked up again, molten eyes were glaring at her.

Shannon laughed. "Are you gonna stare at me until I crack?"

"That's the plan!"

"Okay, okay." Shannon patted the air with her hands. "Sarah hasn't said anything to me, but Lucy Lewis…"

"Lucy Lewis!" Her mother spit out the name as if it had been a mouthful of sour milk because she couldn't stand Lucy or her gossiping mother, Mandy, the snooty president of the PTA.

"Do you want to hear this or not?" Shannon inquired.

"Yes, yes, go ahead."

Just as Shannon was about to explain, they heard the haughty horn of Chet's BMW.

"Ugh, it's Chet," Shannon said.

"Now, now," her mother admonished her. "He's a good guy."

"Well, then why doesn't he just come to the door like everybody else?" the teen snapped. While her frosty words were still clinging to the air, they heard three soft knocks in the vestibule.

Her mom gave her a told-you-so smile and walked out of the room. Despite the fact that he was an arrogant jock with a brain the size of a pea, their mother liked Chet because she knew that he had been molded like a piece of clay by the hands of his supercilious parents. When her mother opened the front door, the boy was standing on the stoop in a Burberry coat covered in a dusting of snow with a poinsettia in his hands.

"Merry Christmas, Mrs. Delaney," he said, handing her the festive plant.

"Merry Christmas, Chet!" she replied cheerfully. "Come in, come in." Then she walked into the kitchen with the soon-to-be snob and said, "Shannon, look who's here!"

"Hi, Chet." Shannon forced a smile. "Want a cup of hot chocolate?"

"No, thank you," he said, scanning the room.

"Sarah's still getting ready." Her mom put the poinsettia on the counter, then practically pushed the boy into a chair. "Now what kind of cookie would you like?"

Chet opened his mouth to decline the offer, but Shannon's mother cut him off. "We have peanut butter blossoms, pecan snowballs, and ginger snaps."

Realizing she wasn't taking no for an answer, he said, "I'll have a ginger snap. Thank you."

"So you're going to Phoebe's huh?" Shannon's mother inquired.

"Yes, Mrs. Delaney." Chet bit into cookie with a wooden expression on his face.

"Fancy schmancy!" she cried. "I hear they have caviar nachos there. Is that true?"

The boy turned crimson with embarrassment and said, "I'm not sure, Mrs. Delaney."

Before their mother could ask another awkward question about their dinner plans, Sarah ran down the stairs and came into the kitchen wearing an oversized blush sweater and a midi pencil skirt with a front slit. She had put her hair in braids, and with her blue eyes shining, she looked like a cover girl. Staring at her daughter, her mom remembered something that her own mother used to say about Irish girls: *When they're pretty, they're really pretty, and when they're not, they're really not.* However, she knew that Sarah fell into the "really pretty" category, and it made her proud. But she also felt a sense of sadness because it seemed like only moments ago this goddess standing before her was a cheeky runt with skinned knees, and soon she'd be living somewhere else with her own heartaches and disappointments.

"Okay, I'm ready," Sarah said, snatching a pecan snowball off her sister's plate.

"Thank you for the cookie, Mrs. Delaney," said Chet.

"Oh, you're welcome, dear," she replied. "And thank you for the poinsettia!"

The couple hurried out of the room as Sarah shouted, "Bye, Shannon! Bye, Mom!" Then the front door closed, and the house filled with silence. Shannon started to leave, but her mom stopped her.

"Not so fast, missy."

"Mom, I have to pee," Shannon objected.

"Okay, but make it quick. I want to hear what Lucy said."

When Shannon returned from the bathroom, she told her persistent parent everything she'd heard about Chet at Harrison's Jewelry Store and the rumor that he was going to propose to Sarah on Christmas Eve. Their mother listened with interest, but a dubious expression slowly formed on her face when the tale ended.

"What do you think?" Shannon inquired.

"Not sure," she replied.

"Not sure about what?" her daughter pressed.

"Well, I've just never seen their relationship going very far because of their..." her mom paused, looking for a polite word, and then she said, "differences."

"You mean because Sarah's super smart and Chet's an airhead?" Shannon asked.

"Well," her mother considered her assessment, "something like that. But hey," she changed the subject, "we still have a lot of stuff to do!"

"Like what?" Shannon inquired.

"We've got to hang the stockings, put the presents under the tree, make a plate of cookies for Santa, and watch *Scrooge!*" While there were numerous film adaptations of Dickens' Christmas classic, their mom preferred the 1951 version starring Alistair Sim. Although her daughters had to prop their eyes open with toothpicks during the show, it had become an integral part of their Yuletide celebration.

For the next hour, mother and daughter stuffed stockings with stationary, lipstick, nail polish, headbands, hairpins, and Hello Kitty socks. Then they put a pile of presents beneath the tree, left a tray of cookies for Santa by the fireplace, and turned on *Scrooge*. Shannon couldn't imagine why anyone would watch an achromatic movie when there were plenty in color. In fact, there was a colorized version of *Scrooge*, but her mom felt that digitally tinting frames that were meant to be black and white was akin to vandalism, and she wouldn't allow it in her house.

When they got to the part where Ebenezer meets the

Ghost of Christmas Present, Shannon heard a soft whirring sound, and turning, she found her mother snoring. As she gazed at the quadragenarian curled up on the couch, she felt a rush of nostalgia. Before, it had always been her and Sarah that had crashed during the movie, and now the roles were reversed. In the past, their mom had carried her drowsy daughters upstairs. However, Shannon had no intention of carrying an adult, so she turned off the movie, locked the front door, and went to bed.

The snow started to fall heavily while Shannon was sleeping. Thick, downy flakes the size of cotton balls covered the streets and the houses, and she awoke to the sound of her mother stumbling up the stairs and closing her bedroom door. Shannon tried falling back to sleep, but something on the floor caught her eye. Looking down, she saw shafts of blue light moving across the carpet. At first, she reasoned that the beams must be from a passing snowplow. But she quickly realized that the luminous display was coming from her closet. When Shannon got out of bed and opened the door, the glass ball she had put on the shelf was ablaze with a blinding light. After a moment, her eyes adjusted to the glare, and she saw fierce winds blowing sapphire raindrops across the glass. Soon, the mystical downpour began to diminish and blue clouds circled the perimeter. Then the clouds dissolved as two silhouettes emerged beneath a faint yellow glow. Slowly, the frail light turned into the streetlamp outside, and like before, the two hazy figures became Frankie and Sarah wrapped in a loving embrace.

This time, however, she noticed something that hadn't occurred to her until now—in the visions, there were always braids in her sister's hair. But Sarah hadn't worn her hair like that until tonight. Pressing her face closer to the sphere, she examined the twin mahogany plaits falling down her sister's neck. When the ball suddenly went dark, Shannon rose like a marionette brought to life by the implacable strings of fate and went to the window. A feeling of dread crept across her heart as her eye slowly roamed the dark landscape, and there beneath the streetlamp surrounded by a golden halo of light stood Sarah and Frankie. They were desperately clinging to one another as if, within the luminous ring that enveloped them, they had found the last source of oxygen on the planet. Shannon had often dreamed of being held like that by Frankie, and now she realized that, after years of yearning, that would never happen. Her heart broke into a thousand pieces. She gripped the windowsill for support, but her legs couldn't maintain the weight of her pain, and she collapsed on the bed.

Shannon lay there for an hour trying to stifle her sobs by burying her face in a pillow. The boy she loved since fifth grade, the boy she cherished and called her own, had been stolen by her sister who had already robbed her of attention, dignity, and confidence. When Shannon's tears finally subsided, she stared up at the phosphorescent stars her mom had pasted on the ceiling when she was a kid. She remembered how the lambent constellations had comforted her when she was afraid of the dark. Now they were merely Band-Aids on her wounded world.

An eternity later, she got out of bed and looked out the window. The snow had stopped falling except for a few stray flurries, and the only thing beneath the streetlamp was a yellow stain of light where the lovers had stood. When the wreath on the front door jingled, she knew that Sarah had come inside. For a moment, Shannon considered waiting until morning to confront her sister. However, she couldn't contain her resentment. She put on her bathrobe and crept downstairs. Sarah was in the vestibule brushing snowflakes off her coat with a faraway look in her eyes when she noticed her sister.

"Oh, hey, sis. What are you doing up?"

"You lied to me," Shannon hissed.

"What?" Sarah looked baffled.

"You lied to me about Frankie." She let her words hang in the air like rotten fruit. Then she said, "I saw you two out there."

"Oh." Sarah's voice broke. "Well, I didn't lie—"

"Bullshit!" Shannon barked. "I asked you what happened the day of the Math Marathon, and you made it seem like there was nothing between you and him."

A few tears formed in Sarah's eyes, and she said, "Well, I didn't realize it then."

"That is such garbage." Shannon took a step forward. "And this whole month you've been pretending to be my friend."

Sarah stammered, "But you *are* my friend!"

"Really? Do you lie to your friends? Do you take away the one thing that they—" Shannon formed the missing verb with her hands and started to cry.

"Listen, Shannon, I didn't realize that you felt that way about Frankie." Sarah began to embrace her sister.

"Get away from me!" Shannon pushed her back. "I hate you!"

Sarah stood there for a moment with wilted arms. Then she ran up the stairs.

5

───────────

When Shannon was eight years old, Billy Medico, a psychopath down the street who liked burning worms with a magnifying glass, told her that Santa Claus wasn't real. She was crestfallen because if Billy was right, it meant her mother had been reading the letters she had written to the old elf. It also meant that her father had been eating the cookies they always set by the fireplace. On top of that, it implied that her parents had been lying to her, but more than anything, it meant that there was no magic in the world. When she approached her father with her doubts, he told her that Billy was mistaken and that Santa Claus was indeed very real. When Shannon pressed him for proof, he said there was no way he and her mom could possibly know the contents of her Christmas letters because she always sealed the envelopes and put them in the mailbox right away. Furthermore, he reminded her about the tiny boot prints they always found near the empty cookie plate. Feeling a little better, Shannon decided that the only way to really know was to wait up for Santa on Christmas Eve.

So after Tilly, the old tippler, had gone home and their stockings were hung by the fireplace, she made a pillow fort on the living room floor and waited. At one point, she thought she heard something creak on the roof but realized it was the box spring in the bedroom above her reluctantly receiving her father's weight after he returned from the bathroom. Then Shannon thought she heard sleighbells, but this turned out to be the wind playing with the bell wreath. After an hour, disappointment began to set in, and it occurred to her that waiting up for someone who didn't exist was a fruitless endeavor, so she abandoned her post, ran up the stairs, and hopped into bed.

When the sky turned lilac the next morning, Sarah ran into her sister's room and jumped on the bed, screaming, "Get up! Get up!" Then the two girls rousted their sleepy parents and dragged them down the stairs. Now that Shannon no longer believed in Santa, a gray cloud of sadness was wrapped around her heart. However, she pretended to be happy because she didn't want to disappoint anyone. Within fifteen minutes, the siblings tore open the presents it took their parents a month to wrap, and soon the living room was a mishmash of shredded paper and discarded ribbons. After playing all morning, they had to get ready for church. So they collected their toys and went upstairs. As Shannon was putting on a sweater Tilly had knitted for her, something shiny outside snagged her attention. When she looked out the window, there was a little silver bell with a leather strap caught on a branch. Her somber heart suddenly filled with light because she knew that Santa had been there, and she began screaming, "He was here! He was here!"

When her family came running into the room, they found Shannon pointing out the window. Within minutes, the twins were on the snowy lawn watching their dad climb up a ladder. After extricating the bell from the branch, Paul Delaney came down and handed it to Shannon.

"Must've fallen off the sleigh," her dad said, looking up at the tree.

"Can I keep it?" Shannon asked.

"I don't see why not," he replied.

Shannon ran upstairs to her room and examined the bell on her bed. The straw-yellow hue along with the myriad nicks and scratches made it seem very old. Additionally, the frayed leather strap, as well, bore the marks of many years. Of all the gifts she had received that day, this was by far the most precious one because it had restored her faith in Santa Claus.

JUST WHY SHANNON had taken the bell out of her closet on that depressing Christmas Day ten years later, she couldn't be sure. But it had always reminded her of her dad since he had crawled up a ladder with a bell he bought at an antique shop because his little girl was growing up and he wanted to push back the hands of time.

Shannon stared out the window at the snow-covered branches. Then her eye wandered over to the streetlamp where Sarah and Frankie had stood last night, and pieces of her broken heart tore into her flesh. Remembering the orb had predicted last night's events, she picked it up with trembling hands and sat down on her bed. The cold glass contained only a muted reflection of the gray sky behind her. But one thing on this muddled morning was clear—this ball possessed a powerful magic.

A strange feeling of calm slowly spread throughout her

body. It was as if a cool rain was caressing her wounds, and somehow Shannon knew that the comfort was coming from the ball in her hands. She also knew that if she asked the sphere a question, it would answer her. After sifting through her mind for inquiries, Shannon finally whispered, "What's going to happen next?"

Instantly, the ball trembled as wisps of blue vapor rose inside it and gathered at its crest. Then, as if struck by a fierce wind, the vapors scattered and a hazy image began to appear. At first, it looked like a pale star caught in branches. But when the picture came into focus, it was Frankie's treehouse lit up by a frail source of light from within. Just then, there was a soft knock on the door. Someone walked in, and the ball went dark. Shannon was so startled by the intrusion that she barely recognized the woman standing in front of her, and when her mother wished her a Merry Christmas, it sounded like the voice of a stranger.

"You still have that old thing?" Her mom pointed to the ball fastened between her daughter's fingers as she sat down on the bed.

"Yes." Shannon put the orb on the nightstand. However, as soon as it left her fingers, the cool rain that had soothed her soul dispersed, and her eyes welled up with tears.

"What's the matter?" Although her mother's query came from a place of love, it made Shannon even more sad. How could she tell her, or anyone for that matter, about the prophetic visions in the orb? Then a string of panic wrapped around her throat because she had to account for her mood but couldn't think of anything. Fortunately, her mother saw the Christmas bell on the bed and assumed that Shannon had been thinking of her dad.

"Shannon, your father loves you very much."

"I know it, Mom," Shannon replied.

"You can call him later today. Okay?"

"Okay."

"Hey," her mother grabbed her hand, "let's wake up Sarah and see what Santa brought us."

Shannon followed her mother down the hall. When they stopped in front of Sarah's room, their mother placed an index finger on her lips to indicate silence. Then she slowly opened the door and tiptoed across the floor. The moment Shannon saw her sister's beautiful sleeping face, a wave of fury rose up inside her, and it took all her strength to suppress it.

Sarah's eyes popped open when her mom whispered, "Merry Christmas." As if something in a nightmare had been chasing her, she scanned the room for traces of the illusory fiend. Slowly, fragments of reality formed a picture, and recognizing the faces hovering above her, a dagger of guilt punctured Sarah's heart.

"Merry Christmas." Her voice sounded rusty as if it hadn't been used in years.

"Come on," their mom said. "Let's go see if Santa came."

The two girls avoided one another's eyes as they walked downstairs. Seeing the pile of presents beneath the shimmering tree, both realized that they needed to sweep their feelings away and pretend, at least for today, that last night hadn't happened.

"This one has your name on it." Sarah handed a present to her sister.

"Thanks." Shannon accepted the gift.

"Oh, look!" their mom bellowed. "Here's one for both of you."

Knowing she wanted her daughters to unwrap the gift simultaneously like they used to when they were small, each pulled at a small fold in the colored paper until a box of baking utensils was revealed.

"Santa must want you girls to bake him some more cookies," their mom said.

Unable to maintain her spurious mirth, Shannon reached under the tree and pulled out a gift. "This one is for you, Mom." As she watched her mother open the package, another sorrow swelled inside her because this was the sweater she and Sarah knitted together. Her sister must have felt the same thing because as soon as the red garment emerged from the box, Sarah burst into tears and ran upstairs.

"What's the matter with her?" Their mother looked at the ceiling in astonishment.

"I don't know," Shannon fibbed.

"Oh my goodness!" her mother suddenly gasped. "I forgot to ask her how last night went with Chet!"

Feeling a tinge of satisfaction in knowing what her mother didn't know, Shannon offered, "Why don't you go ask her?"

"Did she say anything to you?"

Shannon thought about the secrets Sarah had kept over the past month and said with a twist of irony, "Nope. She didn't say *anything* to me."

"Hmmm." their mother stood up. "Don't open up anything else, okay? I'm gonna talk to her."

"Okay, Mom," Shannon replied.

Listening to her mother's footsteps going up the stairs, a mischievous grin appeared on her face, because, while Sarah had proven adept at duplicity, Shannon wondered how her sibling would hold up against blunt questions from their inquisitive mother. Would she tell the truth about Frankie? Or would she try to maintain her charade? Then something occurred to Shannon that filled her with smug satisfaction— Sarah, the straight-A student, the apple of her mother's eye, the brightest star in the sky, had finally fallen from grace. And regardless of how one chose to view the narrative of her decline, she was, at the very least, a liar because she continued to date Chet while holding a candle of love for Frankie. Furthermore, Sarah had persuaded her former beau to choose Cal over Syracuse, spurning the hometown faithful in favor of a bunch of deadheads in Berkeley whose idea of tailgating was roasting tofu on solar stoves while drinking spinach smoothies. Adding to the salacious intrigue was the fact that a spat between the clandestine lovers had cost her school the prestigious Math Marathon Award, because if Frankie hadn't deserted his team, they probably would have won.

Once Shannon had pulled apart, strand by stand, her sister's web of deceit, she sat back and smiled because now everyone, including her mother and the students at Baldwin High, would see Sarah for what she truly was—a treacherous, two-timing bitch. As she was savoring the impending damage to her sister's once-pristine reputation, Shannon heard footsteps on the stairs, and her mother appeared.

"What's going on?" Shannon inquired with a barely discernible trace of duplicity in her voice.

"Well," her mother sat down, "it's over."

"What's over?" Shannon asked.

Her mother picked up the Christmas sweater her daughters had knitted for her and put it on.

"Mom," Shannon urged, "what's over?"

"Sarah and Chet," she finally replied. "They broke up."

Shannon feigned surprise and then asked, "Did she say why?"

"Oh, come on." She threw a severe look at her daughter. "You know as well as I do."

Her mother's comment knocked Shannon off balance for a moment because she thought her mom could sense the spiteful pleasure she was enjoying at her sister's expense. Eventually, Shannon mustered, "What do you mean *I know?*"

"Because Chet's… what did you call him last night… an airhead? Anyway, I need a cup of coffee," her mom said and left the room.

Shannon breathed a sigh of relief, realizing that her progenitor had only been referring to the cognitive differences between Sarah and Chet. Then it occurred to her that if Sarah hadn't told her mother the real reason for breaking up with Chet, she had no intention of telling anyone else. Which meant that Shannon was the only person, outside the paramours, who knew the truth. Suddenly, she felt giddy knowing that she held Sarah's golden-girl status in her hands. Furthermore, it occurred to her that she also held Frankie's life in her hands because if Chet found out Frankie had been seeing Sarah, he'd probably kill him. A smile stretched across Shannon's face as she marveled at the difference only a few hours could make. Last night, she'd felt as if she'd lost the love of her life and her sister in one fell swoop, and now they were coins in her pocket.

Later that day, her dad called. Shannon heard her mother giving him a brief synopsis of the day's events in hushed tones before handing her the phone. Last year, when he had called on Christmas, the miles separating them had seemed like light years, and Shannon had wept inconsolably. This year, however, although she missed him, it was more of a nostalgic longing for a bright moment in her past that could never return. As he talked about his new job in the Windy City and seeing the Giants crush the Bears at Soldier Field, Shannon heard platitudes, not the warm words of her father, the man whose voice had once stirred the deepest currents of her heart.

6

Gossip spread like manure through the halls of Baldwin High School when classes resumed in January—Chelsea Miller was pregnant, Spider Rizzo got a DUI, and Snooky Jackson dyed her hair bright green. But by far the juiciest piece of chatter was the breakup of Sarah and Chet. Apparently, Lucy Lewis's older brother, Lance, a bartender at Phoebe's, had seen the whole thing. The couple eating crème brûlée by the window on Christmas Eve, Chet getting down on one knee, and Sarah fleeing the restaurant in tears. Additionally, Lucy's mother, Mandy, found out through Karen Smith, the owner of the restaurant, that a stunned Chet had sat there for thirty minutes after Sarah left, completely oblivious to the busboys cleaning up around him and the irritated customers waiting for the table.

Although nobody really knew why Sarah had rejected Chet's offer, speculation abounded. Some said it was because Sarah didn't like Chet's overbearing mother. Some said it was because Chet wasn't smart enough for her. A few said that Sarah was intimidated by Chet's money, while others maintained it was because Chet had a small dick. And as was often the case when social cataclysms occurred, people felt compelled to pick sides. Musicians, math nerds, and science geeks supported Sarah, whereas the jocks, cheerleaders, and rich kids supported Chet. The Drama Club, of course, remained neutral because they only cared about themselves. Furthermore, because Sarah and Chet no longer ate lunch together, the upheaval changed the complexion of the cafeteria. Sarah's allies now sat in the tables by the entrance while Chet's chums commiserated by the buffet line.

In the past, Shannon usually ate a bagged lunch by herself in the art room or the library. However, now she sat perched on a windowsill in the cafeteria and watched the inglorious spectacle of social discord around her. Because she hated Baldwin High School, she enjoyed the strife that had upset the hierarchy and sent the students scurrying into factions. Furthermore, Shannon loved the fact that Sarah, the perfect one, was now the beneficiary of disparaging glances and the subject of sordid bathroom conversations. In fact, she had even seen a vulgar depiction of her sister drawn in lipstick on a mirror that she almost wiped off. However, she didn't want to deprive others of their amusement, so she left it alone. But what Shannon most cherished was the idea that she held these students like puppets on a string. One word to Lucy Lewis about Sarah and Frankie's romantic embrace beneath the streetlamp would turn them into an angry mob. She envisioned them throwing food at her sister and driving her out of the school like some harlot in biblical times. She pictured Chet kicking Frankie's ass, then throwing him into a dumpster filled with garbage and flies. As Shannon was enjoying these reveries, she felt a tap against her knee. Looking down, she saw Miss Parish with her clipboard.

"Get down from there, Delaney!" the old lizard hissed.

Shannon promptly hopped down and faced the principal. Normally, she would have felt intimidated by the reptilian eyes, but she returned her glare with cool detachment. Sensing Shannon's indifference, Miss Parish snapped, "Seniors! Think you own the place!" and walked away.

After surveying the cafeteria one last time, Shannon decided to go to her next class early and hang out until the bell rang. On the landing of the stairs, she looked outside and noticed exhaust fumes pouring out of Frankie's red F-150 in the parking lot. Because the truck was covered in a dusting of snow, she couldn't see what he was doing, and she began to imagine possible scenarios. Shannon knew that he and Sarah weren't stupid enough to meet there, but perhaps they were planning a rendezvous via text message. Even though the bell was about to ring, curiosity got the better of her, and she rushed outside. When the inquisitive teen knocked on the window, she thought she heard voices, but it turned out to be music.

"Hey, Shannon," Frankie said, opening the door.

"What are you doing out here?" she asked, climbing in.

"Nothing," he replied.

Shannon noticed the untouched sandwich next to him. "Not hungry?"

"Nah, not really," the boy answered in a gray voice.

They heard the school bell ring.

"Well," he zipped up his jacket. "We better get going."

"Not so fast, Frankie," she said. "We need to talk."

He sat back and sighed like a man that had just been condemned to death.

"Why didn't you tell me, Frankie?"

"Tell you what?" he asked.

"About you and Sarah." She felt a swell of sadness gathering inside her.

"There's nothing to tell." He turned off the ignition. "Come on. I don't want to be late for class."

"Frankie!" she screamed. "Don't lie to me!"

He faced her, and his eyes were pools of lava. "I love Sarah, okay?!" he shouted. "Is that what you wanted to hear?!"

Shannon had known that Frankie was in love with her sister, but when the words came out of his mouth, it felt like he had punched her in the face.

"But it doesn't matter." His voice softened.

"What do you mean, it doesn't matter?" she heard herself ask.

"Because it's over," he said. "Over before it ever started."

"You mean because of Chet?"

"Yeah, Chet, and she's leaving for California in a couple of months and doesn't need any complications." The tardy bell punctuated the end of his sentence. "Come on," Frankie said. "We're late."

When Frankie and Shannon entered the school, they joined a crowd of frantic students racing up the stairs and went their separate ways on the second floor. Fortunately, Mrs. Castillo, Shannon's Spanish teacher, was fumbling with the document camera and hadn't seen her slip in after class had started. Shannon immediately checked to see what her classmates were doing. Then she took out her workbook, and while pretending to conjugate verbs, she contemplated the situation. Now that Sarah had severed ties with Frankie, Shannon could assume her familiar role as savior since she had always consoled him after his breakups. Yet this was a much more promising situation since his past romances were mere dalliances, and he hadn't required her comfort for very long. Now, however, his heart was broken, and she could bask in his convalescence. But one flaw in the fabric of her plan became apparent when she recalled the poignant tableau beneath the streetlamp—two souls stitched together, stars pouring out of their eyes. Even though Frankie said it was over, Shannon knew it wasn't.

ALTHOUGH IT WAS ONLY three o'clock when Shannon walked home from school that day, the houses were already warped by another hopeless dusk. Adding to the gloom were dead Christmas trees on curbs waiting to be hauled away with the trash. The bell wreath on her front door reminded her to put the decorations away since nobody else would do it, and she didn't want to see mistletoe in March.

After getting the boxes out of the attic, Shannon began pulling ornaments off the tree, wrapping them in tissue paper and packing them away. While finishing the task, something small on one of the branches caught her eye. The object turned out to be a ceramic snowflake Sarah had made. Consequently, a memory blossomed in her mind. Back in second grade, when the students created Christmas decorations, Miss Klim, the art teacher, told everyone to poke holes in their pieces before firing them so the heat could escape. However, headstrong Shannon ignored the teacher's advice and put a Santa as dense as a dwarf star in the kiln. When her figurine exploded, destroying every other piece in its vicinity, the furious instructor kicked her out of class. She was devastated because she wouldn't be able to hang an ornament on their eight-foot Douglas Fir at home. However, on Advent Sunday, the day her family trimmed the tree, Shannon noticed a tiny present on her pillow. When she pulled off the paper, it was Sarah's snowflake.

Tears welled in her eyes while recalling the act of kindness and feeling an unexpected wave of love for her sister, and she decided to keep the ornament in her nightstand drawer upstairs. However, when she entered her bedroom, another storm was raging inside the orb. Indigo clouds raced around the circumference as shards of silent lightning broke against the glass. The second Shannon took the ball in her hands, the tempest dispersed, leaving a soft, cerulean mist. Slowly, a picture began to emerge in the center of the sphere. At first it looked like a snowball, but after a moment, it turned out to be the cherry tree in her backyard covered in flowers. Then the vision faded except for one of the white blossoms, which slowly became a Pink Moon above the maple in Frankie's yard. Tucked into the branches was the treehouse she had seen in the previous vision lit from within by a frail light. Through the slats in the cedar planks, she could see shadows moving around inside. Then the vision blew out like a candle, and Shannon was by herself in the darkness waiting for the Pink Moon to rise in another sky.

7

When the cold arrives in December, there's a pervasive excitement in Central New York as moms pulled jackets, hats, and mittens out of closets and kids prepared for sledding, ice skating, and hopping cars. When the first snowfall painted the world white, there's an atavistic sense of joy even old people could feel in their rickety bones. Adding to the bliss, there's a shift in cuisine from banal meals such as pork chops and string beans to skillet lasagna, split-pea soup, and cornbread casserole. Moreover, the cozy early evenings lent themselves perfectly to impromptu holiday parties rife with Bordeaux, Malbec, and luscious amber ales.

However, after Christmas and New Year's swirled down the toilet, the holiday buzz became a horrendous hangover when the bills showed up like subpoenas in the mail and the relatives from out of town decided to stay another week. Furthermore, mornings became a horrid routine as adults scraped ice off their windshields with frozen hands as children huddled together like penguins on bus stops. But what made this situation absolutely hellish was its interminable nature since January had just begun, and February was waiting around the corner like some frozen corpse in a nightmare. To deal with their depression, some people drank more booze while others watched reruns of *Law and Order* until their eyes felt like they were going to fall out.

Shannon struggled with the winter blues, but hers wasn't caused by the weather. Rather, it was an acute case of disappointment. She had planned on nursing Frankie through his emotional crisis, but he wasn't receptive to her aid. When inquiring about his wellbeing through text message, he'd reply with a thumbs-up emoji. But the boy was clearly lying because he looked like a wafer-thin prisoner with lifeless eyes. Additionally, Shannon had expected him to latch onto some well-endowed trollop to soothe his wounded heart with sex and then run to her for salvation when the futile affair ended. But apparently, the promiscuous dingbats no longer provided solace to him. With her plans foiled, Shannon's soul felt like the hearth of an abandoned house filled with ashes and soot, and she needed something to soothe the growing emptiness inside her.

The remedy for her spiritual malaise arrived one morning in a totally unexpected way. Mr. Michaels, her precalculus teacher, asked Shannon to bring his attendance sheet to the office and then pick up some copies for him. Because Shannon hadn't been in the Dragon's Lair since Miss Parish chastised her the day of the Math Marathon, she was a little nervous about going. However, only feeble-minded Mrs. Mahoney was there, so she was able to drop off the document without incident.

Normally, someone in the copy room would hand her a sealed envelope stuffed with papers. However, today nobody was there. Which meant that Mr. Michaels' tests on polynomials were sitting in the catch tray along with the answer sheet. Shannon had never been good at math. She had barely passed algebra and geometry, and now she was languishing in a precalculus class required for graduation. In the past, the idea of cheating would have filled her with anxiety. Nevertheless, a sudden calm took possession of her, and she made a copy of the answer sheet for herself. Then she put Mr. Michaels' papers inside an envelope that was on the counter, fastened the string around the button, and went back to class.

For the next few days, while her classmates suffered through grueling review sessions, Shannon reclined in a cloud of contentment. However, she would ask a lot of questions and assume a worried expression when Mr. Michaels was near to maintain the illusion of effort. She even went for help after school one afternoon, and the portly pedagogue lauded her resolve. Curiously, while engaged in these shenanigans, Shannon's loneliness disappeared, and her soul was filled with an intoxicating energy that made her feel as light as a balloon. Additionally, sometimes at night, the euphoria would follow her into sleep, and she'd become a comet with a bright blue tail.

On the day of the test, students were only allowed to bring a pencil, calculator, and scrap paper. iPhones, Apple Watches, and AirPods were strictly forbidden, but Shannon didn't need these devices because she already had the answers. To keep up appearances, she filled her scrap paper with an incomprehensible mishmash of coefficients and variables. However, the correct responses resided in her memory. And as she sat there watching her beleaguered classmates scratch symbols on their tests or punch buttons on their calculators, she felt as if she was a kite flying above them.

The next day when Shannon got her test back with an A+ written in Mr. Michaels's splashy cursive at the top of the page, she let it sit on her desk until class ended. Even though students weren't supposed to look at one another's grades, all of them did, and she wanted everyone to see how smart she was. Shannon was especially happy to see Becky Blum's jaw drop when she caught sight of Shannon's score because Becky was an insufferable sycophant who Shannon detested. However, the cherry on the cake came at the end of class when Mr. Michaels praised her for getting the highest grade, and the perfunctory clapping that followed was music to her soul.

After a few days, however, the intoxicating buzz of her escapades began to wear off, and the loneliness crept back in. Her heart felt like a stone in her chest, and her dreams were void of color. Furthermore, she could no longer cherish her sister's fall from grace because high school gossip has a brief shelf life, and Sarah and Chet's saga had grown stale. Additionally, Frankie stopped returning her texts, and when she tried talking to him at school, he was either hurrying off somewhere or engaged in a conversation with Spider Rizzo or some other loser. Meanwhile, Shannon's grade in her fourth-period government class had deteriorated because she wasn't doing her homework, and her progress report merited a call slip from her counselor.

While waiting in the guidance office for Miss Walker, she overheard a conversation between two faculty members in the nearby staff lounge that would form the basis of an elaborate scheme and bring iridescence back to the barren landscape inside her.

"Miss Parish wants to see our midterms," said Mr. Felice,

a freshman comp teacher with a few stray hairs swept over a shiny bald spot.

"Not only that," replied Miss Britten, a slovenly health teacher who wore the same sweatshirt every day, "she wants to see all of our tests in advance from now on."

"But why?" the man asked. "Doesn't she trust us?"

"I think she's concerned about the rigor. There were a lot of A's last semester."

"And that's a bad thing?" he inquired.

Miss Britten chuckled and said, "I just feel bad for the people in the copy room. Can you imagine how many print requests they're going to get?"

"Yikes," Mr. Felice responded. "Wouldn't want to be them. Well, see you around."

"Yup, see you around."

As Shannon was digesting the crux of their conversation, Mrs. Walker's door opened and Bobby Billings, a slacker who lived on her street, walked out.

"Hey, Shan," he said in a colorless voice.

"What's up, Bobo?" She used the moniker assigned to him by his younger brother, Nathan.

"Well," the boy looked at the yellow slip of paper in his hand, "I guess I'm failing everything."

"Oh, that sucks," Shannon replied.

"Yup, and if I don't turn things around, I'm not gonna graduate."

Just then, Mrs. Walker stepped out of her office. "You've got to do your work, young man," she said with her strong, urban vernacular. "And you've got to get to school on time."

"Okay, Mrs. Walker," the boy said.

"Here you go." She handed him a hall pass.

After Bobo walked out, Mrs. Walker turned to Shannon. "And how are you today, missy?"

"I'm fine," she replied.

"Well, come on in." The counselor went into her office, and Shannon followed her.

Once they were seated, Mrs. Walker put her pink tortoise shell glasses on and looked at a paper on her desk. "So, you're failing government?"

"Yeah," Shannon sheepishly replied.

"You need to pass that to graduate," Mrs. Walker said.

"Yup, I know it."

"Well, if you know it," her counselor rejoined, "then how come you're failing?"

"I really don't have a good reason," Shannon said.

"Then let's hear a bad reason," Mrs. Walker pressed.

"Well, it's super boring," Shannon said. "Bills, amendments, checks and balances. I mean, nobody cares about that crap."

"Well, you better start caring about that crap or you're not going to graduate." Then a look of consternation spread across the counselor's face as she squinted at the paper. "Wait, you've got a B+ in precalculus?"

Shannon felt a snake of fear slither down her spine. "Yeah, I guess so."

Mrs. Walker took off her glasses and said, "This doesn't add up."

"What do you mean?" Shannon asked.

The counselor opened a file on her desk, plucked out a white piece of paper, and held it in the air. "See this?"

"Yeah, I see it," Shannon replied.

"This is your transcript." The counselor put it down and

looked at it. "You passed algebra and geometry by the skin of your teeth and now you've got a B+ in precalculus?"

"Well," Shannon scanned her brain for an excuse, "I studied for the last test."

Mrs. Walker sat back and looked at her. "What's going on with you, girl?"

"I don't know," she replied. "Senioritis, I guess."

"Senioritis explains the government grade, not the precalculus grade."

Shannon summoned a wave of defiance. "I thought we were here to talk about my bad grades and now I'm in trouble for my good grades?"

"You're not in trouble, Shannon," the counselor's voice softened, "but I'm worried about you."

"Why? Because I have a good grade?" Shannon quipped.

"No, it's not about the grade, but you're starting to get that look you had two years ago when your father left. Remember?"

Shannon reflected on her turbulent sophomore year rife with transgressions when Miss Parish wanted to expel her. "Yes, I remember, but I'm fine."

Mrs. Walker studied her for a moment and then looked back down at the papers on her desk. "Okay, so you're gonna turn things around in government?"

"Yes," Shannon replied. "I'm missing a few homework assignments, but I think Mr. Cameron will accept them for partial credit."

"Well, let's hope so," she said, still perusing the documents on her desk. "Have you taken your midterm in there yet?"

"Nope," Shannon said, recalling the ten-page review packet Mr. Cameron had given them. "It's next week."

"Well, then you better start studying. Oh, and you're missing a credit because you never did your community service," Mrs. Walker added. "How are you gonna make that up?"

Just then, a glorious idea unexpectedly dropped into Shannon's mind. "Actually," she sat up, "I was wondering if they needed any help in the copy room."

"What made you think of that?" Mrs. Walker looked up at her with a mixture of curiosity and intrigue.

"Well," Shannon replied, "I was in there a couple of weeks ago and there were all these copies in the catch trays, and nobody was around, so I just figured maybe they could use some help."

"That's amazing," said Mrs. Walker, "because I just got a message this morning about needing student helpers in the copy room."

Shannon was surprised because her budding plan was working better than expected. "Really? That's so cool! Do you think I could get a credit if I helped out in there during my free period?"

"Girl, you've got the job!"

As Shannon went back to class, her heart felt as light as a feather because she had found a resolution for her failing grade in government and her missing community service credit in one fell swoop. Now that teachers were required to show Miss Parish copies of their tests prior to exams, there was a good chance she could intercept Mr. Cameron's midterm before it reached the principal's desk.

When Shannon arrived at the copy room the next day, she was delighted to find the dimwitted school secretary squinting at the control panel of a gigantic Xerox machine.

"Good morning, Mrs. Mahoney," she said. "Need any help?"

"Oh, good morning, dearie," the secretary replied. "Do you know how this darn thing works?"

"What's the problem?" Shannon asked.

"Well," the old lady took a step back, "nothing's coming out."

"Let me see." Shannon opened the trays and saw that they were empty. "It's out of paper."

"Oh!" Mrs. Mahoney covered her mouth with a hand. "I thought I broke it!"

"No, no, you didn't break it." The teen grabbed a ream of paper and began filling the trays. "It will be working in a second."

"I don't know why they want me in here." The secretary looked at all the other machines in the room as if they were enigmatic monsters from another planet.

"What do you mean?" Shannon asked as she closed the trays.

"Well, I'm supposed to supervise, but I don't know how any of this stuff works."

When the copier began shooting out paper, the dingbat declared, "Well, I'll be," as if she'd just witnessed a miracle.

"Don't worry, Mrs. Mahoney. I'll take care of everything."

"Are ya sure? Because I'm supposed to be…" She paused, and Shannon could tell by the moist light in the old lady's eyes that she was trying to remember something important. "Oh! I'm supposed to personally bring all exams to Miss Parish."

"That's perfect," Shannon rejoined. "I'll set the exams aside, and you can bring them to the principal. Sound good?"

"Oh, that would be lovely, dearie. Just lovely."

Shannon was amazed at how smoothly her plan was working out. It was as if pieces of a sidewalk were falling into place before she took each step. Furthermore, having Mrs. Mahoney at the helm was perfect because she was as dumb as a flamingo. The first day, she mainly sorted worksheets, cleared paper jams, and replaced ink cartridges. But things got exciting when the midterms began to appear because she knew Mr. Cameron's was bound to come soon.

Just as she was about to head to government on a bright and cold Friday morning, paper began shooting out of the copier. Shannon knew it was her government midterm because the ten pages of questions could only be the handiwork of Mr. Cameron, who claimed to be related to Roderick Cameron, a member of the Four Hundred, a list created by Lady Astor in the Gilded Age to distinguish old money snobs from the arrivistes. After making sure the coast was clear, Shannon made a duplicate of the document and stuffed it in her backpack. Five minutes later as Mr. Cameron made threats about next Tuesday's test, Shannon smiled because she had the bastard's midterm in her bag.

When Shannon perused the answer key in her bedroom after school, she realized there was no way she could memorize all the answers and would have to find another way. After sifting through a number of different schemes, she looked into the glass ball on her nightstand for an answer. However, it only contained a reflection of the turquoise sky outside. She considered writing the answers on her blue jeans, but Mr. Cameron might grow suspicious if she kept looking down at her lap. Then she thought about taking pictures of the answers and surreptitiously checking her phone. But electronic devices were strictly forbidden.

Feeling discouraged, Shannon considered the grim possibility of actually studying for the exam—the essay section wouldn't be bad. As long as she bullshitted for two pages about popular sovereignty and sprinkled in a few facts about the three branches of government, she'd be fine. However, the multitude of matching and multiple-choice questions gave her anxiety because she'd never know the difference between administrative adjudication and appellate jurisdiction, and gerrymandering sounded like a word invented by Dr. Seuss.

Worn out by her musings that led nowhere, Shannon lay down on her bed. Soon, she fell into a semi slumber where the fading daylight illuminated the curtain of her eyelids. Slowly, her thoughts traveled into Mr. Cameron's classroom— she could vividly see the whiteboard with her teacher's inscrutable scrawl, the faded portrait of FDR by the window, and the dusty copies of Plato on the bookshelf felt close enough to touch. Then she saw the surface of her warped wooden desk scarred by penknives and nailfiles, and when she saw the name "Bobo" etched into a corner, her eyes popped open with an epiphany. She could write the answers on the desk! Given the number of nicknames, initials, and obscenities bored students had carved over the last hundred years, nobody would notice the tiny letters written in pencil.

Shannon felt an electric current rush through her fingertips as she copied the answers into her notebook because Monday during midterm review while Mr. Cameron was helping the pretty girls, she could write them down. Then, the following day, she could erase them after acing his exam. Suddenly, something occurred to her. Although Bobo probably carved his name into her desk a while ago, she hadn't noticed it before her phantasmal journey into Mr. Cameron's classroom. Now she knew that the deadbeat sat there during the afternoon government class.

Just then, Shannon heard a car door close, and when she looked outside, she saw their pickup in the driveway. With her arms as light as air, she flew downstairs, expecting to find her mother in the kitchen. However, entering the room, her limbs turned to liquid when she saw Sarah putting groceries away. Although they lived in the same dwelling, the sisters hadn't been in the same room since Christmas Eve. She tried to flee, but the creaky floor gave her away.

"Oh, hi, Shannon," Sarah said, turning around.

"Where's Mom?" Shannon asked.

"She's still at work. I'm going to pick her up later," her sibling replied.

"Okay." Shannon turned to leave.

"I'm making chili." Sarah stopped her. "Want to help me?"

Shannon knew that her sister was holding out an olive branch, and a tiny flame of forgiveness began to blossom in her heart. But then she recalled the lovers beneath the streetlamp, and the pale light was extinguished. "Sorry. I'm studying for my government midterm." After Shannon went upstairs, dusk dropped like a hammer on Sarah's hopes of reconciliation.

8

———

As Shannon walked to school on a weirdly warm morning past forgotten toys and mittens in the shocking green grass, she recalled days like this in her youth that tricked her into thinking spring had finally come. She remembered getting her bike out of the garage only to have her hopes dashed when a cold front brought another three weeks of winter. This recollection didn't depress her, however, because she now realized that people couldn't count on nature, family, or friends to make them happy. They had to manufacture their own joy. For instance, she had the answers for tomorrow's midterm in her backpack, and this was a happiness she could count on and control. Shannon was in such a good mood, in fact, that she even found Mr. Reed's lecture on situational irony slightly interesting. Additionally, Mr. Michael's PowerPoint on rational functions didn't put her to sleep. During third period, she compiled worksheets and replaced the toner in one of the copy machines. When the bell rang, her skin glowed with excitement because phase one of her scheme was about to begin.

When Shannon entered her government class, she encountered the same atmosphere of apprehension created by Mr. Cameron's suffocating superiority and mirthless wit, but today she felt like a spectator and not a prisoner of his mood. As the rest of the class worked on the remaining portions of their review sheets, Shannon began copying the answers onto her desk. At first, she paid close attention to her teacher's whereabouts. However, when it occurred to her that the tiny letters blended in with the sea of scribbles on the scarred wooden surface, she proceeded with confidence. Her task was completed with plenty of time to spare, so she opened her textbook, and while she was pretending to read a chapter on judicial review, a shadow suddenly darkened the pages.

"Any questions, Delaney?" asked Mr. Cameron, who was standing beside her.

Fear gripped her throat because the answers to tomorrow's exam were in full view.

"No sir," she replied in a shaky voice, "but thank you."

She thought he would go away, but he stayed by her side, and the pungent potpourri of stale cigars and aftershave made her queasy.

"What's this?" he said, looking down at her desk.

When he took off his glasses, Shannon knew she'd been caught. She pictured an angry crowd heckling her as she walked through the halls with expulsion papers stapled to her chest.

"Oh, Delaney. Of all the dumb…" Mr. Cameron stopped himself, and she felt curious eyes of students like leeches on her skin. "Why didn't you just ask for help?"

"I'm sorry, sir," she stammered.

His hand moved slowly through the air like a ghost in a nightmare, and she thought he was pointing to the answers on her desk, but he simply flipped a few pages in her textbook. "Judicial review isn't even on the midterm," he said with condescension. "Here." His thick finger rested on a picture of James Madison. "Start with the Bill of Rights."

"Okay, sir. Thank you."

When he walked away, Shannon's nerves were ablaze because she almost got caught. She considered erasing the answers, but then a cool rain swept through her soul and brought a comforting thought—Mr. Cameron hadn't seen the answers and he had been standing on top of them. Granted, her open textbook had obscured some of the letters, but unless someone was looking for them, they'd remain hidden. Then she recalled Mrs. Walker's skepticism about her grade in precalculus and decided to get a few answers wrong on tomorrow's test. Because if she, a poor student, suddenly aced her midterm, Mr. Cameron might suspect foul play, and even though she was planning to erase the letters after the exam, there was no need to stir up suspicion.

On her way home after school, Shannon looked at all the dead leaves on the sidewalk revealed by the melted snow, which caused her to reflect on the transitory nature of seasons —when she was a child, winter, spring, summer, and fall seemed to last forever. Now they quickly expired like milk left on the counter.

Just as she was turning the corner onto her street, she heard someone calling her name. Turning around, she saw a figure slowly approaching. After scrutinizing the AC/DC hoodie, the untied shoes, and the sluggish gait, she realized that it was Bobo. Regardless of whether he was walking home or fleeing a burning building, he always moved at the same plodding pace.

"What's up, Shannon?" he inquired when he finally caught up to her.

"Not much, Bobo," she replied. "What's up with you?"

"Nothing," he said, and they began walking together.

Shannon recalled their last meeting in the counseling office and decided to inquire about this to strike up a conversation.

"Last time I saw you was with Mrs. Walker, remember?" she said.

"Yeah," he replied in a drab voice.

"So how are your classes going?"

"Speaking of classes," he switched gears, "what are all of them letters on your desk?"

Shannon felt as if her world, which had been softly spinning in its own orbit, had suddenly slammed on the brakes because Bobo had infiltrated the atmosphere.

"What letters?" She was instantly disappointed by her feeble reply.

"Them letters you drew," he pressed. "They look like answers or somethin'."

"How do you know where I sit?" she asked.

"Cuz Snickers sits next to you," he said, referring to Nicky Sanchez, who had earned the shameful sobriquet by shitting his pants in elementary school.

"Well, I haven't seen any letters," Shannon said with rising annoyance.

"But it's your handwriting," the boy insisted.

A sudden storm of anger surged inside her. "Listen!" she screamed. "I don't know what the fuck you're talking about! Now get away from me!"

Shannon quickly walked away, but after passing a few houses, she turned around and saw that Bobo was still standing there. His eyes were pinned to the sidewalk, his shoulders were shaking, and she realized he was crying. A faint ray of compassion pierced her turbulent heart, and she went back to him.

"What's the matter?" Shannon asked when she reached him.

"They're, they're," he stammered through sobs, "gonna kick me outta school."

"Why?" she inquired.

"Cuz I'm failin' everything," he said, and now it was clear why he was so interested in the letters on the desk. "I'm sorry, Shan. I didn't mean to make ya mad." He dragged his shadow down the sidewalk.

"Bobo, wait!" Shannon caught up to him. "Okay, listen. I'm going to help you, but you have to promise not to say anything to anybody."

He wiped his cheeks and looked up at her. "I won't say nothin'."

"Okay," she whispered. "Those letters *are* the answers for tomorrow's midterm."

Bobo's eyes brightened. "I knew it!"

"Be quiet!" Shannon cautiously glanced at the trees as if they were listening. "We have to be careful."

"Sorry, Shan." His shoulders drooped.

"Now listen to me," she whispered. "Don't rush through the exam. Okay?"

"Okay," he replied.

"Because if you finish quickly, Mr. Cameron will be suspicious," she cautioned.

"K." Bobo nodded in agreement.

"But now I'm going to tell you the most important

thing." Shannon paused to make sure he was paying attention.

"Okay," he looked around and then whispered, "what's the most important thing?"

"You have to erase the letters when you're done."

"Erase the letters when I'm done," he repeated.

She continued, "Because if Mr. Cameron finds them, we're screwed. Got it?"

"Got it."

"Bobo…" Shannon wondered how to phrase this. "Do you know what it means to be discreet?"

"You mean like careful?" the boy asked.

"Yes, careful because you don't want to draw any attention to yourself."

"K," he said.

Even though he intimated understanding, Shannon wanted to reinforce the point.

"How do you normally act in there?" she inquired.

"Me?" He pulled a small Swiss Army Knife out of his pocket. "I usually carve crap on my desk with this."

"Okay, well, go ahead and do that, but don't forget to take your time on the test and don't forget to erase the answers when you're done."

"K. Thanks, Shan. You're the best." He put the knife in his pocket, pulled up his sagging pants, and started to walk away.

"Oh, Bobo, one last thing," she said with a severe tone that made him turn around. "If you get caught, don't throw me under the bus. Okay?"

"But, Shan," he walked back with moist eyes, "I'd never snitch on you."

"But if you get caught," she continued, "they're going to want to know where you got the answers."

"Yeah, I know," his voice cracked, "but I wouldn't tell 'em."

"Well, what would you say?" she asked.

"Nothin'," he said. "I promise."

"Okay." Shannon produced a comforting tone. "I believe you."

They walked in silence until they reached Bobo's house.

"Let's walk home again tomorrow, okay? I'll meet you by Mr. B," she said, referring to the effigy of Syracuse's first mayor in front of the school.

"K," Bobo replied.

After exchanging phone numbers, Shannon watched Bobo trudge across his front lawn. She felt a twinge of guilt as he disappeared into a darkened porch because she'd hurt his feelings by suggesting he might snitch, which to high school students was a crime worse than selling drugs to toddlers or sleeping with a sibling. But she had to be sure he wouldn't rat her out.

DURING PRECALCULUS THE NEXT DAY, Shannon was beset by anxiety. Because if Bobo, someone with the mental alertness of a tombstone, had noticed the letters on her desk, that meant someone else might have. Maybe Suzy Connelly, the kiss-ass who sat behind her in government, had seen them. Or maybe Mr. Cameron had only pretended not to notice them and now he was waiting to catch her in the act. Or perhaps Mrs. Mahoney saw her making a copy of the exam, and at this very moment Miss Parish was typing up her expulsion papers. The same parade of anxious thoughts circled her mind during third period. But when she got to government, her fears receded because exams were already face-down on the desks, and Mr. Cameron was taking attendance.

Even though she had the answers, Shannon dutifully read through each question before circling the correct choice. Additionally, she looked up at the ceiling several times with a bemused expression to keep up appearances. In the matching section, she deliberately picked the wrong definition for treason to be ironic. Furthermore, she botched "marble cake federalism" in the multiple-choice section because it always reminded her of the dreadful fare at PTA Bake Sales. Lastly, in the essay section, she only used two facts to support her flimsy thesis because Mr. Cameron thought girls were stupid, and she didn't want to burst his opinion. After finishing, Shannon tallied up her score and estimated a B+, which was just enough to avoid suspicion and pass the class. She considered erasing the letters to remove all traces of her crime. But she had to trust that Bobo would keep his promise.

Shannon looked for the boy at lunch to give him one last pep talk, but he wasn't around. So she ate her bagged meal in the art room and scrolled through her various social media accounts. During Spanish, she knew Bobo was taking the test and tried to picture him being discreet, but the mental strain gave her a headache, so she abandoned her endeavor.

When school let out, Shannon waited by the statue of Harvey Baldwin, an early proponent of public education who had fought in the War of 1812. Sadly, some miscreant had spray-painted nipples on his chest. Though maintenance tried to efface the graffiti, the faded tits remained. Therefore, the school's namesake looked more like a tribute to Hermaphroditus, the gynandrous child of Hermes and Aphrodite, than an elder statesman. She tried calling Bobo, but it went straight to voicemail, and her texts went unanswered. After fifteen minutes, she decided to leave because the weather had turned colder, and she only had a sweater. On the walk home, an array of reasons for Bobo's absence tumbled around in her mind like clothes in a dryer. Maybe he forgot they were supposed to meet; maybe he was home sick. After all, Shannon hadn't seen him in his usual spot in the foyer at lunch, but deep down she knew something was wrong.

A cold front from Canada brought a mixture of sleet and howling winds that knocked over trees and pulled down power lines during the night. Shannon hoped for a snow day but quickly abandoned her wish because in Central New York they didn't cancel school unless there was ten feet of snow. Furthermore, she wanted to make sure the letters on her desk had been erased.

Downstairs, she noticed her mother's Scout II in the driveway and the keys on the kitchen table, a sign that their mother had worked the nightshift and she could take the truck to school. Shannon heard Sarah getting ready in the bathroom upstairs and wondered if she should endure an awkward ride with her sister or brave the cold. Shannon was leaning toward walking, and even had her coat in her hand, until a fierce wind rattled the shutters and toppled a garbage can. Then Shannon grabbed the keys, started the pickup, and waited for Sarah, who emerged from the house five minutes later.

"Toasty in here," Sarah said when she hopped in.

"*Now* it is." Shannon's words were colder than the wind outside.

"Thanks for warming it up," her sibling said ebulliently while sipping coffee from her Yeti mug.

The trees, covered in frozen sleet, looked like ice sculptures as they drove down the slick streets. The sisters hadn't been together like this since they baked Christmas cookies last December, and the powerful quiet, broken only by the rattle of shifting gears, was deafening. Normally, in a situation like this, Shannon would speak to repel the tension, but she was determined to hold her tongue. Checking both windows before pulling onto James Street, the main thoroughfare, she caught Sarah looking at the dashboard with a slight smile and knew her sibling was waiting for her to crack. But Shannon dug in her heels, and they rode in silence all the way to school.

After peeling away from Sarah in the parking lot, she went to her first period class, where a convocation of girls was engaged in lively conversation. The din hushed momentarily but then picked up speed again when Shannon sat down. From what she could gather listening to snippets of their dialogue, someone had been expelled. Considering the number of fights and drug busts at the school, this wasn't surprising. Although, when one of the chatterboxes said, "Poor Bobo," her heart froze. However, she couldn't find out more because the bell rang, and the discussion died.

Each minute was a small eternity as Mr. Reed lectured about the insipid symbols and themes in *The Catcher in the Rye*, which he considered a "tour de force," but Shannon didn't give two craps about the exploits of some spoiled brat in Manhattan because she wanted to know what happened to her friend.

By fourth period, the news was all over the school—Mr. Cameron had caught the boy in his classroom after school, and when Shannon saw her desk during government, she realized why Bobo had returned. Only a small section of the answers were gone, and she guessed that the boy had forgotten to erase them and returned when his blunder occurred to him. However, there was no time for suppositions because class was about to start and the answers to yesterday's test were in plain view. So she put her backpack on the desk and waited until Cameron doused the lights for one of his boring PowerPoints. Then Shannon took a Wet Wipe out of her bag and carefully scrubbed the wooden surface until the evidence of her crime was gone.

Scattered feelings and botched schemes plagued her mind for the rest of the day. Moments of pity were washed away by waves of resentment. Thoughts of confessing were crushed by selfish alibis until fate stepped in. Even though there was still ten minutes left in fifth period, students began packing up, a sign that they were done for the day, and her exhausted Spanish teacher acquiesced to their tacit demand. Then the familiar crackle of the loudspeaker filled the air, and Mrs. Mahoney's voice said, "Please send Shannon Delaney to the principal's office." The classroom grew silent for a moment as Shannon finished packing up her things, and then menacing murmurs followed her out of the room.

In the green stairwell, Shannon felt as if she were heading to the gallows because she was certain Bobo had squealed on her. Even though Baldwin High School had been a place of dread, she realized in this moment how much it meant to her. Not the pep rallies, dances, football games, or classes. Rather, the vibrant stream of life pouring through the halls, the gravitational forces that kept her life in orbit. And when they kicked her out, she would be as motionless and insignificant as a dead star on the outskirts of the universe.

"Oh hello, dearie!" Mrs. Mahoney said when Shannon entered the office.

"Did Miss Parish want to see me?" she said with a knot in her throat.

"Oh, yes, that's right." The old secretary stood up and knocked on the principal's open door. "Shannon Delaney's here to see ya."

"Tell her to come in," a cold-blooded voice said.

When Shannon walked into the Dragon's Lair, Miss Parish was signing a document that she assumed were her expulsion papers.

"Have a seat," the old lizard said without looking up, so Shannon took off her backpack and sat down. After a solid minute of silence, the principal looked up. "You're friends with Robert Billings?" Even though this was phrased as a question, it came across as an accusation.

"You mean, Bobo?" Shannon asked benignly.

"Yes, Bobo," Miss Parish snapped.

"Well, I wouldn't say we're 'friends,' but he lives down the street from me." She was trying to distance herself from the boy.

Without taking her eyes off Shannon, the dragon carefully folded the paper in her hands and placed it in an envelope. "I suppose you've heard the news?"

"What news?"

"Oh, come on, Delaney!" the lizard hissed. "Don't sit there and pretend you don't know what's going on."

"You mean with Bobo?" she asked.

"Yes!"

"Well, I heard he's in trouble," Shannon said.

"Good!" Miss Parish shrieked. "We're finally being honest."

The dismissal bell rang, and the principal sealed the envelope. "I don't have time to play games, so I'm going to get to the point."

Shannon took a deep breath as she prepared to receive her expulsion papers, but the next thing that happened surprised her—Miss Parish produced a smile and said in a sugary voice, "You live down the street from Robert?"

"Yes," she replied.

"Can you drop this off on your way home?" The principal handed the envelope to Shannon. "It's imperative that he gets this."

"And you want *me* to bring it to him?" Shannon asked incredulously.

Miss Parish took off her glasses. "Yes. See, we can't get a hold of his mother," she made a mocking expression indicating her opinion of Sandy Billings, the town drunk, "and Robert's not allowed on school property, so you're our only hope."

"Can I ask what it is?" Shannon asked weakly.

"It's none of your—" the principal began but stopped herself. "It's confidential." She tried to reconstruct the smile that had fallen off her face, but the outcome was a grotesque smirk worse than any frown.

"Sure, I'll bring it to him." Shannon stood up.

Without saying anything, Miss Parish turned toward her computer, and the blue light on her face revealed deep crevices created by a lifetime of scowling.

ASHEN CLOUDS STRETCHED across the sky when Shannon left school. Walking down the sidewalk, she thought of Bobo's life—even though the Billings lived down the street, they were from the wrong side of town. They were the embar-rassing family that stuck out like a sore thumb with the snow-covered steps in the winter, untrimmed grass in the summer, and broken-down cars in the driveway year round. Tommy Billings, Bobo's dad, had the dubious honor of owning the city's first meth lab, and he was currently serving a life sentence in Five Points for fatally stabbing someone in a bar fight. Sandy Billings, his mom, was an infamous alcoholic who had driven her '73 Buick Rivera through the bay window of the house across the street from them. Although she came away without a scratch thanks to the 455-cubic-inch engine in front of her, the English Tudor never recovered. Because even though the window had been replaced, the new bricks around the frame didn't match the original ones, and a pale outline of the damage remained. Consequently, the owners of the Tudor decided that the neighborhood had gone to shit and moved to the suburbs, and since nobody wanted to buy a house with such an aesthetic defect, it stood vacant for a decade, a monument to Sandy's addiction.

However, her brawl with the house was not her most shameful moment. Rather, it was an incident in Shop City, the local strip mall, that inscribed her fame in Syracuse lore. On a Saturday afternoon in May, Sandy went out to buy milk but stopped in a bar and drank five Long Island Iced Teas beforehand. By the time she reached the store, she was a blithering, belligerent mess. After she passed out in the cereal aisle, the manager and two cashiers dragged her outside and tossed her in the bed of her pickup truck like a sack of fertil-izer. Because their dad was in prison, Bobo and his younger brother, Nathan, had to go retrieve her, and since both boys were too young to drive, they borrowed a shopping cart and rolled her home. Unfortunately, this happened to be the same day as the neighborhood block party, so the brothers had to wheel their catatonic mother through a gauntlet of thorny stares and deadly comments. But this was only the beginning of the fallout. Bobo had to fight the multitude of fifth-grade punks who called Sandy a drunk, and due to his small stature, most of these battles ended badly for him. When the school year concluded, the physical harassment subsided, but the social persecution began.

Slowly but surely, Bobo and Nathan were excluded from playdates, and now the boys merely watched the whirlwind of children sweeping by on their bicycles or climbing trees in nearby yards. In fact, Shannon clearly recalled her mother's callous indifference about Bobo's birthday party that summer. When an invitation had been received, her mom held the card behind her back and quickly changed the subject. Then on the day of the celebration, Shannon went to a baseball game with her dad, but disappointment ruined the walk-off win because her parents had joined the public lynching of the Billings.

Approaching Bobo's house, Shannon cursed her neighborhood for rejecting this family that desperately needed their help, especially the two boys who had basically raised themselves. And now here she was delivering Bobo's expulsion letter, the final nail in his coffin. After walking onto the dark-screened porch, she rang the bell and breathed the imprisoned air that smelled like damp rugs and dead dreams. After waiting a few minutes, Shannon realized the doorbell was broken and knocked. Finally, the muffled sound of footsteps split the silence and Bobo opened the door.

"Hey, Shan," he said with the hum of a television behind him.

"Hey, Bobo," Shannon replied.

"I'd invite ya to come in, but my mom's asleep."

"Oh, that's okay," she responded. "I just wanted to come by and see how you were doing."

Bobo stepped out onto the porch and closed the door. "Cameron caught me," he said in a dejected voice.

"I know, I heard," Shannon replied.

Bobo looked at Shannon. Then his eyes dropped to the floor.

"Bobo," she said, "why didn't you erase the letters after the test?"

"Well, I kinda forgot," he answered.

"You forgot?!" she erupted. "How could you forget?"

"Well," Bobo took a deep breath, "me and Snickers smoked a bowl before class," he said, again referring to the kid who once pinched a loaf in his pants. "And it kinda slipped my mind."

"But why did you get high before a test?"

"Well, I had the answers," he replied. "It wasn't like I had to concentrate."

Shannon was about to scold him for his lack of judgment, but remembering the letter Miss Parish gave her, she slowly unzipped her backpack and handed him the envelope. "This is for you," she said grimly.

Without opening it, Bobo said, "I been expecting this."

"Bobo, they're going to expel you."

"I know it." He looked out at the solemn dusk that had settled on the street.

"But it's my fault," Shannon said with tears in her eyes.

"Na, it ain't your fault," Bobo consoled her.

"But, Bobo, if I didn't give you the answers, you wouldn't have cheated."

"But they ain't expelling me for cheating," he said.

"Wait, what?" Shannon wiped her cheeks.

"They're sayin' I stole keys off a maintenance cart and broke into his room to steal stuff."

"Steal what stuff?" she asked incredulously.

Bobo answered, "I guess someone nabbed Cameron's MacBook, and now they think it was me."

"Wait," Shannon tried to wrap her mind around his words, "did you take the keys?"

"Hell no," Bobo replied. "I didn't need keys cuz Mr. McCrory forgot to lock the door."

Mr. McCrory was a sixty-seven-year-old custodian who was notorious for his blunders, including the one time he crashed a Zamboni into a bake sale. Another time he used Christmas decorations for a Halloween dance and students bobbed for apples beneath mistletoe. But the kids adored him, and he was an institution at Baldwin High School.

"But did you tell them that the door was unlocked?" Shannon inquired.

"Yeah, but they didn't believe me," he answered.

"Well, did you tell them you were just trying to erase the letters?" Shannon asked. "I mean, cheating isn't as bad as stealing."

"Nah, I didn't tell 'em," he replied.

"Why?" she pressed.

Bobo took a deep breath and then said, "Cuz then they'd want to know where I got the answers, and that would lead to you."

Shannon felt terrible because she got him kicked out, and *he* was protecting *her*.

"Bobo," new tears collected in her eyes, "we have to tell them. This isn't fair."

"But if we tell 'em then we'll both be expelled," he reasoned.

"Yeah, but…"

"Shan," Bobo interrupted her, "look around." His hand swept across the dark porch littered with broken furniture, faded toys, and a broom missing most of its bristles. "This is all I'll ever be, and no diploma's gonna change that."

"Bobo, no," she stammered through her tears.

"You're smart," he continued, "and you need that diploma."

They both heard a muted groan followed by footsteps inside the house.

"I gotta go, Shan." He opened the door and stepped inside. "I'll see ya around."

Shannon stood looking at the "13" affixed to Bobo's front door. As if it wasn't enough for The Fates to spin a tragic tapestry around this hapless family, the goddesses also had to add some situational irony by branding them with a cursed address. Upon hearing the clatter of dishes from inside, she left the gloomy porch and felt relieved to breathe the fresh air beneath the first stars of the evening.

AFTER GETTING HOME, Shannon thought about what Bobo had said about his doomed existence. While there may have been some truth about the trajectory of his life, she didn't want to play the part of Atropos by cutting his throat like a piece of thread. She decided to confess her crime because then Bobo's reason for being in Cameron's room would make sense, and maybe he wouldn't be kicked out. Surprisingly, a wave of relief washed over her. Even though her disclosure meant expulsion, Shannon was thinking about someone else for a change, and after a month of myopic machinations, this felt strangely exhilarating.

Walking up her driveway, she was greeted by a burst of blue light—turquoise branches swayed, and the snowy lawn glistened like a carpet of sapphires. At first, she thought it was winter lightning. Or perhaps, she reasoned, someone had stumbled across some leftover fireworks. But the sky was as dark as soil. After scanning the firmament, Shannon realized, to her amazement, that the phantasmagoric display was coming from her bedroom window as shards of blue light leaped through the glass like flames in search of oxygen.

Upon entering her bedroom, the bright orb almost blinded her, and she had to shield her eyes to navigate the distance to her nightstand. Instinctively, she knew that if she held the ball, the severity of the storm would recede. And she was right, because the moment her fingers touched the glass, the light show diminished, and vague images began to form. Shannon was expecting to see the Pink Moon above Frankie's treehouse that appeared the last time. However, a very different vision emerged. At first, it looked like hazy planets surrounding a twinkling star, but the star became a birthday cake and the planets slowly turned into party hats. When a clear picture finally formed, a young Bobo was blowing out ten candles as kids sat around a table with eager expressions. Mookie Meltzer was there along with Frankie, Snickers Sanchez, Lucy Lewis, and Becky Blum, the sycophant in her math class. The last guest was facing Bobo, but Shannon knew from the golden rope of hair hanging down her back that it was Sarah.

This vision of Bobo's birthday party back in the summer of fifth grade made her sad because she had thought her parents boycotted the celebration, but now it was clear they lied to her. It had been a carefully orchestrated con job where Shannon played the part of the hapless patsy. Furthermore, the baseball game with her dad had simply been a ruse to get her out of the house. Unraveling their duplicity was like peeling an onion because the scaly leaves only revealed more layers of lies beneath. She remembered her mom and Sarah listening to her recap of the tenth-inning affair with bated breath which was odd because neither one gave a crap about baseball. Now she knew they had been putting the finishing touches on their masquerade. Recollections of how nice her dad had been at the game also paraded through her mind—normally, she was allowed to get one cotton candy and maybe a box of popcorn. However, on that day, Shannon received cotton candy, Cracker Jacks, an ice cream cone, and a Syracuse Chiefs hat. What she had thought were tokens of affection were merely consolation prizes.

As Shannon continued to examine the vision, it occurred to her that the hoax went far beyond her family. Because if Lucy Lewis, the school gossip, never blabbed about the party, that meant she was part of the plot. So was Frankie, Mookie Meltzer, Snickers, and Becky Blum. The faces inside the orb melted into a pool of flesh except for a pair of eyes that stared into her soul, and for a moment Shannon felt the bone-chilling horror of being buried alive. However, the vision faded when headlights painted her windows yellow. Shannon flew downstairs like a storm in search of destruction, but her momentum died when she entered the kitchen. Somehow the woman standing in front of the open refrigerator seemed smaller than before, and for the first time in Shannon's life, her beautiful mother looked old.

"Hi, Mom," she said.

"Looks like we're having spaghetti again." Her mother's words were like wilted flowers. "Sorry."

"That's okay." Shannon took out a pot and filled it with water. "I'll take care of it."

Her mother began taking plates out of the cupboard, but Shannon stopped her. "I got this."

"Are you sure, kiddo?"

"Of course. Just sit." She led her mother to a chair and asked, "Want a cup of tea?"

"Well… sure, but you don't have to—"

"Cinnamon spice or chamomile?" Shannon asked.

"Chamomile, thanks, honey," her mom said as she sat down.

When Shannon put the kettle on the stove, she noticed the residue of recent tears in her mother's eyes. "Is everything okay, Mom?"

"Oh, yes," she replied. "Just a long day."

Shannon knew that "just a long day" was the Irish way of saying, "I don't want to talk about it." So she respected her mother's implicit request and put a box of spaghetti into the boiling pot. As she watched the noodles bending and squirming in the bubbling water, she thought of different ways to broach the subject of Bobo's birthday, because it occurred to her that her sudden interest in the past event would seem downright strange.

"Where's your sister?" her mother asked.

"Oh, I don't know," Shannon replied. "Probably at the library."

Just then, the kettle whistled. Shannon poured two cups of tea and brought them to the table. "Mom, do you remember Bobo?"

"Of course I do," her mom replied. "The boy down the street."

"Yeah, so anyway—"

Her mother cut her off. "I heard all about it."

"You heard about what?" Shannon asked incredulously.

"He's getting kicked out of school, right?"

Because Shannon was so fixated on Bobo's birthday party, she forgot all about his looming expulsion. "Oh, right," she played it off. "But how did you hear about it already?"

Her mother put her tea down and looked at her daughter with raised eyebrows.

"Mrs. Lewis?" Shannon guessed her mother's thoughts. "You've got to be kidding me!"

"None other than Mandy the Mouth." her mother laughed. "That's what we called her in high school."

"Well, we call her daughter Lucy Lips," Shannon countered, "so I guess the apple doesn't fall far from the tree."

"No, it certainly doesn't," her mom agreed.

"So, did she call you or what?"

"Yup. She told me to make sure to keep the car doors locked because we had a 'thief' living down the street." Her mother sipped her tea, and then said, "What a bitch."

When the full impact of her cheating scheme dawned on Shannon, the guilt and shame she felt this afternoon returned. Not only would Bobo be expelled for a crime he didn't commit, but this scandal would destroy a family name already smeared with dog shit. In a small town like Syracuse, word traveled fast, and although her community had trouble remembering good things, their memories were steel traps when it came to remembering bad things. So any chance Bobo had of escaping the shadow of his convict dad and alcoholic mom had shattered when he'd been branded a thief.

"It's totally ludicrous anyway." Her mother's words roused Shannon from her painful thoughts.

"What, Mom?" Shannon asked.

"I said it's totally ludicrous. Bobo isn't a thief."

"Yeah, I know." Shannon's eyes grew misty.

Her mother sipped her tea. "But why was he in the classroom after school? Any ideas?"

This question stunned Shannon, and images of her crime flew through her mind like a flock of startled birds. She saw herself making a copy of the test, writing the letters on her desk, putting the bogus document in Mr. Cameron's hands, and then handing Bobo his expulsion papers.

"What's the matter?" her mom asked.

"Oh," Shannon realized tears were streaming down her face, and she wiped them away, "I just feel bad about Bobo."

"Really?" her mom asked skeptically. "I didn't realize you two still hung out."

"Well, we don't." Shannon felt as if her guilt was a fragrance that her mother could smell, and she felt relieved when the timer for the spaghetti gave her a reason to leave the table.

"Oh, well, Shannon, there's nothing you can do about it, so don't let it get you down."

But there was something she could do about it, and she vowed to walk straight into Miss Parish's office tomorrow and tell her the truth.

"That poor family," her mom said. "Always one bad thing after another."

As Shannon was rinsing off the spaghetti in the sink, she looked out the kitchen window at the cherry tree that and remembered the vision of Bobo's birthday party in the orb, and her anger returned.

"Hey, Mom," she said as she brought two steaming bowls to the table. "Speaking of Bobo, do you remember me and Sarah got an invitation for his party a while ago?"

"An invitation from the Billings?" her mom asked as she went to the refrigerator for Parmesan cheese.

"Yeah. For a birthday party," Shannon replied.

"No, I don't remember that." Her mother returned to the table and sat down. "I haven't heard from those people in years." Then she sprinkled the condiment on her food and began eating. "This is delicious! Thanks, honey."

"You're welcome, Mom."

During the gentle hush that falls over a gratifying meal, Shannon tried another attempt at cracking open the past. "Well anyway, it was a long time ago, but I thought you might remember."

"Remember what, honey?" her mother asked.

"Bobo's birthday party."

"Bobo's what?" her mom put her fork down.

"His birthday party. Me and Sarah got an invitation a while ago."

"Does this have something to do with his expulsion?" her mom asked with a bewildered expression carved into her face.

"No, no," Shannon returned. "I was just wondering if you remembered."

"When was it?"

"Like I said," Shannon replied, "it was a while back."

"What does *a while back* mean?" Her mother's tone had the unmistakable hue of burgeoning frustration.

"Oh, forget about it." Shannon forced a laugh. "It's stupid."

"No, I want to know. How long ago?"

Now forced to tell the truth, Shannon realized she was

behaving like a petty, vindictive bitch. "Really, Mom," she started to get up. "I'd rather not—"

"Sit!" her mother commanded. "Tell me when this party was!"

"Um," Shannon stammered. "It was like seven years ago."

"Seven years ago!" Her mother burst out laughing. "Why in God's name are you thinking about something that happened seven years ago?"

Somehow her mother's laughter brought back all the pain of her family's duplicity, and Shannon grew bold. "Well, I just found out you guys lied to me."

"Who lied to you?"

"You, Dad, and Sarah!" Shannon snapped.

"What?" her mother inquired in abject bewilderment. "When?"

"Like I said, seven years ago," Shannon affirmed. "Bobo invited me and Sarah to his birthday party, but only Sarah went, and you guys pretended she didn't."

Finally, the light of recognition grew in her mother's eyes.

"Dad even brought me to a baseball game just to get me out of the house," Shannon continued. "Now do you remember?"

"Yes, I remember, but Shannon, why are you bringing this up now?"

"Like I said," Shannon responded, "I just found out."

"Did Bobo tell you?" her mother asked.

"No," Shannon replied. "Bobo didn't tell me."

"Sarah?" her mother pressed.

"No. Sarah didn't tell me."

"But who—"

"The real question is," Shannon interjected, "why did you guys lie to me?"

"Well," her mother's eyes closed like curtains as she revisited the event, "we didn't want to hurt your feelings."

"Well, that didn't work, *did it?*" Shannon snapped.

"No, it didn't."

"But I still don't understand why Sarah got to go and I didn't," Shannon continued. "Were you afraid I'd embarrass you or something?"

"Of course not, honey."

"Send Goldilocks and keep the Ugly Duckling home?"

"Shannon!" her mother shouted.

"Well, then tell me the truth!" Shannon shouted back.

Her mother stared at her food for a moment and then said, "Bobo put us in an awkward position."

"Bobo what?" Shannon asked.

Her mother took a deep breath and said, "He only invited Sarah."

Shannon felt as if an eighteen-wheeler had just run over her heart. "He *what?*"

"He only invited Sarah," her mother repeated. "I'm sorry, honey."

The room filled with the suffocating presence of an exposed lie, and it felt as if the tables, walls, chairs, and cupboards had suddenly been pushed together.

"But that doesn't make any sense," Shannon said. "Bobo was friends with me, not Sarah."

"I know it, honey." Her mother steepled her fingers. "At first we decided neither one of you should go, but…"

"But what?" Shannon enjoined.

"Well, that was when Tommy Billings had just gone to prison and we knew other parents wouldn't let their kids go, so we—"

Shannon finished her mother's sentence, "You let Sarah go so Bobo would have some guests at his tenth birthday party."

"That's right."

Just then, the bell wreath, still on the door since Christmas, jingled and Sarah came in with a light dusting of snow on her long blond hair.

"Smells like spaghetti!" she declared in a jubilant tone that only magnified the sorrow in Shannon's heart.

"Hi, sweetie," their mother said.

Sarah took off her coat, got herself a bowl of spaghetti, and sat down. "Thanks for making dinner, Mom."

"Actually, it was Shannon," her mother corrected her.

"Oh!" Sarah smiled at her twin. "Thanks, sis."

Shannon forced herself to say, "You're welcome."

A few moments of silence passed until Sarah asked, "So what were you guys talking about when I came in?"

"What makes you ask?" Shannon leaped at her sister's question.

"I don't know," her sibling replied. "But the room felt heavy. Like maybe someone died or something."

"Oh, we weren't talking about anything in particular," their mother said, hoping that the previous subject would be dropped.

"Actually," Shannon interjected, "we were reminiscing."

"Oh, really?" Sarah got up and poured herself a glass of milk. "Reminiscing about what?"

"A birthday party," her twin replied.

"A birthday party." Sarah sat back down. "Whose?"

"Bobo's," Shannon answered.

"Bobo?" Sarah looked at her mother and then back at her sister. "The boy down the street?"

"That's the one," Shannon confirmed.

"Well," her sibling twirled her spaghetti with a fork, "how was the party?"

"I don't know."

"You don't know?" Sarah asked.

"That's right," Shannon replied.

"How come you don't know?"

"Cuz, I didn't go, but *you* did," Shannon snapped.

Utterly confused, Sarah looked around the room to make sure she had walked into the right house until her mother spoke.

"Sweetie, do you remember Bobo had a birthday party back in fifth grade, and they invited you but not your sister?"

Shannon watched her sister's eyes sifting through pieces of the past until she found the fragment they were talking about.

"Oh, that's right." Sarah cringed. "I do remember that."

"Well," their mother continued, "Shannon just found out about it, and she's upset."

Although Sarah now knew *what* they were talking about, she couldn't figure out *why* they were discussing a party that happened seven years ago, so she simply said, "Oh, okay."

When the blue strobe lights of a passing snowplow danced across the kitchen wall, Sarah commented on the snow. Subsequently, her mother, relieved by the shift in discourse, reciprocated by discussing the temperature. Soon a fresh topic, rife with cheerful platitudes and anecdotes, was underway until Shannon spoke.

"So how was it?"

"How was what?" Sarah replied.

"Bobo's birthday party?"

Sarah looked at her sister to see if she was joking, but Shannon's grim expression let her know she wasn't.

"Honestly, Shannon," their mother inserted, "it was seven years ago."

"I realize that, Mom. I'm just asking her how the party was. Okay?"

"Well, let me see." Sarah made a lackluster attempt at recalling the past but came up empty-handed. "Actually, I remember going, but I can't remember anything that happened."

"Nothing?" Shannon asked.

"Nope. Not a thing," her sister replied.

"Not even what games they played or what presents he got?"

"Shannon!" their mother scolded her. "This is absurd. Can *you* remember anything specific about that day?"

"I remember *everything* about that day," she replied. "The Chiefs played the Mudhens. Peachy Reece had a no-hitter going until Toledo tied the game with a single in the ninth. Then Nick Bottom hit a walk-off run in the tenth, and Dad bought me a bunch of crap because he felt bad about Bobo's party. Okay?" Shannon looked at her astonished listeners and continued. "Now if I can remember all that, Sarah should be able to remember something."

"Like what?" Sarah asked.

"Like who was there?" her sister countered.

Sarah was growing tired of Shannon's antics, but she decided to cooperate to avoid further strife. "Okay, let me see." This time, she closed her eyes and scoured her memories. "Actually, I might be able to remember who was there."

"Really?" their mother asked, slightly astonished.

"Yes, I think so."

While the orb had predicted the future with precision, it had yet to prove its knowledge of the past, and if Sarah's list matched the faces in the vision, then Shannon would know the orb was omniscient. However, it occurred to her that if *she* rattled off the guests and not her sister, the same thing could be accomplished with the added benefit of displaying her own sagacity. "Wait!" she screamed as Sarah was about to speak.

"Wait for what?" her mother and sister said at the same time.

"What if *I* tell *you* who was there?"

"Hold on," their mom said. "Shannon, how could you possibly know who was there?"

"I told you before, I remember everything about that day."

Sarah, now totally sick of her sister's bullshit, said, "Okay, then tell us."

"Let me see." Shannon looked at the ceiling for dramatic effect. "Mookie Meltzer, Frankie, Snickers, Lucy Lewis, and," here she closed her eyes and squinted as if probing the shores of her mystical powers, "Becky Blum." When she looked at her captive audience, Sarah's mouth was hanging open in amazement, but her mother's face was frosted with skepticism.

"She's right," Sarah spoke first. "That's amazing."

"What's amazing about it?" their mom asked. "Someone told her. That's all."

"Nobody told me," Shannon said defensively.

"Not even Lucy Lips?" their mother replied.

"Nope," Shannon countered. "I just knew."

"But I thought you just found out about the party," Sarah added.

"I did!" Shannon exclaimed.

"Oh, Shannon," her mother took her plate to the sink, "stop lying."

"*Me* lying?!" Shannon protested. "*You* guys lied! Not *me*!"

Sarah raised her hands in surrender. "We lied to you, and we're sorry, okay?"

"Don't patronize me, you bitch!"

"Really, Shannon?" her sister remarked in a condescending tone. "Are you going to pull my hair now, too?"

"You deserve it!"

"Well, here." Sarah spun around and displayed a golden ponytail. "Give it a nice tug. You'll feel better."

"Stop it!" their mother screamed, and when they looked at her, they realized she was crying.

"Mom, what's the matter?" Shannon asked.

"You're acting like a bunch of brats!" their mother sobbed. "That's what's the matter!"

Given the situation, her ire was predictable, but the tears running down her cheeks were peculiar, and both daughters knew that something else was wrong.

"Mom's right." Sarah looked at her sister and said, "Sorry I was being a jerk."

"That's okay," Shannon replied. "I'm sorry, too."

When they looked back at their mother, she was leaning against the counter like a broom someone left behind.

Shannon stood up. "Hey, come and sit down, okay?" She put her hand on her mother's back and led her to the table.

Once the three of them were seated, Sarah said, "Let's see what we have for dessert," and began to rise, but their mother put her hand on her daughter's arm.

"Sit," their mom said in a solemn voice. "I have something to tell both of you."

They looked at each other and then back at their mother. "What is it?" they asked in unison.

"Your father's getting married."

As the words hovered in the air like snowflakes too delicate to land, Sarah put both hands on her mouth and began to cry while Shannon became incredulous. "When did you find out?"

"He called me today," their mother replied.

"Well," Shannon stammered, "why didn't *he* tell us?"

"I don't know—" Their mother's answer was cut short by Sarah, who let out a harrowing sob and ran out of the room. When a bedroom slammed and the springs of a bed squeaked, their mom stood up and looked at Shannon. "I'm sorry, honey." Then she followed her disconsolate daughter upstairs.

By herself in the kitchen, Shannon braced herself for the storm of sadness that would render her helpless, but the deluge never came. After that, she looked around the room and marveled at the irony of her surroundings. The walls were the same lemon yellow, the refrigerator was still plastered with pictures and Post-it Notes, and a crude rendering of the Erie Canal remained by the window. But the familiarity belied the fact that everything was different because her father was gone forever.

9

February brought the worst winter storm in fifty years. Subzero temperatures, frightening windchills, and fifty inches of snow pummeled the city. Cars, trucks, and buses were scattered along the road like forgotten toys, and twenty-seven people died from exposure to the cold, including a busload of senior citizens coming back from a casino. However, the frigid conditions comforted Shannon because they matched the frozen landscape in her heart.

After learning about her father's impending marriage, she felt forsaken and hopelessly depressed. In the past, she would have reached out to Frankie. But ever since Sarah dumped him, he hadn't returned any of her texts. Furthermore, she couldn't lean on her family because her mother's eyes looked like open wounds, and she still hated Sarah for stealing Frankie's heart. However, there was an unexpected source of comfort that Shannon discovered one afternoon when the weather finally softened.

She was walking home from school, and the sky, which had been as gray as a gravestone for days, was a light blue that made Shannon think of the curtains that used to hang in her room when she was a child. They were cerulean with white airplanes on them, and she used to lay on her bed and fly around in those planes until sleep pulled her into other skies. The memory filled her with happiness, but she cradled the feeling cautiously because approaching dusk would soon swallow the color forever. However, upon entering her bedroom, she was surprised to see that the orb on her night-stand was the same shade of blue—not cerulean dimmed by time, but the color she had seen thirty minutes ago. It was as if the ball was in tune with her feelings. Shannon quickly reasoned that the pigment was simply a reflection in the glass, and the rest was her imagination.

It snowed the next morning, and the world was the color of dirty socks all day. Yet, when Shannon got home, the ball was cerulean again, and now she knew that the orb was trying to make her happy. In fact, the more time she spent in her room, the more blue the ball became—in her bed at night or in the morning, the ball was radiant. However, if she watched a movie with her mother or did her homework downstairs, she'd return to find it dim as a distant star. Additionally, it became clear that the luminous performance was meant for Shannon alone because whenever her mom popped in, the ball turned black. Yet, as soon as her mom left, it became blue again.

One afternoon when the temperature climbed to forty degrees and sunlight pierced the iron clouds, Shannon found a storm raging inside the orb when she got home from school. But after she sat down on her bed, the tempest subsided and blue drops slipped down the side of the glass. Somehow, Shannon instinctively knew that if she asked the ball a question, it would answer her, so she put her face close to it and whispered, "Who are you?" This query elicited no response, but when she asked, "Where did you come from?" an incredible transformation occurred. The blue drops evaporated, and a row of hazy, undulating lights appeared. As the picture became more clear, the lights became lanterns swinging back and forth in a warped wooden room filled with suitcases, bunkbeds, and shadowy faces. A damp, suffocating feeling pervaded the atmosphere. However, when Shannon muttered, "What is that?" the vision plunged into darkness because an amorphous figure had opened her door.

"Who are you talking to, sweetie?" her mother's voice sounded strange, and for a few frightening moments, Shannon didn't know where she was.

"Me?" Shannon responded with a shaky voice. "I'm not talking to anyone."

"Really?" her mother replied incredulously. "I could've sworn I heard voices."

Finally, the scattered pieces of reality formed a picture, and she recognized her surroundings. "There's no one else in here." Shannon gestured toward the walls, the empty chair, and the dark orb. "See?"

"Listen, kiddo," her mom sat next to her on the bed, "you've been spending a lot of time in here lately, and I'm worried about you."

Even though her mother's tone was warm, Shannon got defensive. "I'm fine, Mom."

"Well, that's good to hear, but I'd understand if you weren't."

"What does that mean?" Shannon asked.

"It means that your father's plans came as a surprise to all of us," she said, referring to her dad's imminent marriage.

"Oh," Shannon replied. "I don't care about that."

"Of course, you do, sweetie." Her mom rubbed her back.

"Why should I care?" She scooted to avoid her mother's reach. "If he wants to marry some bimbo, he can."

"He's still your father…"

"No, he's not!" Shannon erupted.

"Shannon!" her mother put her hands to her mouth. "How can you say that?"

"I can say it because it's true! A father is supposed to make his kids feel safe and always be there for them, right?"

"Well, yes," her mother began.

"Then someone who's never around and only calls on Christmas and birthdays doesn't fit the definition of a father, right?"

Her mother's eyes grew misty. "Well, it's not that simple."

"Actually, it *is* that simple, and that's why I'm not upset about him."

She studied her daughter's face and then said, "But you two used to be so close."

"Yes, we *did*," Shannon countered. "And whose fault is it if we're not close anymore?"

"Well—"

"He doesn't care about me, so I don't care about him." As these words left her mouth, Shannon had a startling moment of metacognition. She had just forsaken her father, and it hadn't aroused the slightest bit of feeling. In the past, even the mere thought of saying something like this would have made her sob, but today she felt nothing. Her eyes sought out the branch where he'd put the sleigh bell years ago with the hope that it would bring a tear, but her eyes stayed dry as the desert. This frightened her.

She was about to share her epiphany when her mother stood up and said, "Well, I'm sorry you feel that way."

"Wait, Mom, I—"

"Adults aren't perfect, you know," her mom said bitterly. "Inevitably, we'll disappoint you."

"Mom—"

"Are you going to stop loving me if I make a mistake?" Shannon was stunned by the force of her question.

Her mother replied, "It's easy to judge other's mistakes when you don't have the courage to make your own."

"What's that supposed to mean?" Shannon asked.

"Look at you!" her mother's sadness had turned to anger. "You sit up here like some princess in a tower casting judgment on the minions below."

Shannon started to speak, but her mother cut her off again.

"No friends. No job. No responsibility. Nothing."

"I have responsibilities, Mom," Shannon said feebly.

"Like what?" her mother inquired.

"Like school, homework…"

"Homework, huh?" her mother scoffed.

"Yes." Shannon pointed to the books on her nightstand.

"Well, maybe you should try opening them once in a while," her mother rejoined.

"What does that mean?" Shannon asked.

"I just got off the phone with Mrs. Walker." Her mother stood up. "You're failing three subjects."

The words hit Shannon like bricks. "I'm… what?"

"That's what I came up here to talk to you about."

"Mrs. Walker is wrong. Tell her—"

"You can tell her yourself. She wants to see you tomorrow at ten."

When her mother left, Shannon looked out at the dusk that had fallen like a hammer. Although she felt like she could reach out and touch the bruised sky, it seemed far away. In fact, everything seemed distant—the trees, the houses, her mother, her father. However, the blue vapors that began spinning around the base of the orb soothed her. It was as if they were saying, *When the world disappears, I am here for you.*

That night, Shannon had a terrible dream. She was wrapped in coarse linen and trapped inside a dark space with very little air. Her skin was burning, but her bones were cold, and the pungent smell of rotting pine made her nauseous. When her eyes adjusted to the murky light, grainy patterns appeared above her, and she realized she was in a coffin. Pounding on the lid was impossible because her arms wouldn't move and her screams were as silent as stones. Then the box suddenly shifted, and Shannon heard the sound of heavy feet as daylight sliced through the seams in the wood along with salty air. Prayers were mumbled as the box tilted back. Then she slid through a trap door, and for a few terrifying seconds the sun chased her until she shattered the surface of a glass sea and descended into the darkness.

Normally, Shannon would perform the minimum tasks necessary for school—a cursory brushing of her curly locks and some eyeliner to obscure the bags beneath her eyes. However, for some reason, this morning she had a strong impulse to embrace the day. So she showered, put on makeup, and left for school on time for a change. Warm breezes slipped through the weakening fingers of winter as Shannon walked to school surrounded by memories of past springs when she and Sarah got their bikes out of the garage and flew around the neighborhood with only their shadows beneath them.

At school, Mr. Reed, her supercilious English teacher, assigned *A Tale of Two Cities* because he liked to save the most boring books for second semester. The entire class groaned when copies of the five-hundred-page novel with small print were passed out, and they gasped when they heard about the five-page essay due at the end of the year. But as Shannon began reading, she immediately related to the character haunted by a specter. Even though she had done her best to shake off last night's dream, the nightmare had been following her all morning—she could feel the coarse linen against her skin and smell the decaying coffin. The sensory phenomena, she speculated, was probably anxiety caused by her impending meeting with Mrs. Walker because the woman had a knack for peering into her soul, and Shannon didn't want anybody looking in there right now.

After sifting through different excuses for her poor grades during precalculus, she decided to tell Mrs. Walker about her dad's imminent marriage since she didn't know why she was failing and this seemed like a good excuse. Furthermore, Shannon feared that her counselor would find out about the orb, and a primal urge to protect her sole source of comfort rose up inside her. When second period ended, she went to the copy room to tell Mrs. Mahoney about her appointment with her counselor. However, the old secretary wasn't there. Fortunately, there was a paper jam in one of the machines and fixing it would prolong her appointment with Mrs. Walker. So she opened the tray, and after pulling out a mangled document, a heartless voice turned her hands to ice.

"What do you think you're doing over there, Delaney?"

Realizing it was Miss Parish, Shannon quickly turned around. "I was just fixing a paper jam."

"Give me that!" the principal snapped.

When Shannon held out the twisted paper, Miss Parish snatched it out of her hands. "What are you doing in here?"

"I work in here this period," the teen replied.

"You *what?*" the dragon asked incredulously.

"I work in here, and I just came in to tell Mrs. Mahoney that I have an appointment with Mrs. Walker, but she wasn't here, and then there was a paper jam—"

"Enough!" The principal's command cut through Shannon's words like a chainsaw. "What time is your appointment in the counseling office?"

"Ten," Shannon replied.

The old lizard looked at her watch. "Well, you have thirty seconds to make it, so I suggest you get going."

"Yes, Miss Parish." Shannon grabbed her backpack. "Thank you."

The bell rang, and as Shannon stepped into the hallway, she was nearly trampled by a clamorous knot of students racing to class. However, their voices were soon swallowed by the closing doors, and only the hum of the fluorescent lights above could be heard. Suddenly, a clicking of heels on linoleum emerged, and she knew Miss Parish was behind her because nobody else wore pumps in the dead of winter. In fact, her principal wore variations of the same outfit every day—monochrome pant suits with heels the exact same color. If her suit was maroon, so were her shoes. If her suit was mauve, her shoes were, too. Shannon almost admired the woman's style that was both bold and progressively ugly. Being that the Dragon's Lair and the guidance office were both at the other end of the building, Shannon wondered if she should slow down and let the old hag catch up. But then it occurred to her that maybe Miss Parish wanted to follow her so she maintained the same pace. Upon reaching her destination, the clicking of the heels had stopped, and when she turned around, the principal was gone.

The couch by the window in the waiting room looked inviting, but the second Shannon's bottom touched the seat, Mrs. Walker's door opened and a warm voice said, "Come on in, girl." When Shannon entered the room, her counselor was wearing a caramel-and-black crinkle blouse with her hair in lemonade braids. The juxtaposition of this stylish lady and the frumpy principal made her laugh.

"Well, look at this beautiful girl with a big smile!" Mrs. Walker said. "Did you get all dolled up just for me?"

"No," the teen replied. "I just felt like making an effort today."

"That's good!" Mrs. Walker smiled. "You should make an effort more often because a pretty girl like you shouldn't always hide beneath hoodies and baseball hats."

"Okay, Mrs. Walker. I'll try more often." Though Shannon had no intention of repeating this morning's toilette, she wished she liked herself enough to dress nicely every day.

"So," Mrs. Walker began, "speaking of making an effort, what is going on with you, girl?"

"Oh." Shannon blushed. "You mean the four classes I'm failing?"

"Failing!" Mrs. Walker chuckled. "Girl, fifty-nine percent is failing. You're flunking these classes."

"I know," the teen admitted.

"Well, if you know, then how come you're flunking?" her counselor asked.

"I mean, I didn't know," Shannon replied, "but my mom told me, so now I know."

Mrs. Walker sat back, put on her pink tortoise shell glasses, and looked at her computer screen. "A fifty percent in Spanish, a thirty-five percent in English," she cringed, "and a fifty percent in government."

"I know," Shannon said. "I'm planning on talking to my teachers today."

"Talking to them about what?" her counselor asked.

"About what I need to do to pass," Shannon replied.

"Girl, you already know what you need to do—go to class, do homework, apply yourself."

"I know." Mrs. Walker's concern made Shannon feel bad about not feeling bad.

"Okay." The counselor closed her laptop. "Now we know what you *haven't* been doing. Now tell me what you *have* been doing."

"What do you mean?" Shannon's walls went up because the conversation had shifted to her personal life.

"Like who have you been hanging out with?" Mrs. Walker inquired.

"Nobody," Shannon replied.

Mrs. Walker pressed, "No friends?"

"Nope."

"What happened to that boy you used to chill with?" her counselor asked. "The musician?"

"Frankie?" Shannon asked.

"Yeah, Frankie," Mrs. Walker replied.

"We don't hang out anymore," Shannon said grimly.

"Why not?" Mrs. Walker inquired.

"It's a long story," Shannon answered.

"I got time."

"Well…" Shannon thought of the embrace beneath the streetlight that shattered her world. "It's complicated."

"Honey, most things in life are complicated," her counselor offered.

"Not like this," Shannon said with conviction.

"All right, then." Mrs. Walker took off her glasses. "So is he the reason you're not doing your schoolwork?"

"No!" The word flew out of Shannon's mouth like a pebble out of a slingshot.

"Hmmm." Mrs. Walker steepled her fingers. "Your mom says that you been spending a lot of time in your room."

At the mention of her room, Shannon felt that sooner or later she'd trip up and say something about the orb, so she shifted the topic. "My dad's getting married."

"I know," Mrs. Walker's voice softened. "Your mom told me."

"Well, maybe that's why I've been so withdrawn."

"Maybe it is," her counselor replied, "but listen, honey, your parents got divorced two years ago."

"Yeah, I know." Shannon was disappointed because her excuse hadn't derailed Mrs. Walker's line of inquiry.

"And divorced people get remarried sometimes."

"So you don't think that has anything to do with my *flunking*?" Shannon stressed the slang term to show her disdain for Mrs. Walker's diction.

"Well," her counselor, unfazed by Shannon's vitriol, said, "it probably has something to do with it, but knowing you, there's more."

"Knowing me?" Shannon was clearly annoyed now. "What's that supposed to mean?"

"Well," Mrs. Walker replied, "during your rough patch two years ago, you were telling a lot of lies."

"Yeah, but what does that have to do with now?" Shannon asked.

"Because when you don't like your reality, you create another," Mrs. Walker said.

Mrs. Walker's reply was like a slap in the face since Shannon hadn't seen this pattern in her own behavior until now.

"And," her counselor continued, "I'm just waiting for the walls of your made-up place to come crashing down again."

Although the shrewd diagnosis made Shannon admire Mrs. Walker even more, it also made her sad because it closed the door on ever confiding in her about the orb. If Mrs. Walker ever said the visions were a product of her imagination, Shannon might start to hate her. And she didn't want to hate her. Just then, the fourth-period bell sliced the room in half.

Shannon rose from her chair. "Well, I gotta get to class and get my grades up."

"Sounds like a plan." Mrs. Walker got up, too.

"Sorry we didn't get to finish," Shannon said.

"That's okay. We'll pick up where we left off next week."

"Next week?" Shannon asked.

"Yup," her counselor confirmed.

"Wait… when?"

"Same bat time, same bat channel." The reference to the 1960s TV show somehow wasn't lost on Shannon.

"But I have to work in the copy room," Shannon protested.

"They'll be okay in there for a while."

"For a while?" The teen groaned. "How often do I have to come?"

"Until you're passing everything. Weekly counseling is

standard procedure for at-risk students, especially seniors *flunking* three classes." Mrs. Walker underscored the verb to show Shannon she wasn't fooling around.

"Okay, got it," Shannon conceded. "So once I get my grades up, I don't have to come here?"

"Don't you like coming here?" Mrs. Walker pouted.

"I like *you*," Shannon said, "but no, I don't like coming here."

The counselor laughed and clapped her hands. "Honey, I don't blame you one bit." She walked Shannon to the door.

"Okay, see you next week." Shannon started to walk away, but Mrs. Walker gently touched her sleeve.

"Just remember, honey," she said in a barely audible voice, "the truth will lead you out of the pain, so focus on what's real."

As Shannon walked to Mr. Cameron's class, she considered Mrs. Walker's parting words but realized they didn't apply to her. Because, after all, who would believe *her truth*? What was the likelihood someone trusting a lousy student with a history of lying when she said she possessed a magical orb that showed her visions of the past and future? The answer was simple—nobody would. Yet, though she couldn't change her reality, she could change people's opinion of her. Which began with school because a nobody with bad grades was a freak. But a nobody with good grades was a bookworm, and bookworms didn't attract attention like freaks did. So she resolved to pass her classes since she feared Mrs. Walker's perceptive prowess and wanted to get off her radar before she found out about the orb.

When Shannon asked teachers for missing work, most were empathetic. However, Mr. Reed refused to give her any slack. He said she needed an A on every assignment from now on, including the essay and the final exam, in order to pass. Previously, this would have knocked the wind out of her sails. Yet somehow the snob's reaction fueled her desire to succeed. So when she got home, rather than looking at SparkNotes, she actually read the assigned chapters and got an A on her first reading quiz. Furthermore, she began doing her government homework—the Naturalization Act, the Chinese Exclusion Act, the Alien Contract Labor laws—not exactly interesting reading but getting off the "at-risk" list meant she'd have to cowboy up and study. Even boring crap like this.

By March, Shannon was passing four out of her five classes. She was still failing English with a fifty percent, but acing next week's test on *A Tale of Two Cities* would put her within striking distance of a D. Which meant her meetings with Mrs. Walker would soon be over. In fact, her progress changed the tone of her weekly counseling sessions. Now they talked about academic goals and study strategies. Not personal stuff, which was a relief.

However, in the event that Mrs. Walker did inquire about her vacant social life, Shannon had her bases covered. As much as it pained her, she sat with Lucy Lewis at lunch, and the blabbermouth relished the company, because, even though Lucy was editor of the school newspaper and president of ASB, everyone hated her. However, Shannon realized that a circle of friends would look even better, and two more pals fell into her lap.

Unlike the rest of her classes, maintaining her grade in precalculus required more than effort because she didn't understand math. To Shannon, the symbols and themes of literature were simple. Additionally, the myriad acts and statutes in government, though boring as hell, stuck in her mind like flies in a spiderweb. But complex numbers, polar coordinates, and conics were more baffling than nuclear pasta. Fortunately, the brainy Meltzer twins who lived down the street were more than happy to help. As it turned out, Mookie'd had a crush on Sarah since kindergarten, and he would do anything to be close to her, even if meant sitting in her kitchen. And Echo did everything Mookie did.

Shannon's burgeoning social life meant she was spending less time in her room, and the orb expressed its displeasure in myriad ways. The first time she came home late, the ball turned pale blue and stayed that way until she fell asleep. But after her delinquency became a pattern, the orb stayed dark when she came home. In fact, it only glowed at inopportune moments. For example, one night when Shannon was sound asleep, she was awakened by a strident mixture of static and found her room ablaze with sapphire crystals. However, the second she sat up, her room collapsed into darkness. After similar incidents, she threatened to put the orb in the closet, but it continued to misbehave. The last straw was the night before her big English test. She was trying to finish a chapter, and Dickens' verbose prose required acute concentration. Yet every so often the ball would blind her with a sudden blast of light, and Shannon would forget everything she had just read. At the end of her rope, Shannon said, "If you distract me again, you're going in the closet." Instantly, the ball turned purple as if it was truly penitent, but the moment she began reading again, shards of light flew into her eyes. Out of patience now, Shannon picked up the ball, put it on the shelf in her closet, and slammed the door.

Because she stayed up studying until three a.m., the chirping alarm clock became a bird in her dreams. Fortunately, the hydraulic screech of a garbage truck woke her at seven-thirty, which meant she still had twenty minutes to get to school. After slipping into a pair of Uggs and putting on a hoodie, she ran out the front door. Luckily, Mookie and Echo, driving by in their mom's Subaru, saw her and gave her a ride. By the grace of God, Shannon got to class just as the first bell was ringing.

When Mr. Reed passed out the tests, he smiled and said, "Good luck," to the pretty, popular girls. Yet he dropped Shannon's on her desk as if he was throwing down a gauntlet. With an inexplicable surge of confidence, she picked up the test and smiled at him. When he walked away, the teen blew lightly on the tips of her pencils and went to work. Though her teacher supplied more possible answers than terms in the matching section to trip students up, Shannon sailed through this portion with ease. Furthermore, the short-answer questions were pathetically easy because they were all plot based. She dreaded the essay because Mr. Reed was known for his gnarly questions, and given the required length coupled with the time constraints, one could see why. But after reading the prompt, Shannon snickered because if you couldn't talk about three examples of the resurrection motif in *A Tale of Two Cities*, then you were a dumbass.

Shannon finished before anybody else did. When she dropped the test on Mr. Reed's desk, he gave it a cursory glance and then returned to his computer screen as if she hadn't been there. But when she returned to her seat, Shannon noticed him looking at it again. As if struck by an insatiable fit of curiosity, he put on his glasses, picked up his red pen, and began grading it. His face ran the gamut of emotion. He squinted, glared, smiled, and pondered. Finally, she saw him make a notation at the top of the first page and then something astounding happened Mr. Reed, the biggest snob on the planet, who had never offered her a kind word or any type of encouragement, gave her a thumbs-up. Shannon felt as if she'd died and gone to heaven. What made it even better was that Piper Martin, the most insufferable teacher's pet of all time, saw the interaction, and her perpetual smile fell off her face.

Shannon practically floated into precalculus on the wings of her recent success. Even the pop quiz on vectors didn't kill her buzz because Mookie had just gone over these with her, and she got the answers right. More importantly, she was totally prepared for her meeting with Mrs. Walker. Now that she had just aced a test in English, putting her in range of a D, with a little pleading, perhaps, she could get out of her counselor's doghouse today.

Mrs. Walker's door was closed when Shannon arrived, so she sat on the couch by the window and took her government textbook out of her bag. However, as she was trying to read about immigration policies, she kept getting distracted by a flash of red outside. At first she thought it was a reflection of the traffic. Then she noticed a robin hopping around on the barren branches, and her heart filled with joy because the bird meant the return of spring was around the corner. In the midst of her musings, Mrs. Walker opened her door and said, "Come on in, girl."

Shannon gathered her belongings and walked into the office.

"Sorry about the wait," her counselor said, sitting down.

"Oh, no worries," Shannon replied.

"Girl," Mrs. Walker looked her over, "you look like something the cat dragged in."

"Oh." Shannon sat down and looked down at her hoodie and her Uggs. "I was cramming for an English test all night."

"Well, how did it go?"

"I aced it," Shannon responded. "And you'll never guess what happened!"

Mrs. Walker leaned forward. "Well, don't leave me hanging."

"Mr. Reed gave me a thumbs-up."

"He what?!" Mrs. Walker sat back as if someone shoved her. "Girl, I think I better call the pope because this is a miracle."

They both laughed at the thought of the stuffy, pseudo-aristocrat stooping to such bourgeois behavior.

"And what made it even better was that Piper Martin saw it," Shannon added.

"Oh, my goodness!" Mrs. Walker clapped her hands. "Girl, you hit the lottery."

"And," the teen continued, "if my calculations are correct, that means I now have a fifty-seven in there."

"I'm proud of you, Shannon." The counselor reached across the desk and patted her hand. "Now let me take a look." She punched a few keys on her computer and then looked at the screen. "You're passing everything except English."

"But it's now a fifty-seven, and it was a thirty-five," Shannon interjected.

"That's good, that's good." Mrs. Walker was still looking at the screen.

"And you said once I was passing everything, we wouldn't have to have these meetings anymore."

"That's right." her counselor looked at her. "Once you are passing *everything*, we're done."

"Oh." Shannon looked down. "I thought a fifty-seven was close enough."

"It's way better than a thirty-five, but it still isn't passing, and you're stuck with me until you are passing. Comprende?"

"Si entiendo," Shannon replied.

"But I'll tell you what." Mrs. Walker's softened. "Since you're doing so much better, I'll let you go a little early today. How does that sound?"

"That sounds great!" Shannon stood up.

"Anyway, I think they could use you back in the copy room because the new girl needs a little help."

"You mean they got someone else?"

"No, no, you've still got the job," Mrs. Walker replied. "This girl's filling in till you come back."

When Shannon walked into the copy room, she was surprised to see Maryanne Newman, the student she had manipulated the day of the Math Marathon, putting a ream of paper in the copy machine. Then, when her eye swept across the rest of the room, she saw Miss Rossi, the beloved teacher's aide, stuffing envelopes.

"Hi, Maryanne," Shannon said.

Maryanne looked up with a smile, but when she saw who it was, her eyes turned cold. As it turned out, although she was cognitively impaired, there was apparently nothing wrong with her memory.

"Can I help you with that?" Shannon asked.

"Oh, she doesn't need any help." Miss Rossi winked. "She knows everything about copy machines."

"That's right," said Maryanne as she closed the drawer and looked around the room triumphantly.

"But she does need help with the teachers' names." Miss Rossi pointed at the staff mailboxes.

"No, I don't," Maryanne protested.

"Oh, I can help with that." As Shannon started walking

over she tripped on a recycle bin and tried to break her fall by grabbing the counter. But she accidentally pulled down a stack of papers that fluttered to the ground around her like a flock of pigeons.

Maryanne rushed to her side. "Are you okay?"

"I think so," Shannon said while getting to her feet.

Once they were facing each other, Maryanne could no longer contain her suppressed mirth and burst out laughing. As the coldness evaporated from her eyes, Shannon knew the girl had forgiven her.

Miss Rossi came over and brushed lint from the gray carpet off Shannon's back. "Are you hurt?"

"No, Miss Rossi." She laughed. "I'm good."

"You sure?" the aide asked.

"Yes," Shannon answered. "I'm sure."

"Well," Miss Rossi looked at the floor littered with papers, "we better get this place cleaned up."

Within a few minutes, they had the room back in order.

ON HER WAY to government class, the fatigue created by four hours' sleep coupled with the morning's dramatic events finally caught up with Shannon, and walking up the stairs felt like scaling Mount Everest. Fortunately, Mr. Cameron was showing a documentary about the first wave of immigration to America, and she would be able to sleep, because it was understood that he only showed videos when he was behind in his grading. Therefore, kids could do anything they wanted as long as it didn't disturb him. She began watching the archaic footage of people walking across planks into awaiting ships and waving goodbye forever to families on the shore.

Then the video shifted to some boring shmuck wearing a bowtie, and Shannon put her head down. At first, she could hear the dinging of text messages and the chatter of her classmates, but then Shannon fell into a dream— *She's in her bed looking up at phosphorescent stars. Slowly the stars became grainy faces in a wooden sky. Then she falls like a rock toward a glass sea, which shatters as her body is pulled into the darkness.*

THE OLD-FASHIONED SCALE with the weighing ruler and height rod brought back memories of annual physicals at Salem Hyde Elementary School. This was a festive occasion because it meant a temporary reprieve from the white-haired witches who posed as teachers during the day before flying back to hell on their brooms at night. Furthermore, while the students stood in poorly supervised lines waiting for the nurse, all kinds of mischief ensued, including spitballs, wedgies, writing on the walls, writing on each other, and plugging the drinking fountain drain with paper.

As Shannon lay on the examination table with an icepack on her forehead, she felt a sense of longing for elementary school when days were filled by simple things like recess and art projects. Laminated leaves, paper owls, ceramics in the kiln. Now she wanted to crawl inside a kiln because she'd just had an experience more mortifying than Snickers Sanchez shitting his pants and more traumatizing than Patsy Clark's bloody tampon falling out of her shorts during gym.

"You gave us quite a scare." Shannon's thoughts scattered like mice when the school nurse spoke.

"How long have I been here?" Shannon asked.

"Oh," the nurse looked at her watch, "about an hour."

Shannon removed the ice pack and sat up. "Can I go back to class now?" Going to Spanish was actually the last thing she wanted to do, but it was better than being in here with Mrs. Hawkins, who had long nose hairs and a mole on her cheek the size of Kansas.

"In a little while, but let's get you checked out first."

The nurse inspected Shannon's eyes with a pen light. Then she asked her to walk in a straight line. Finally, she asked her what day it was, and when Shannon's answer matched the calendar, she was allowed to leave. Because there were only fifteen minutes left in fifth period, Miss Hawkins sent her home. Walking down the sidewalk, Shannon reflected on what happened in Mr. Cameron's class. One moment she was asleep; the next she was on the floor with a circle of terrified faces above her. Apparently, she had fallen out of her chair during the video and let out a bloodcurdling scream. Aside from being mortified, she was confused because this was the second time she dreamed about being trapped inside a coffin and then dumped into the ocean. In her ninth-grade health class, she had learned that dreams were tangled interpretations of past experiences. However, this vision had no connection to anything in memory. Aside from taking the ferry to the Statue of Liberty, she'd never been on the ocean. Also, she was pretty sure that she'd never been inside a coffin (unless being in the back seat of her dad's Mustang counted). And although it defied logic, Shannon couldn't shake the feeling that she'd been in someone else's dream.

Nobody was home, which meant a brief calm before the storm. Certainly, the school had called, and it was only a matter of time before Shannon had to face her mother's interrogation. She entered her bedroom, and a pool of sluggish light crept out of her closet. When she opened the door, the ball was filled with pendulous lights, which quickly became the swaying lanterns she saw in a previous vision. Then the warped wooden room with shadowy faces appeared. After Shannon picked up the ball and sat down on her bed, the scene shifted and a rectangular shape emerged. At first, it looked like a crate, but the torpid light revealed a small coffin crudely slapped together with pine boards. Then the scene tilted, and the ocean appeared as two small hands reached for the sun that unraveled like a ball of yarn.

Her mother's pickup truck pulling into the driveway signaled the end of the vision. Because once its roar destroyed the silence, the illusion disappeared. But a few things made sense. Due to the size of the coffin and the small hands, she knew the spirit in the orb was a small child. Moreover, due to its possessive, mercurial nature, she knew it was a girl. Finally, Shannon knew in her bones that the spirit was trapped and she needed to set her free.

10

The harsh interrogation Shannon expected never happened. They talked for a long time, but her mother wasn't judgmental or reactive. Rather, she listened with open ears and an open heart. Even when it was clear that Shannon was giving circuitous replies, her mother respected her privacy. However, a line was drawn in the sand when it came to counseling because Shannon's troubling behavior merited more than a mother's love. At first, Dr. Murdock, the shrink Shannon had seen back in tenth grade, was suggested. But she had a strong antipathy for the quack who prescribed antidepressants that only made her problems worse. And when her mother began rattling off names of other doctors, Shannon felt hopeless until Mrs. Walker's face popped into her head. When she mentioned her counselor as a possible option, her mother was skeptical since Mrs. Walker was "a guidance counselor, not a psychologist." Furthermore, Shannon had already been seeing Mrs. Walker once a week and "it clearly wasn't enough." However, Shannon objected to her mother's assessment because in the four weeks she'd been seeing her counselor, her grades had improved dramatically, meaning she was no longer at risk of not graduating. Unable to refute her daughter's line of reasoning, her mother agreed to the plan with the stipulation that any more troubling behavior meant more "intensive supports."

Shannon was anxious about her next meeting with Mrs. Walker, who would certainly want to talk about her meltdown in government class. But that was still two days away, which gave her time to focus on the trapped spirit. However, this brought a new anxiety. Because if Shannon wanted to get to the truth of the orb, she'd have to start at its origins, which meant talking to Frankie since it had once belonged to him. Only a few months ago, a conversation with him would have made her happy. Now, however, after processing everything that happened, her resentment had turned to shame, and she avoided him like the plague. Yet the orb had come from his house, and if she was going to help the ghost, she needed to talk to him.

Because her mother didn't have to work the next morning and Sarah got a ride with a friend, Shannon drove the truck to school. Going down the gray streets, she braced herself for a shitstorm of gossip. Before the days of cell phones, only certain cliques would have known about her humiliating episode in government. But with Facebook, Snapchat, and TikTok, the incident had already been posted, liked, and disliked by thousands of teens with nothing better to do than prey on the one another's sorrows in a landscape littered with tears and damaged reputations. In fact, when she sat down in first period, Spider Rizzo, the most obnoxious boy in school, manufactured a mocking scream, and a few boys laughed. Although, when Shannon gave them a scalding glare, their mirth dissolved.

Unless she wanted to endure more ridicule, eating in the cafeteria was out of the question, so she bought a slice of pizza and sat on a bench outside. Although winter put up a valiant fight, spring had finally arrived. The barren landscape had been defeated by crocuses, snapdragons, violets, and pansies. As Shannon was enjoying the bright and crisp day, she heard the rapid click of an engine that wouldn't start. Looking up, she saw Frankie in his truck. Fear assailed her, but she had to find out about the orb and this was her only chance. Walking over, she saw him hop out of the cab and open up the hood.

"What's the matter?" she asked.

"Oh, hey Shannon." He gave her a cursory glance, then looked back down at the engine. "Not sure."

"Is it the battery?" Shannon inquired.

"Nah," he replied, "the lights and radio are working. I think it's the starter."

"Sounded like the battery to me."

"So you're a mechanic now?" Frankie asked with a playful edge.

"Nope, and apparently neither are you," she parried, "but you're in luck because my mom's truck is over there and I have jumper cables."

"That's great, but it's not the battery," he insisted.

"Five bucks says it is."

"You're on!" he bellowed.

Shannon got her pickup, and they connected the cables. After Frankie's truck started with a satisfying roar, she hopped into his cab with her open palm held out.

"Five dollars, please," she said.

He reluctantly opened up his wallet and handed her a fin. "Thanks."

"Anytime." She folded the bill and put it in her pocket.

"Listen, Shannon," Frankie said after a tense silence. "I know why you're here."

"Gave up your dream of being a mechanic and now you're a mind reader?"

"Seriously." He looked at her. "I haven't talked to Sarah in two months."

Without knowing why, she said, "Why not?"

"Sarah forbid me to talk to her." His eyes grew misty. "She won't even look at me."

Shannon felt her wound opening and switched the subject. "Believe it or not, that's not why I'm here."

He pointed to the clock on the dashboard. "Well, you better get to the point, then."

She took a deep breath. "Do you remember the glass ball you gave me?"

He searched his memory for a moment and then said, "The Palantir?"

"Yes," Shannon replied.

"Sure, I remember," Frankie said. "What about it?"

"Do you know where it came from?" Shannon inquired.

He squinted at her in disbelief. "Are you serious?"

She held his eyes with hers. "Dead serious."

"Well," he looked away, "it was in a box of my Aunt Mary's stuff in the attic, remember?"

Shannon recalled admiring it in the dusty loft in Frankie's house. "Yes, now I remember. So it belonged to your aunt?"

"Yeah. Then my mom turned that space into her office and threw all that crap away."

"But you saved the ball for me," Shannon said as she affectionately recalled the kind gesture.

"Yeah, I rescued it from the curb cuz you liked it."

Shannon realized in this moment how much she had

missed Frankie—her life with his friendship was technicolor. Without him, it was charcoal. Just then, they heard the bell indicating the end of lunch.

"Listen, Frankie. I still need to talk to you. Can we talk after school?"

"I work after school," he replied.

"Well, how about tonight?" Shannon pressed.

"Well—"

"Please." She grabbed his hand. "This is important."

"Okay," he agreed.

As she pretended to conjugate verbs in Spanish, anxiety wrapped around her throat like a scarf. She hadn't planned on talking to Frankie this soon, and she didn't know what she would say. Should she be honest about the visions in the orb? Should she tell him about his illusory embrace with Sarah beneath the streetlamp or the Pink Moon above his treehouse? If she did, he'd think she was nuts. But if she didn't, she'd never get to the truth.

They planned to meet at Frankie's house at seven-thirty, which meant she'd have to get all her homework done that afternoon. Her mother was working the night shift, so Shannon didn't have to bring the truck back right away. This made her happy because she had to read two chapters of government before solving twenty precalculus problems, and she didn't want to be distracted by the temperamental orb in her bedroom. So, after texting her mom, Shannon drove to the White Branch Library on Butternut Street, one of the oldest buildings in Syracuse. After reading about ruined financiers jumping off the Brooklyn Bridge and seeing pictures of soup kitchens and lines of moribund men in front of employment agencies, Shannon realized why they called it the Great Depression. However, nothing at the moment was more depressing than the twenty parametric equations staring back at her. Additionally, what made it frustrating was knowing that she could easily google the answers, but she had to show her work. So this was not an option. Fortunately, the Meltzer twins had been tutoring Shannon, so her understanding of the material was developing.

However, something far more glorious was also happening. In the past, maintaining mediocrity with Cs and Bs was second nature to her. Yet when she began failing several classes and was in danger of not graduating, she reached into pockets of potential that turned out to be secret treasures.

Over the years, Shannon told herself she was stupid. Yet the quizzes and tests she'd been acing recently belied that notion. Consequently, she was beginning to realize that Sarah's shadow, which had been her permanent residence, was merely an invention of her own mind. Sure, she'd never get a perfect score on the SATs or win a scholarship to Berkeley. Still, she could feel a long-dormant intelligence beginning to bloom. Moreover, whereas Sarah excelled at academics, it was Shannon who, early on, had been praised for her creativity. In fact, her painting of Gandalf, the wizard from *The Hobbit* and *The Lord of the Rings*, had been in the display case at Salem Hyde Elementary. Additionally, she had won a poetry contest in middle school. However, a combination of puberty, high school, and her parents' crumbling marriage created a storm of insecurity, and she sought refuge beneath a shroud of indifference. But her hiding place wasn't working anymore, and she needed to come out.

The sun began to sink into Onondaga Lake, the most polluted lake in the United States, as Shannon was finishing her last problem. Though her head hurt, she was proud of herself for weathering a storm of parabolas and coefficients.

The clock on her phone said seven-fifteen, which meant it was almost time to meet Frankie. Although she still hadn't figured out what she was going to tell him. Driving down Butternut Street, past crack houses that used to be nice homes, she considered circuitous explanations of the magical orb. However, these tales sounded just as crazy as the truth, so she decided to be honest.

When Shannon pulled up to his house, a crescent moon was beginning to rise. Walking up the driveway, she saw him working on his truck in the garage with a clip light dangling from the hood.

"Need any help?" she asked.

"Nope. I got it," he said, attaching cables to a brand new battery.

An awkward silence filled the space between them, so she pointed to the treehouse. "Remember we used to chill up there?"

"Bagshot Row," he said, referring to the row of Hobbit holes beneath Bag End.

"That's right!" Shannon shouted. "I thought you had forgotten."

"Nope, I didn't forget." He wiped his hands on a rag. "So, what's up?"

His question implied a time limit on their conversation, and it flustered her. "Well, first of all, do you think we could be friends again?" She hadn't planned on asking this, but now she couldn't take it back.

"I thought we were friends," he replied dispassionately.

"Come on, Frankie," she countered. "We haven't talked in months."

He folded the prop rod, and the hood closed with a bang, "Listen, Shannon, I don't have time for this."

"Time for what?" she asked.

"Time for your crap!" he snapped. "I mean, do you even realize how selfish you are?"

She heard herself ask, "How am I selfish?"

"You want me all to yourself like one of your precious baseball cards," he continued.

"What do you mean, Frankie?"

"According to you, my friends are losers, and all the girls I date are bimbos. You don't want me to have any life outside of you, and when I finally find someone—" He stopped. "Just leave me alone."

His words hurt, but they were accurate. When he started to walk away, Shannon said, "Frankie, you're right. I've been a clingy, selfish, demanding bitch, and I'm sorry."

He stopped for a second and then continued toward his house.

"But listen, Frankie," she continued, "I still need to talk to you."

When he walked up the back stairs and started to open the screen door, panic set in, and Shannon screamed, "PLEASE!"

"Shannon, be quiet." He thrust his thumb toward the house. "My folks."

Knowing she had to lasso him before he went inside, she said, "Frankie, I don't think your Aunt Mary is crazy."

He closed the door and faced her. "What did you say?"

"Remember you said she saw visions in that ball you gave me?" Shannon asked.

"Yeah?"

"Well, I've seen them, too," she admitted.

"You saw my uncle crash into a tree?" Frankie scoffed.

"No, but I've seen other stuff."

"Like what?" he asked incredulously.

"Will you please come down here and talk to me?" she pleaded.

"Listen, Shannon," he put his hand on the doorknob, "I heard about your dad getting married, and I'm sorry you're having a hard time."

"Yeah, but this has nothing to do with—"

"And I also heard about your little scene in Cameron's class," a strain of contempt had crept into his voice, "but I can't be a part of this."

"Part of what?" Two small tears slipped down her cheeks.

"Part of your attention scheme," he answered.

"My—"

"Like pulling the fire alarm back in tenth grade, remember?"

When Frankie walked inside and closed the door, Shannon stood there for a moment, looking up at the treehouse. There was a time, she reflected, when he would have believed her. But those days, like a lot of other things, were gone. As she drove home, the familiarity of her neighborhood had somehow vanished. Although the streets and houses were the scenery of her youth, everything seemed strange and hostile.

Her mother had a billion questions about the ancient library that had been saved from the wrecking ball several times. When Shannon informed her that everything looked the same, including the murals of Cinderella and the Pied Piper on the first floor, the inquiries transitioned to homework. While her mom's interest was genuine, Shannon also sensed a subtle interrogation because she had never gone to the library before. So she decided to extinguish all doubts by having her mom check her precalculus homework with one of the one free pencils the branch gave out. Unfortunately, she had forgotten everything about parabolas, but at least now she believed her daughter's story.

When her mom left for work, Shannon began ruminating about her encounter with Frankie. After beating herself up for a while, she decided to finish reading *A Tale of Two Cities* because she had a paper due on it the next week. The poignant ending left her feeling raw—Sydney Carton, a cynical, self-loathing drunk, had flipped the script of his existence by literally giving his life for someone else. Even though he was just a fictional character, Shannon wondered if she would ever be capable of doing such a selfless thing. Considering her recent behavior, the odds were against it. But a tiny flame in her soul, like a trembling star on a winter night, told her she could attain a similar grace. Just then, the bell wreath on the front door jingled, meaning Sarah was home. However, rather than taking a step toward magnanimity by mending fences with her sister, she scooted up the stairs like a frightened mouse and went into her bedroom.

The orb was clearly happy to see her because it was the color of spring skies and childhood curtains. As it turned out, Shannon was strangely happy to see the glass ball as well. After changing into pajamas, she grabbed one of the cheap romance novels she loved to read at night and sat in her beanbag chair. However, the hackneyed plot wasn't keeping her attention, and her mind kept drifting all over the place. She thought about her baseball cards, her dad, the crescent moon in the sky, the orchid in Mrs. Walker's office, and the coffin in her dream.

When she heard Sarah come up the stairs, brush her teeth, and then close the door of her bedroom, Shannon looked at the clock; it was eleven-thirty. As if a hand reached out and grabbed her thoughts, she wondered where her sister had been. In fact, her twin had been coming home late recently, which was odd for a girl who was usually in bed by nine. In the past, Sarah had stayed out late with Chet sometimes, but since they'd broken up, it was highly unlikely that she was with him. While sifting through myriad possibilities of her sister's whereabouts, she noticed that her windows had turned pink. Thinking, perhaps, that a light had gone on next door, she looked outside. However, her neighbor's house was as black as ink. With a shudder, Shannon realized that the source of the light was behind her.

After turning around, the Pink Moon she had seen in a previous vision was drifting around the perimeter of the orb like a balloon without a string. When Shannon sat on the bed, the moon dissolved, and Frankie's treehouse appeared with light seeping through gaps in the cedar planks. Slowly, the gaps grew wider, and she could see a candle stuck in a Coke bottle with wax dripping down the sides. A small breeze bent the flame toward a dark corner where recumbent figures stirred. As the hazy shapes came into focus, the frail light shifted to a trail of clothes scattered on the floor. As she began to perceive a yellow thong and bra, the flame tilted back and the vague figures became naked bodies wrapped in a libidinous embrace. Because the girl was beneath the boy, Shannon couldn't see her face, although the strands of blond hair leaking onto the floor let her know it was Sarah. Unable to endure anymore, Shannon whispered, "STOP," and the ball went dark. Now she knew where her sister had been at night. Furthermore, she also knew that Frankie, who supposedly hadn't seen Sarah in months, was a lying sack of shit.

As she looked out the window at the crescent moon that was sinking in the horizon, an idea flew into her mind: She would catch them! She'd burst in on them in the act of their sin and drive them out of Eden with a flaming sword like Jophiel in the Bible. After googling lunar phases, she realized that the next Pink Moon was due to arrive on Friday. All she had to do was wait.

EVEN THOUGH SHE woke up to a bright blue sky and birds chirping, Shannon wished she could wave her hand and blot out the morning. Because today was her first meeting with Mrs. Walker since her embarrassing scene in government, and she wasn't looking forward to it. While she could evade her mother with roundabout replies and evasive anecdotes, her counselor saw right through her machinations. If Shannon wasn't honest, she'd be filleted like a fish.

During English class, a debate erupted about *A Tale of Two Cities*. The dispute centered around Sydney Carton's motivation for saving Darnay's life. Piper Martin, the obnoxious know-it-all, said that it was simply a device to reiterate the theme of resurrection. Annie Belmont, another bigmouth, said that it was a hackneyed ploy to show the continuing carnage of the French Revolution. Normally, Shannon never spoke up during class, but these two windbags were driving her nuts.

"Guys, you're missing the point."

When Shannon spoke, Piper gave her an incredulous glance and said in a haughty voice, "Well, then please enlighten us, Delaney."

"Happy to," Shannon shot back. "He did it because he loved Lucie and her child, and he didn't want their lives destroyed by the death of Darnay. There weren't any *devices* or *ploys.*" She made imaginary quotes with her fingers to mock their crude attempts at erudition.

"On the surface, that's why he did it," Annie Belmont chimed in, "but his deeper motivation—"

"Deeper?" Shannon cut her off. "What can be deeper than loving someone so much you give your life for them?"

"Spare us the sermon," Piper said. "You're not grasping the subtext."

"Maybe not," Shannon replied. "But at least I'm not regurgitating things I read on SparkNotes."

After Shannon's comment, one person started to clap. Then another joined in, and soon the room was filled with applause. Rather than stopping it, Mr. Reed started clapping, too.

Her next class was math, and the most annoying thing about the subject was the incessant cycle of new material. Every time Shannon started to grasp a concept, the teacher moved onto something else. It was like leaving a city the minute you made friends. She had just begun to feel good about parabolas and now they were beginning inverse functions, which sounded as pleasant as root canal. While taking notes, images of Sarah and Frankie naked on the treehouse floor flooded Shannon's mind, and her pencil snapped in half. This elicited stares from startled classmates. Fortunately, however, someone's phone chimed, and as everyone watched Mr. Michaels confiscate the device, she calmly dropped the wooden remains into her bag and grabbed another pencil.

They were given the last fifteen minutes of class to start their homework. Normally, Shannon cherished this opportunity because it was less she had to do later. However, her meeting with Mrs. Walker was drawing near, and she wasn't sure how to handle it. Deep down, the teen wanted to tell her counselor about the orb. But Frankie didn't believe her, and she couldn't bear the thought of another door slamming in her face. Furthermore, she didn't want Mrs. Walker to think she was insane.

When the bell rang, Shannon grabbed her books and headed to her appointment. Since the marking period ended today, there was a swarm of upset kids in the guidance office, which made Shannon ponder an interesting paradox—bad students only cared about their grades when report cards came out. They goofed around in class and happily failed tests, but when they received an F, these same kids screamed and cried like banshees. At least when Shannon was bombing her classes, she was aware of it. However, her thoughts shifted when she saw Bobo's younger brother, Nathan, leaving Mrs. Walker's office.

"What's up, Big Nate?" Shannon asked.

"Not much," he replied. "Gotta get my grades up."

Shannon remembered having this same conversation with Bobo there last January, and the coincidence made a chill run down her spine.

"How's your bro?" she asked.

"He's good," the boy replied. "He's working at Mickey D's."

It occurred to her that Bobo would be here right now and not shoveling fries for minimum wage at McDonald's if she hadn't pulled him into her plot.

"Okay, Mr. Nathan." Mrs. Walker came up behind him. "Time to get those grades up."

"Okay," he said. "I'll try."

"Don't try," the counselor rejoined. "Just do it."

"Okay, Mrs. Walker," the boy answered.

As he was leaving, someone bumped into Nathan, and he

dropped his books. Shannon, in a vain attempt to repair her broken karma, helped him collect the fallen texts.

"Thanks, Shan," he said before walking out the door.

"Well, missy, how are you today?" Mrs. Walker asked.

"I'm good," the teen replied.

"Well, come on in, girl."

Shannon followed her counselor into the office and sat down. She had thought Mrs. Walker would start grilling her about the incident in government last week. But her counselor simply turned toward her computer and clicked a few buttons on the keyboard. "Well, well, well," she said. "You still got a B in Precalculus?"

"Yes." Shannon blushed. "I've been working my tail off in there."

"What's the secret of your success?"

"Well, Mookie and Echo have been tutoring me, and I'm doing my homework," Shannon replied.

"It's paying off," her counselor perused the screen again. "And you're finally passing English!"

"Yeah, I know." Shannon smiled. "I'm actually starting to like that class."

"Will miracles never cease?" Mrs. Walker faced her. "Girl, you're passing everything, which means you're out of my doghouse."

"Wait... what?" the befuddled teen asked.

"You're off my at-risk list, so you're free to go."

Though Shannon should have been delighted, a feeling of dread wrapped around her like a damp blanket because she wanted to tell her counselor about the orb.

"Mrs. Walker," Shannon began.

"Yes?"

"Did you hear about what happened to me in government?"

"Oh, I hear lots of things." She took off her glasses and cleaned them with a tissue.

"Well," Shannon continued, "I sort of freaked out in there."

"Tell me about it," her counselor urged.

"Well, I want to, but—"

"But what?" Mrs. Walker asked.

The coffin from the vision blossomed in her mind, and suddenly Shannon felt trapped in it again. After a moment, she said, "I don't want you to think I'm crazy."

"Do you think you're crazy?"

"No… but—"

"But what?" her counselor pressed.

"Sometimes I'm not so sure."

"Listen, honey," Mrs. Walker put her glasses back on, "crazy people don't wonder if they're crazy. They're just crazy. Now tell me what's going on."

Shannon's mind exploded with images—Frankie and Sarah beneath the streetlamp, the Pink Moon above the treehouse, Bobo's birthday. It was as if the orb was daring her to tell.

"Mrs. Walker," she began. "Do you believe in magic?"

"Of course I do!"

"Wait." The images in Shannon's mind retreated. "You do?"

"Sure!"

"Well," Shannon slowly began as if testing the temperature of water with her toe, "like what kind?"

"See that orchid over there?" Mrs. Walker pointed to the flower with the floppy purple blossoms by the window.

"Yes," Shannon replied. "I love that plant."

"Guess how old it is."

"I don't know." Shannon considered. "Ten years old?"

"Guess again," Mrs. Walker said.

"More or less?" Shannon asked.

"More," the counselor urged.

Shannon thought about her mother's fern, Alice, that had lived twenty years and said, "Twenty?"

Mrs. Walker shook her head.

"Older than twenty?!"

"That plant is a hundred years old," her counselor said.

"Get out of here!" Shannon erupted.

"I kid you not. My grandmother brought it over from Jamaica."

"But wait." Shannon shoved the air with her hands. "How can it be that old?"

"Magic," Mrs. Walker said.

"Well, what kind of magic?"

"See that little pouch over there?" Her counselor pointed to a little white bag at the stem of the plant.

"Yes," Shannon affirmed.

"That's my nana's scapular."

"What's a scapular?" Shannon asked.

"It's a charm."

"Well, what's in it?" Shannon inquired.

"I'm not really sure," Mrs. Walker replied. "Herbs, I think." She stood up and walked over to the orchid.

"Do you really think it works?" Shannon asked.

"Girl, my nana wore it and she lived to be one hundred and fifteen years old." The woman brushed one of the blossoms with her hand. "And now her orchid wears it."

"Well, why don't you wear it?" Shannon asked.

"Cuz, I don't want to live to be one hundred and fifteen."

"Okay, well," Shannon took a deep breath, "would you believe it if someone told you they saw stuff?"

Her counselor came back and sat down. "What kinds of stuff?"

"Mrs. Walker," Shannon stared at her own hands that seemed separate from her body and said, "it's gonna sound so weird."

"Any more weird than magic charms and hundred-year-old plants?"

Although she wanted to tell her counselor about the orb, Shannon hesitated because she didn't want to be carted off to Hutchings, the local loony bin. But more importantly, disclosure meant an end to her private world, a world of beauty and power that was all her own. However, as she was about to divulge her secret, there was a knock at the door signaling the arrival of Mrs. Walker's next appointment.

"Mrs. Walker," Shannon stood up, "can we still meet every week even if I'm not on the at-risk list?"

"Of course we can, honey." Mrs. Walker walked her to the door. "In fact, you don't have to wait till next week. Come see me anytime."

11

April was usually a muddy time in New York. However, the month brought abundant sunshine this year, and many flowers, including azaleas and marigolds, bloomed ahead of schedule. Additionally, new buds painted Shannon's cherry tree pink, and she fondly remembered playing with Sarah beneath the glowing canopy of branches in her backyard. However, this memory was quickly tainted because the rosy hue reminded her of the phantasmal moon above Frankie's treehouse and the naked lovers on the floor. Because it was psychotic and creepy, she had all but abandoned her plan of bursting in on them until something happened that sealed her date with fate.

On Friday morning, Sarah came bouncing down the steps in a strangely cheerful mood, and as she bent over to put on her shoes, Shannon caught a glimpse of her yellow thong and remembered the underwear in the vision. A snake of jealousy coiled around her heart when she realized Sarah's good mood was due to her date with Frankie tonight. Additionally, while the deceit and treachery of the lovers infuriated her, it was the location of their rendezvous that angered her the most. The treehouse was a sacred place containing Shannon's precious memories of Frankie. It was a map of all the places they visited, including the Shire, Bree, and the Misty Mountains. Additionally, it was where they unwrapped the beautiful gift of their friendship. Consequently, Sarah and Frankie having sex there was an act of heresy. It was akin to vandalizing a statue of the Virgin Mother, and Shannon wanted revenge.

The day crawled by like a snail on a hot sidewalk. Because most teachers had run out of patience and enthusiasm by the end of the week, they usually assigned busy-work like practice problems or worksheets. So Fridays were not only long, they were also boring as hell. However, as Shannon completed a review packet in government about the public trials and social executions during McCarthyism, she had a diabolical idea. She would take pictures of the lovers with her phone and post the images on Snapchat so that their lives would be destroyed like all the "commies" blacklisted during the Red Scare.

When the last bell of the day finally rang, Shannon packed up her things and headed home. Though night was still a few hours away, she tasted vengeance on her tongue. She immediately headed into her bedroom to see if the Pink Moon had already risen in the orb. Yet it merely reflected the sky filled with wispy clouds, so she lay down on her bed and waited. Her mother was at work, Sarah wasn't home, so the house was as quiet as a tomb. Despite her merry-go-round of thoughts, she dozed off. After a short trip through the netherworld of sleep, the sound of laughter pulled her back to consciousness. At first, Shannon thought the mirth had been part of a dream, but while staring at the ceiling, she heard the giggles again.

After a quick glance at the orb, which was silent and blue,

she looked out her window and saw her five-year-old neighbor, Annabelle, playing with a friend in her yard. The two were encased in a shaft of sunlight that had slipped through the trees. The scene pierced Shannon's heart because it recalled her childhood when her backyard was the world and places like the store and post office were on other planets.

She remembered playing a game with Sarah call "Miss" where they took turns being grownups. Sometimes, one sibling would be a doctor and the other would be her patient. Other days, they drove fire engines or sailed over the mountains in a plane. She smirked at the bitter irony because both girls were in such a rush to leave the tranquility of childhood for the shark-infested waters of adolescence.

As the sun started to sink in the horizon, Shannon began planning her mission. Judging by the brightness of the moon in the last vision, she figured that the lovers would be wrapped in sin around nine. Which meant she'd have to leave the house at eight-thirty because Frankie lived a few blocks away. However, it occurred to her that her mother would be home by then. Therefore, she had to have some kind of reason for going out. The library was a possible destination, but then her mom would offer her the truck, and she couldn't take that rattling shit-box since Frankie and Sarah would hear it a mile away. While making frittatas, Shannon pondered other alibis, but they all seemed spurious.

When her mother came home, the lovely aroma of asparagus, roasted red peppers, and feta cheese that Shannon had waiting made her smile. After eating, they talked for a little while. But because her mother had just finished a twenty-four-hour shift at the hospital, she began hiding yawns with her hand. Although Shannon suggested she go to bed, her mom wanted to watch a movie since this was what they normally did on Friday nights. Moreover, her mother probably felt guilty for not spending enough time with Shannon. Anxiety assailed Shannon while making popcorn because it was almost eight-thirty. However, her fears receded when she found her mother asleep on the couch in the living room.

Warm breezes stirring the dark leaves sounded like applause. Feeling compelled by the ghostly sound, Shannon took a shortcut through the park. The Pink Moon hovering above Sunnycrest Hill made her heart leap as if the gravity of the sphere was pulling her entrails out, and she ran down the summit. By the time Shannon got to Frankie's house, she was drenched in sweat. With luminous shards seeping through the cedar planks, the treehouse was exactly the way it appeared in the orb.

Walking up the lawn, only the hum of distant traffic could be heard. After opening the camera on her phone, she began climbing the wooden ladder nailed to the big maple's trunk. On the last step, Shannon looked up at the Pink Moon and took a deep breath. Then she pushed open the door, pressed the shutter button, and the small room exploded with light as frightened eyes and naked limbs flew around like a flock of startled birds. Because the candle had tipped over, darkness descended once the flash disintegrated. However, after a momentary hush, a girl's cry crept out of the gloom— it was sorrow, shame, and dread rolled into one pitiful sound that made Shannon flee. By the time she reached the street, the lament had become a series of shrieks that shredded the night sky like a pair of scissors.

At the top of Sunnycrest Hill, Shannon stopped to catch her breath as the reality of her actions set in. The Pink Moon still hovered above the city, and the lights of houses still punctured the darkness. Yet everything had changed because her psychotic deed had lifted her from the pages of normalcy and placed her in the annals of psychopaths that lived in the city. There was Canine Pete on Salina Street who lived with a hundred dogs and Matches Mahoney on Rugby Road who lit her husband on fire. Now there was Crazy Shannon, the peeping tom who stole souls with her camera. However, the worst part was knowing that the screams that tore the night apart hadn't come from Sarah.

On the front steps of her house, Shannon decided to delete the picture. But before burying it in the cemetery of cyberspace, she needed to look at it. A second after touching the photo app with her thumb, Ali Clark's terrified face lit up the screen—the flash filled the girl's open mouth with lightning; her eyes were red pools of terror. Looking at the image, Shannon recalled Ali's sad past. Her parents were killed by a drunk driver coming back from a Super Bowl party three years ago. Apparently, a man with a blood alcohol level of 0.4 driving a Hummer hit their Toyota Corolla from behind going ninety miles per hour. Because the couple weren't wearing any seatbelts, both flew through the windshield, and their broken bodies were found on opposite sides of the road. After that, Ali moved in with her grandmother, Delilah, a shiftless septuagenarian enjoying a carefree life of bingo, book clubs, and painting lessons at the senior center. The old lady resented the teenager she'd inherited (if the truth be told, Delilah had been a lazy, lousy mother, too, but now her age provided an excuse for her shortcomings). Shortly after this, Ali began wearing skin-tight T-shirts and lots of makeup, and rumors about her spread as often as her legs did. However, Shannon remembered the little girl who wore a pink dress to Easter Mass. While others saw a floozy, Shannon saw a soul crushed by tragedy, but rather than comforting this damaged person, she had terrorized her.

Her mother was still asleep on the couch when Shannon came inside. Though it felt as if she had traveled to hell and back, she had only been gone thirty minutes. Suddenly, a bout of nausea drove her into the bathroom. After vomiting copiously, she looked in the mirror, and the zombie staring back at her with bleached skin and blood-red eyes sparked an epiphany—the orb had tricked her.

Shannon had expected to see the ball ablaze with scornful images when she went into her bedroom. However, it merely reflected the necklace of stars hanging in the sky outside. Then she sat down on the bed, looked deeply into the glass, and said, "Why did you lie to me?" At first, the orb remained unchanged as if it were oblivious to its own machinations. But when Shannon threatened to throw it against the wall, images started swirling inside the glass. First, hazy curtains turned into shirts as her closet slowly emerged from the mist.

"Okay, so you're mad at me for putting you in the closet?" As if ignoring her question, the clothes became cedar planks, and the inside of the coffin appeared again. Then came the heavy feet, the muted prayers. But before the trap door could open above a glass sea, Shannon picked up the ball and screamed, "I swear to God I'll smash you if you don't tell me what the fuck you want!" After she yelled, the chimerical coffin smashed against the glass with such force that the ball slipped out of her hands and landed on the bed. After rolling across the blankets, the orb settled by her pillow and went dark. Once her heart stopped racing, Shannon sat down as a parade of faces swept through her mind—Maryanne, Bobo, Sarah, Frankie. All relationships damaged by the orb. But

Shannon knew these people were appetizers and that the ball wouldn't be satisfied until it devoured her.

12

———

The bright sunshine pouring through her window the next morning annoyed Shannon because it contradicted her miserable state of being. When our hearts are sour, we want the rain to wrap us in its damp embrace. Yet the weather follows its own moods, not ours. When she looked at her phone, there was one message from Frankie that said, *WTF,* and another from a cell she didn't recognize saying, *please call me,* which she assumed was Ali. The last thing she wanted to do was talk to the girl she had wronged. However, the sooner she owned her shame, the sooner it would begin to fade. Before calling, Shannon thought about putting the orb back in the closet, but she didn't want to anger the spirit again.

After dialing the number, a frail voice answered. "Hello?"

"Hi, Ali, it's Shannon."

"Hold on." A whisper followed by footsteps and a closing door. "Shannon," Ali finally said on the verge of tears. "Why did you do this to me?"

"Ali." Pain gripped Shannon's heart. "I'm so sorry. I didn't realize it was you."

"Yeah, but," her voice trembled, "why would you do that to anyone? It's so horrible."

"I know. It's a long story," Shannon said, realizing that no excuse could justify such a hideous act. "I didn't mean to hurt you."

"But you *did* hurt me." Ali's voice finally broke, and a torrent of muffled sobs filled the phone.

"Listen, Ali, I deleted the picture right away, and I promise I will never, ever tell a living soul."

A voice finally emerged from the snivels. "If my grandmother finds out, she'll kick me out and I'll have no place to go."

"Ali," Shannon said, "your grandmother will never find out. I swear to God."

"Okay." Ali's voice finally calmed. "You promise?"

"I swear to God on my mother's life."

"Okay. Shannon, can I ask you one thing?" Ali inquired.

"Of course!"

"Who did you think was in there with Frankie?"

For a moment, the world stopped spinning because Shannon couldn't answer this honestly, but she was so sick of lying that she felt compelled to tell the truth. However, the truth was not only bizarre, it also incriminated Sarah, so she gave an evasive reply.

"To be honest with you, Ali, I don't really know what I was thinking."

"Okay," Ali replied. "Thank you for calling me. Goodbye."

After putting her phone on the bed, Shannon looked at

the orb filled with the morning sky and said bitterly, "Are you happy now?" However, the ball remained silent and blue as if she hadn't spoken at all.

Her mother and Sarah were at the kitchen table with a letter and untouched pancakes between them when Shannon came downstairs. She could tell they were talking about something serious because the air felt like cement.

"Good morning, kiddo," their mom said. "Want some breakfast?"

"Sure," Shannon replied. "What's going on?"

"Sarah has some news," their mother said while walking over to the stove.

"What is it?" Shannon asked.

"Oh, it's not a big deal," Sarah answered and sipped her coffee.

"Sure, it's a big deal." Her mother came back with Shannon's pancakes. "Well, if you won't tell her, I will."

"Go ahead then," her sister urged.

"Sarah's leaving the nest a little sooner than we thought."

"What do you mean?" Shannon asked. "When?"

"May 27th," Sarah said without looking up.

"But graduation is June 2nd," Shannon protested.

"She already graduated." Her mother picked up the letter and waved it.

"But how did you already graduate?" Shannon asked.

"She's been doubling up with night classes," their perturbed parent continued, "and I didn't even know about it."

Shannon felt stupid because she had been wrong about her sister's whereabouts, and a shard of pain went through her heart because the reality of her sister leaving finally hit her. "But why would you want to leave sooner?" she asked.

"I want to get some of my prerequisites done before the fall term begins." Although Sarah's excuse was plausible, Shannon could tell that her sister had ulterior motives for leaving sooner, and getting away from her bitchy twin was probably one of them.

"But," Shannon pressed, "don't you want to walk across the stage? I mean, you'll never get another high school graduation."

"Oh, I've been on that stage enough times," Sarah replied.

"But it's not just about you," her mother interjected. "I want to see both my girls walk across that stage, and your dad is planning on coming, too."

"Dad already knows what I'm doing."

"What?!" Her mother screamed. "You told your dad but not me?!"

"You're never home!" Sarah yelled back. "When the hell am I supposed to talk to you?"

Without saying another word, their mother threw her plate and cup in the sink and tramped upstairs. After the sound of her stormy exit receded, Shannon said, "You should have told her."

"Listen," Sarah stood up, "the last thing I need right now is a lecture from Cruella De Vil, so spare me."

Shannon began to speak, but her sister cut her off. "But I'm sure you, especially, are thrilled I'm leaving, so don't pretend you're not." Then she tossed her untouched pancakes into the garbage, dropped her dishes into the sink, and walked out the door.

Looking at a faded square on the wall where a calendar used to hang, Shannon thought about how hard this year had been for Sarah—leaving Chet, finally finding love, and losing that, too. No wonder she wanted to go away. Shannon had sabotaged her sister's chance at happiness and vowed to fix her mistake. But the haunted orb had to be resolved first, and this, ironically, started with the person whose name appeared on her ringing phone.

She pressed the talk button. "Hi, Frankie."

"Shannon!" he barked. "Are you fucking crazy or what?"

"Yup," she replied. "Totally fucking crazy. How about you?"

"Why did you fucking do that?"

"Because I'm crazy," she answered, "but I thought we already established that."

"Listen, Shannon," he growled.

"No, you listen! You're the reason we're in this mess, and you're gonna help me clean it up!"

"I'm not gonna help you do anything," he said.

"Oh, yes you are," Shannon countered. "You're going to meet me at Mr. B's statue in thirty minutes or I'll post that picture on TikTok." Although she had already deleted the picture, she knew the threat of exposure was the only way to get Frankie to cooperate.

"You want me to meet you at school?" he asked.

"Yes," she replied.

"But why?" Frankie sounded disoriented.

"Because it's Saturday and nobody will be there. See you soon."

It was already starting to sprinkle when Shannon got to school, so she ducked beneath an awning and waited for Frankie. Looking at the statue of Harvey Baldwin (aka Mr.

B), Shannon wondered what this War of 1812 veteran would think of the world today where battles were waged by cowards on the flagitious fields of social media. Amidst her musings, Frankie's F-150 pulled up as it started to pour, and she saw him waving her over. After a mad dash, she hopped into his truck.

"You wouldn't really post that picture, would you?" he asked sheepishly.

"No, Frankie," Shannon replied. "I already deleted it. Here." She handed him her phone. "You can see for yourself."

After thumbing through her pictures, he handed back her device. "Then why did you threaten to put it on TikTok?"

"Because I knew that was the only way to get you here," she admitted.

"Okay, Shannon." He gripped the steering wheel and took a deep breath. "Why did you do that last night?"

"Because I thought you were with Sarah."

"Sarah!" he yelled. "I haven't talked to her since Christmas!"

"I know that now," she said.

"This is so fucked up!" He started the truck. "Have a nice life, Shannon."

"Turn off the truck, Frankie."

"Don't tell me what to—"

"Turn off the fucking truck!" Something in her tone must have scared him because he immediately acquiesced to her demands. "Now listen," she took a deep breath. "you have to help me."

"Why should I help you?" Frankie inquired.

"Because this is your fault," she answered.

"How is it my fault?" he asked.

"Remember the glass ball you gave me? The Palantir?"

"Oh, not this again," he said, recalling the last time she broached this subject at his house.

"Frankie, that fucking ball is haunted!" she screamed.

"Shan—"

"Your great aunt isn't crazy, Frankie! She was telling the truth!"

"You expect me to believe that you saw *visions*." He made quotes with his fingers to display his incredulity.

"How do you think I knew about you and Sarah?" Shannon collected herself.

"She told me you saw us," he replied.

"Yes, I saw you kissing beneath the streetlamp in front of my house."

"Okay, so what does that prove?" Frankie asked.

"Why do you think I was looking out my window at two a.m.?"

"I don't know. Maybe you had insomnia," he replied.

"Frankie," she said, "I saw you two kissing in the ball two weeks before it happened."

"Come on, Shannon," he scoffed.

"And how did I know you'd be with a girl in your tree-house last night?"

His skepticism was shaken by this question, but he grasped for a logical solution. "Who knows? Maybe you've been spying on me."

"Hmmm, yeah," she responded. "From where? A tree? A bush?"

"Who knows? Maybe your mom's truck."

"Frankie, you'd hear that tank coming a mile away."

"Well—"

"Ali had on a yellow thong last night, right?" she asked.

"Shannon," he turned crimson, "I don't fucking know."

"Don't you look at their underwear before you take them off?"

"Okay, okay," he said. "She had a yellow thong, so what? You could have seen that when you took the picture."

"But I didn't!" she cried.

"Prove it!" he demanded.

Shannon was stumped for a moment, but then she remembered that photos weren't completely gone until they were removed from the deleted album. "Fine," she said, pulling her phone out of her pocket. "You can see for yourself."

"But I thought you said you got rid of it!"

"I did, but I just remembered there's still a copy in my deleted files." She opened up the picture and held up her phone. Frankie reached for the device, but she pulled it back. "Not so fast," she said. "Do you see any underwear in that picture?"

"No," he replied.

"Look closely." Shannon held it two inches away from his face. "Do you see a yellow thong?"

"No." He studied the photo with shame etched into his brow. "Now can I please get rid of it?"

"It's all yours." She handed him the phone, and he deleted the picture.

"Shannon, are you sure you don't have another copy?"

"Frankie, I swear to God on my mother's life I do not have another copy."

"Okay, well," he said, still clinging to logic by a thread, "you could have seen her underwear on the floor."

"Yup, and I could have seen the Easter Bunny, too, but I

didn't. Now listen, we need to talk to your Aunt Mary. Is she still at Van Dyke Nursing Home?"

"Yeah but—"

"Well, let's go," she said.

"Wait a second, Shannon," he protested. "We're not going there!"

"Why not?"

"Because she probably doesn't even know who I am anymore," he replied.

"How do you know? When was the last time you saw her?" she asked.

"I don't know. Sometime last year, I guess," he replied.

"Well, Frankie, it's time for a visit."

"Shannon, I'm not going," he said with conviction.

"Fine," she said, opening the door. "I'll walk."

"You're gonna walk there in the rain?" he scoffed. "It's like five miles away."

Shannon faced him with fierce eyes. "That ball has already destroyed my relationship with Sarah. I'm not waiting around to see what it has in store for me next." She started to get out of the truck, but Frankie stopped her.

"Okay, okay," he said. "Let's go."

Van Dyke Nursing Home at the top of Onondaga Hill began as a place for poor people with incurable ailments like tuberculosis and cancer in 1827, but it folded due to lack of funding and became an insane asylum in 1860. However, rumors of abuse, including straightjackets, forced isolation, electroshock therapy, and ice baths, closed the place down in 1924, and it stood empty for nearly twenty years. Then, in

1942, a business tycoon named Noah Van Dyke wanted to get rid of his elderly mother, so he bought the land, turned it into a nursing home, and his progenitor became the first resident.

Frankie's childhood was adorned with painful memories of this place—Christmas Eve, Holy Saturday, and June 15th, Aunt Mary's birthday, were sad days on the calendar because the frail woman in the faded green gown used to be his favorite person in the world. Before her eccentricities became concerns, and before Frankie's mom, a buyer for Nordstrom, began working from home, Aunt Mary was like a second mom to him. She drove him to school, helped with his homework, and read him stories at night on the divan in her bedroom. But when Frankie's mom found her talking to a glass paperweight in the attic (the sphere that now sat on Shannon's nightstand), she put her in Van Dyke.

However, this wasn't the first time Mary Dolan's behavior raised eyebrows. Twenty years before, when her brother, Mike, the neighborhood lush, received his third DUI, she begged him not to drive anymore because she claimed to have foreseen his grisly death in her mother's "cruinne," or globe. And when he crashed his '63 Fairlane into a tree and died, Mary was hysterical because she had warned everyone but nobody listened. For days and days after his death, Mary had sobbed, screamed, and wrung her hands, and they almost had her committed. But after the doctor prescribed a heavy dose of quaaludes, she seemed to find her balance again. Frankie's mom almost threw out the glass ball that had been the focus of Mary's mania, but she decided to keep it in the attic because it had been one of the only artifacts to survive her grandmother's journey from Ireland.

The lobby of Van Dyke had that sinister smell of urine

beneath bleach. Additionally, the long linoleum hallways lined with sedated ghosts in wheelchairs brought Frankie back to those first terrible weeks of Aunt Mary's confinement when she used to scream and cry every time they left. Over the years, however, Mary had learned to accept her fate, and she even looked mildly happy when it was time for her family to leave.

A colossal nurse at the front desk with forearms the size of fire hydrants frowned when Frankie spoke. "I'm here to see my great aunt, Mary Dolan."

"Name?" the corpulent caretaker asked.

"I'm Frankie McCormick."

The nurse studied his face for a moment, and then her steely eyes rolled like coins over to Shannon. "Name?"

"I'm Shannon Delaney, and I'm here with Frankie."

The woman turned to her computer screen, and her face became even more ghastly in the blue light. Then she clicked the mouse and said contemptuously, "It's been over a year since you've been here. She might not remember you."

Frankie felt ire rising in his throat, and he was tempted to assail her with a string of epithets, but his anger dissipated when he realized what she was—a pathetic gatekeeper enjoying a few moments of power in her otherwise ineffectual life.

"I know it's been a while, mam," he said disingenuously. "I sure hope she remembers me."

After giving Frankie and Shannon one more derisive look, the nurse slid the register toward them, pointed at a blank line with her pudgy finger, and said, "Sign here."

An orderly was pushing some old guy on a gurney bed into the only available elevator car, so they decided to take the stairs. As they ascended the three flights, Frankie kept stopping at the windows to point out landmarks of the city below, including the Carrier Dome and Onondaga Lake. Shannon feigned interest in his tidbits of information that she and every other Syracusan already knew. However, it was obvious that he was prolonging the imminent reunion with his great aunt.

As they walked down the hallway illumined by the sickly glow of fluorescent lights, Shannon felt him slowing down, so she grabbed his hand and pulled him the rest of the way. When they entered Room 316, an octogenarian wearing blue rosary beads was watching *The Price is Right* on a small television, and when she saw Frankie in the doorway, her eyes brightened.

"Frankie," she said, holding out her arms. "Is it really you?"

"It's really me, Auntie," he said, bending down and giving her a hug.

"Here." She handed him the television remote. "Turn that damn thing off, will ya?"

"Of course." Frankie extinguished the insipid show.

"And who's this lovely lass?" Aunt Mary asked.

"I'm Shannon, mam," Shannon answered.

"Shannon!" she exclaimed. "That's a river in Ireland, you know."

"Yes, mam."

"I used to fish there when we lived in Limerick. Caught trout this big." She measured a yard with her hands.

"Trout don't get that big, Auntie," Frankie said playfully.

"Oh, hush up, city boy. You wouldn't know trout from a tennis racket."

After they all laughed at her repartee, she said to Shannon, "Come a little closer, will ya, my dear?"

As the girl approached, Aunt Mary said, "Are you any relation to Haley Delaney?"

"Yes," Shannon said, amazed. "She's my mother."

"Glory be to God, you look just like her."

Nobody had ever said Shannon looked like her beautiful mother before, and the comment filled her with joy.

"Okay, Lassie, now pull that chair over and let me catch up with my favorite nephew."

As Aunt Mary and Frankie talked about family, friends, and the local news, Shannon was astonished by the old lady's memory and insight. The old lady remembered that Frankie's older sister, Megan, was a sophomore at Colgate and that the Syracuse basketball team had failed to make the tournament for the second year in a row. Furthermore, she had lucid opinions on everything ranging from transgenders to Donald Trump, and it occurred to Shannon that while this woman might not be able to do somersaults or drive a car, she was extremely perceptive and mentally sound.

After half an hour, a pencil-thin nurse with purple hair came in and fluffed Aunt Mary's pillows. Then she said, "All right, it's almost time for our nap."

"I don't want to take a nap, Sadie," the old woman protested. "I want to talk to my nephew."

"But don't you want to be all rested up for bingo tonight?"

"I don't give a fiddler's fart about bingo!" Aunt Mary insisted.

"Miss," Frankie interjected, "can we please have ten more minutes? I'm being deployed to South Korea tomorrow, and I don't know when I'll be back."

"Oh!" the nurse exclaimed. "Are you in the military?"

"Yes," he lied. "I'm in the Marines."

"Well, if that's the case, of course!" She curtseyed and ran abruptly out of the room like a startled goat.

Aunt Mary slapped her nephew on the knee. "God, I love a good liar," and the two shared a long, hearty laugh.

"But Frankie," Shannon said once the mirth subsided, "what will you say the next time you come? She thinks you're going to Asia?"

"Don't worry about that imbecile," the venerable dame said. "She has the IQ of a goldfish."

After their dwindling conversation became the awkward silence that preceded a painful goodbye, Frankie said, "Auntie, Shannon wants to talk to you about something."

"Oh." She turned her bright eyes on Shannon. "What is it, my dear?"

"Well," Shannon's thoughts were jumbled, "I'm not quite sure where to begin."

"Start at the beginning," the old woman said kindly.

"Well, Frankie gave me something of yours, and I think," she looked around to make sure they were alone, "I think it might be haunted."

Frankie could see that his aunt had no idea what Shannon was talking about, so he said sheepishly, "The cruinne, Auntie. I gave her the cruinne."

When Mary heard this, she turned as white as a sheet and scolded her nephew. "Now why in the hell did you do that?"

"Well," Frankie blushed, "Mom was going to throw it out when she remodeled the attic and—"

"Well, you should've let her throw it out!" the old woman shouted. "I told you how dangerous it was!"

"Yeah but—" He stopped himself.

"You didn't believe me, did you?" Her words were as frail as autumn leaves.

"No, Auntie. I didn't," he said, looking down.

"What's a cruinne?" Shannon asked.

After frowning at her nephew for a few more moments, Aunt Mary said, "It's pronounced *cren-ya*, and it's Irish for globe. My mum bought it from a band of no-good tinkers."

"Tinkers?" Shannon inquired.

"Gypsies," the old woman replied.

"Well," Shannon continued, "what's wrong with it?"

"There's nothing wrong with the cruinne, my dear. It's what's inside it that's the problem."

"Can you guys please tell me what's going on?" Shannon asked.

Aunt Mary looked at Frankie for a long minute because answering Shannon's question meant revealing a family secret, and she wanted her nephew's permission. Additionally, she was reluctant to tell the tale because it meant unwrapping a sorrow that had been tucked away in the fabrics of time. However, Mary realized that she needed to help this girl who was, apparently, being tormented by the same spirit that had plagued her many years ago. Unfortunately, just as she was about to divulge her story, Sadie came back.

"Okay, folks, it's time to go," the nurse said.

"Has it been ten minutes already?" Aunt Mary asked.

"It's actually been fifteen, and it's time for that nap." Sadie fluffed the pillows again.

"I'll come back soon, Auntie," Frankie said as he leaned over and hugged her.

"Fine, fine," the elderly lady said. "Saturdays are the best because I don't have physical therapy, but any day is fine."

"Okay," Frankie said.

"It was nice meeting you, Miss Dolan," Shannon said.

"Call me Mary and give us a hug." She held out her arms.

When Shannon leaned in to embrace her, the old woman whispered, "Her name is Fiona, and Frankie can tell you the rest."

The rain had moved away, leaving fresh breezes behind that accentuated the pungent smell of decay inside Van Dyke, and walking across the lawn, both kids felt an effervescent feeling of freedom. When they got in the truck, Shannon said, "Frankie, who's Fiona?"

"Fiona?" he asked. "I have no idea. Why?"

"Your aunt said, *'Her name is Fiona, and Frankie can tell you the rest.'*"

After starting the truck and pulling out of the parking lot, he said, "I might have heard that name before, but I can't remember who she is."

"Well, what did your Aunt Mary tell you about that ball?" Shannon asked.

He scanned his memory and then said, "She told me about seeing my uncle crash into a tree, but that happened before I was born."

"But what else?" Shannon pressed. "She said you didn't believe her about something."

"Oh." He hesitated. "She told me to stay away from it because it was dangerous."

Shannon could tell he was withholding something. "Frankie, this is important! What else did she tell you?"

He turned on the windshield wipers for a second to remove a few drops of rain from the afternoon storm and finally replied, "She said she saw me die."

"What?!" Shannon cried. "How?"

"Well," he pulled onto the highway, "it's really stupid, but she said I drowned in a car."

"Why's that stupid?" Shannon protested. "People drown

in cars."

"Yeah, but she said I was in my Uncle Mike's '63 Fairlane, but that thing got totaled when he crashed it."

As Shannon stared out at the trees sailing by in the window, she tried to assemble the fragments of information about the cruinne to form a logical picture. Yet, aside from torturing random people, the spirit didn't seem to have a clear motive, and Shannon knew they were missing something.

"Frankie, we need to find out who Fiona is," she said.

"How are we going to do that?" he asked.

"Ask your mom," Shannon replied. "Maybe it's a distant relative or something."

"I can't," he said after a moment.

"Why not?" she inquired.

"Because my mom refuses to talk about Aunt Mary, and she'd be pissed off if she knew I went there today."

"What?!" Shannon cried. "She'd be mad at you for visiting your aunt?"

"Yeah," he responded.

"But didn't you and your mom used to visit her together?"

"Yeah, but last year Aunt Mary refused to give my mom control of her estate, and we stopped coming."

"So," Shannon tried to phrase this delicately but couldn't, "you guys don't visit anymore because of money?"

"Yup." Frankie swallowed.

"But that's not fair to you at all," Shannon said.

"I know," he agreed.

After getting off the highway, they drove down Teall Avenue past houses and yards that used to be nice before pride moved out and poverty moved in. Shannon could still see remnants of the vanquished charm—a bay window covered by plywood, a pawn shop below a faded Schrafft's Ice

Cream sign, and a chapel covered in graffiti. She thought about the insidious nature of time because it didn't appear to be moving, but the moment you looked away, seconds became decades. And when you looked back, everything was either different or destroyed. For example, it seemed like only a minute ago when she and Sarah were inseparable—the "Bobbsey Twins," their grandmother, Tilly, used to call them because they did everything together—and now this stranger who used to be her best friend was moving to California in a month.

As they pulled into her driveway, the truck was filled with sorrow because both had been pondering sad things, and the sudden dusk didn't diminish their gloomy mood. When Shannon looked at Frankie, he was scanning her house with wary eyes.

"What's wrong?" she asked.

"Well," he swallowed, "would it be okay if I came in?"

"Sure," she said, "but what are you looking at?"

"Well, I want to make sure Sarah's not home."

"Oh, she's not," Shannon assured him. "She's never home anymore."

"Oh." He paused, and Shannon could tell by the pain etched into his face that Frankie still loved her sister very much. "I wanted to see something."

"The crumme?" Shannon inquired.

"Yeah," he answered.

"You want to see if I'm telling the truth?" she asked indignantly.

"No, no," he backpedaled. "I believe you, but I want to see it for myself."

"Okay," she accepted his feeble explanation, "but it's finnicky."

"What do you mean?" Frankie asked.

"It only shows things when it wants to."

"Okay, well, can I at least take a look, Shannon?"

"Of course," she said.

Walking up the stairs, Shannon doubted that the orb would show Frankie anything because it had gone dark whenever her mother came into her room. When they reached her door, she put her finger to her lips and motioned for Frankie to go in first. As they entered, the ball stayed blue for five seconds before slowly turning gray. However, Frankie failed to see the significance of its subtle transformation.

"Oh well," he said. "Thought I'd give it a shot."

"What do you mean?" Shannon said. "It was blue. Did you see it?"

"Yeah, but so what?" he scoffed. "It's reflecting the sky."

Shannon tapped him on the arm and pointed out the window at the bloated dusk that had swallowed blue long ago. "Holy shit," he whispered. "It's almost like—" He stopped himself.

"Like it knew you were here?" she asked.

Frankie stared at the dark ball and started to say more, but Shannon whispered, "Come on. Let's go downstairs."

She had planned on making coffee and talking in the kitchen, but a picture of Sarah on the landing made Frankie remember where he was, so he walked outside, with Shannon close behind.

"What are we going to do?" He sat down on the stoop.

"I don't know," Shannon replied.

"So," he said as the streetlamps turned on, "it shows you stuff about me and Sarah. I wonder what it wants?"

"Oh, there's more, Frankie. A lot more." Shannon told him all about the sapphire storms, the swaying lanterns, and the coffin. She told him about her duplicity during the Math Marathon, cheating on the government exam, and the truth behind Bobo's expulsion. Frankie's jaw was in his lap as he listened to her tale. But she could tell that he believed her, and this soothed her heart because for the first time since December, she was not alone in this paranormal labyrinth.

"Frankie, that thing has ruined my life—Sarah, you, all the people I care about are gone." Her eyes welled up with tears. "And look what I did last night," she continued. "I mean, only a real psychopath would do something like that."

"Well," Frankie said facetiously, "you are a bit of a psycho."

"Stop it!" She punched him in the arm as a small smile wrinkled her lips. "I'm being serious. I mean, Ali must think I'm deranged."

"So what?" he replied. "Let her think what she wants."

"But she's going to tell everybody—"

"She's not going to say a thing. Trust me," Frankie said. "Besides, she's not our problem. We have to figure out what we're going to do about that damned cruinne."

"Any suggestions?" Shannon asked.

He paused and then said, "We could smash it to pieces. I have a sledgehammer at my house."

"Yeah, but," she wiped her cheeks with her hoodie, "your Aunt Mary said it's what's inside the cruinne that's the problem, so smashing it won't work."

"Maybe we can mail it somewhere far away, like Pakistan. Whatever's inside couldn't get back from there," he offered.

As Shannon was considering Frankie's solution, the Meltzer twins pulled up in their mom's Subaru. After a moment, Sarah got out of the car. Following a wave goodbye to Mookie and Echo, she turned around. Wrapped in the yellow glow of the streetlamp where she had kissed Frankie last Christmas, Sarah was a tragic tableaux. Then she walked up the front steps and, without looking at them, went inside and closed the door. Without saying a word, Frankie got in his truck and drove away, as Shannon watched his red taillights dissolve in the night.

13

The next morning, Shannon watched her neighbors posing for a picture by their garage. When Annabelle, the youngest daughter, held up a green cross, she realized it was Palm Sunday. Happy memories of this holiday flooded Shannon's mind because it was a special day for so many reasons. First, she used to get a leafy crucifix from the priest, and later that day, after forty days of fish sticks, she'd eat lamb at Tilly's house. However, the most exciting thing about Palm Sunday was the fact that Easter was only a week away. Unlike Christmas, where kids had to behave or else they'd receive a lump of coal in their stockings, Easter was glorious day free of expectations. However, the best part of it was the egg hunt in the morning because a magical trail of bunny footprints (made by her dad with flour the night before) led to plastic orbs filled with Hershey's Kisses and jellybeans. While Shannon was reminiscing, she heard the shower running in the bathroom, which meant that her mother was getting ready for church. It had been ages since she'd gone to mass, and she wanted to accompany her.

Shannon put on her periwinkle dress and planned to get ready in the bathroom downstairs. However, on the landing, she saw Sarah's closed door, and before she could think about it, she was opening the curtains in her sister's room.

"Good morning, Sunshine!" Shannon said.

Sarah sat up and looked around. "What the hell are you doing?"

"Waking you up for church!"

"Go away!" her sister demanded.

Shannon opened the closet and thumbed through her twin's dresses. Then she pulled out a yellow one. "Here." She laid it on the bed. "This one's perfect."

"I'm not going to church with you!" Sarah snapped.

"You have to!" Shannon shot back.

"Why?"

"Because it's Palm Sunday!"

"Go away." Sarah rolled over.

Suddenly recognizing the futility of her demands, she changed her tune. "Listen, it would make Mom happy, so will you please come?"

When Sarah pulled a pillow over her head, Shannon accepted defeat and went downstairs, where she found her mom wearing a red dress for Palm Sunday. She remembered from her First Communion classes that the color represented the blood Christ shed on the cross. However, it wasn't the symbolism of the garment that caught Shannon's eye. Rather, it was the stunning woman standing in front of her. She normally saw her mother in scrubs after a twelve-hour shift and had forgotten how truly beautiful she was.

Shannon let out a piercing wolf whistle, and then she said, "Mom, you look gorgeous!"

"Why, thank you, darling."

"I just have to finish getting ready in here," Shannon pointed to the bathroom, "and then we can go."

"Are you going to mass with me?" Her mom's eyes lit up.

"Of course!" Shannon said ebulliently.

Her mother rubbed her back in circles of gratitude. "Come on, I'll help you."

Because three females lived in the house, the downstairs bathroom was a virtual beauty parlor loaded with mascara, lipstick, rouge, cotton balls, concealer, tweezers, and hairspray. Shannon applied eyeliner as her mother brushed her hair. Just as they were admiring their handiwork in the mirror, a muffled symphony of sounds, including closing doors, running water, and an electric toothbrush, came through the ceiling. Finally, after a few moments of silence, Sarah came running down the stairs wearing a pink dress.

"What happened to the yellow one?" Shannon asked to mask the joy she felt.

"I look like Big Bird in that thing," Sarah replied.

With damp eyes, their mother pulled the girls into a hug and said in a shaky voice, "Thank you." Hearing their mother's sadness made the daughters cry, and soon they were a trembling trio of despair. However, every tear that fell was a liberated sorrow. After five minutes, the sobs turned to sniffles. When they finally looked at themselves in the hall mirror, they started laughing because their makeup was destroyed and the family looked like a troupe of clowns.

"Guys, we need to fix our faces," Sarah said.

"There's no time for that," their mother said, looking at her watch. "We're already late."

"But we can't go to church looking like this." Shannon pointed at their reflection.

"Christ doesn't care what you look like," their mother said.

"But we care!" both girls screamed at the same time.

Their mother grabbed their hands like she did when they were little and dragged them out of the house. Once inside the truck, Shannon and Sarah did their best to salvage their faces, and by the time they reached Saint Vincent's, they were pasty but presentable.

As the family made their awkward journey into a pew, mumbling apologies, parishioners frowned at them because they had violated a secret code of church etiquette. Although people went to mass to be closer to God, most wanted to sit as far away from Him as possible, so the seats by the vestibule were a hot commodity. Consequently, if people came late it was tacitly understood that they would either stand in back or endure the walk of shame toward the pulpit. Therefore, those intruders who had the temerity to barge into the back pews were viewed with the same scorn as lepers and Sodomites.

Tilly had always said that God gave us the answers we needed, so after the silence that followed communion, Shannon steepled her fingers, closed her eyes, and asked Him what to do about the cruinne. She listened for an answer, but all she heard was the clatter of hassocks closing as people stood for the final blessing. At that moment, she felt the cold sting of disappointment. However, on her way out, a shaft of sunlight from the open door lit up a purple orchid in the vestibule, and a feeling of warmth spread through Shannon's body because her prayers had been answered.

~

THOUGH IT RAINED all night and the morning sky was lost in clouds, the orb was as blue as a field of forget-me-nots, and Shannon knew that the spirit in the glass was trying to make amends. But there was no need to fear its supernatural subterfuge today because she was going to talk to the one person who could help her out of this mess. After her mother dropped her off at school, Shannon made a bee line to the counseling office. Fortunately, there were a few spots available on Mrs. Walker's sign-up sheet, so she wrote her name in the ten o'clock slot and went to first period. On her way down the hall, she saw Ali Clark talking to a bunch of girls by the locker. When Shannon approached, they all stopped talking and glared at her. She pretended not to notice their disdain. However, the interaction gave her anxiety because once again she was a painted pony on the gossip merry-go-round.

As Mr. Reed diagrammed sentences on the board, Shannon looked around the room and wondered what everyone would be saying once news spread about her voyeurism. After pulling the fire alarm back in tenth grade, she had been plagued for weeks by names like "Pyro Pam." Additionally, pictures of flames were taped to her locker, and someone wrote "Shannon Was Here" in Sharpie above every fire alarm in the school.

Because taking pictures of naked people was worse than tampering with school property, she shuddered to think about the fallout. These thoughts were making her nauseous, so she decided to focus on something else to pass the time. Of course, listening to Mr. Reed was an option, but Shannon already knew about subjects and predicates. In fact, she felt his efforts were a waste of time because students who didn't know how to craft a sentence by twelfth grade were a lost cause. For a while, she watched the second hand orbit the face of the clock. Then, unfortunately, her eyes landed in the nether regions of Porky Peterson's butt crack. For some reason, this three-hundred-pound boy always sat in front of her, and over the years she had seen his fleshy fissure too many times. When she put her hands over her eyes to repel the vision, Shannon was instantly greeted by a memory.

It was the last band class before Christmas vacation at Salem Hyde Elementary School. As usual, she was sitting behind Porky with only a clarinet to protect her from his ominous crevice. Because he was leaning over to read his sheet music, his crack was bigger than ever, and she prayed that he didn't have a sudden fit of gas. Yet, whereas Shannon saw the appalling aperture as a threat, Neil Huff, the boy next to her, saw it as an opportunity. Thus, with the stealth of a cat, he put a candy cane down Porky's pants without the butterball noticing. After that, Tommy Santos dropped a pencil down there, followed by Roger Miller, who added a straw. Soon the corpulent boy's crack looked like a festive cornucopia. Unfortunately, Timmy Thompson got laughing so hard he fell out of his chair and knocked over the xylophone, and Mr. Straub, the band teacher, screamed at everyone for the last fifteen minutes of class. When Porky got up to leave, the candy cane, pencil, and straw slid into the void of his beefy abyss and were never seen again.

When Shannon returned from her memory, a few people, including Mr. Reed, were staring at her, and she realized that she had been laughing. After apologizing, she grabbed a copy of the worksheet that was being passed around and began the insipid assignment. While circling modifiers and helping verbs, she looked around and noticed that she had gone to school with most of these people her whole life. In fact, Neil

Huff, Roger Miller, and Tommy Santos, the boys who decorated Tiny's butt crack, were in the back row. Though they were taller and had facial hair now, they were still incorrigible clowns. Furthermore, she had gone to kindergarten with Piper Martin and Annie Belmont, the two sycophants in the front row. Then something occurred to her—Shannon had spent the past four years worrying about what these students thought. However, they were the same snotnosed brats who used to cry for their mothers and wet their beds, so she had nothing to be ashamed of.

After precalculus, Shannon headed to the copy room. As usual, the Xerox machine was out of paper, so she went into the supply closet to grab another ream. While opening the box, she heard voices, and looking through a gap in the door, Shannon saw Miss Britten, the health teacher, and Mr. Felice, the freshman comp teacher, enter the room. From what she could gather, they were talking about some incident that happened last week.

"But Miss Parish wouldn't expel a senior second semester," the man said.

"Why not?" Miss Britten replied. "She expelled that Billings kid a few weeks ago."

"Oh, yeah," Mr. Felice said. "But that's because he stole a MacBook."

"No, no," she corrected him. "Turns out those were never stolen. IT took them to install new security and never told anybody."

"But," said Mr. Felice, grabbing a stack of copies off the table, "I thought Cameron caught him in his room?"

"Well," Miss Britten lowered her voice, "the kid might've been in his classroom, but he wasn't stealing MacBooks."

"But then why—"

"Who cares?" she said as they were leaving. "The boy's a piece of trash."

As their voices faded, a cruel truth blossomed in Shannon's mind—Bobo hadn't been expelled for stealing because nothing had been stolen. The MacBook story had been a ruse to get rid of him because Miss Parish didn't like him or his family.

Shannon was furious about Bobo's expulsion, and she wanted to tell her counselor about it, but the cruinne was more urgent business. Mrs. Walker's door was open when she arrived. Without warning, panic assailed her because the moment of disclosure was finally here. She was about to turn around and leave when the purple orchid on Mrs. Walker's windowsill caught her eye. Although the glass behind it was blackened by rain, the purple petals glowed as if the sun were on them, and Shannon felt the warmth she'd experienced in church yesterday.

"You gonna stand out there all day or are you coming in?" Mrs. Walker's voice found her.

"Oh." Shannon walked in. "How did you know I was out there?"

"I know lots of things, girl," her counselor replied. "Have a seat."

After Shannon sat down, Mrs. Walker switched on her computer. "Well, let's see how we're doing." After perusing the screen, she said, "You're still passing everything."

"I know," she paused, took a deep breath, "but I'm not here to talk about my grades."

"Oh, I see." Mrs. Walker turned to look at Shannon. "What can I help you with?"

"Well," Shannon rubbed her kneecaps, "do you remember the last time I was here I told you about seeing stuff?"

"Yup, you started to tell me something," her counselor said.

"That's right, well…" She paused. "I think I'm ready to tell you now."

Shannon told her about the visions in the ball—Frankie and Sarah beneath the streetlamp, Bobo's birthday party, the Pink Moon above the treehouse, and the coffin with the trap door. Then she explained her mistreatment of Maryanne, her deteriorating relationship with Sarah, and the picture she took inside the treehouse. Finally, she relayed the information learned from Aunt Mary.

When Shannon stopped talking, Mrs. Walker leaned back in her chair and took off her glasses. "Girl, you've got a duppy on your hands."

"What's a duppy?" the teen asked.

"It's a ghost," her counselor replied.

"Well," Shannon looked around the room, "what am I supposed to do?"

"Find out what it wants," Mrs. Walker answered.

"I've been trying to." Shannon started to cry.

"Listen, girl," Mrs. Walker handed her a tissue, "the duppy isn't trying to hurt you."

"Could've fooled me," Shannon said.

"Most times," the counselor continued, "duppies are scared and lost, and it sounds like this one needs your help."

"But how can I help a freaking ghost?" Shannon blew her nose.

"If you find out who it is, you can find out what it wants. Now Frankie's aunt said something about a girl—"

"Fiona," Shannon interjected.

"Yeah, Fiona," Mrs. Walker said. "You gotta find out who this Fiona is."

"Well," Shannon wiped her eyes, "the only one who seems to know is Aunt Mary."

"Then you gotta talk to Aunt Mary."

Now realizing her course of action, Shannon stood up. "Thank you, Mrs. Walker."

"You're welcome, Shannon."

"And you don't think I'm crazy for talking about ghosts?"

Her counselor laughed. "Girl, my family's from Jamaica. We got more ghosts there than coconuts."

The rain had stopped by the time Shannon got out of school, but the sky remained as gray and cheerless as a tarnished nickel. Walking into her bedroom, she expected to see the cerulean orb of this morning and was disappointed to find that the glass merely reflected the dour day outside. She talked to Frankie on the phone and told him all about her talk with Mrs. Walker, and they agreed to visit his great aunt on Saturday. After doing a little research on the internet, she found out that *Fiona* came from the Gaelic word *fionn* meaning white or fair. However, the etymology of the moniker did little to unwrap the mystery of the cruinne, so she began her homework.

With only six weeks left of school, Shannon needed to make the final push toward graduation. She had mostly had B's and C's. Although she still had D in English. Meaning she had to ace her remaining quizzes and her final exam. Which meant, once again, abstaining from SparkNotes and actually reading the final book, a collection of Poe's short stories. And there was nothing like a full dose of death, regret, lost love, and madness to lift one's spirits.

First on the list was "The Fall of the House of Usher," a delightful tale about Roderick Usher, a dude who buried his sister, Madeline, in the basement even though she wasn't dead. Navigating the verbose prose packed with excessive adjectives and hackneyed symbols made her sleepy. When she got to the part where Madeline strangled her brother, Shannon slipped into a dream.

At first, her somnial visions picked up where Poe's story left off. Only rather than dying, the sister ran out of the house before it inexplicably crumbled to the ground. In the court-yard, Madeline became a little girl who led Shannon to a cherry tree. The child pointed to the dirt at its roots, and they began digging with their fingers until they reached an open coffin. As Shannon was peering down, the little girl pushed her into the cedar box and slammed the door shut. It was the same coffin from previous visions with the grainy patterns above. But this time there was no murmur of mourners, no tramping feet, only the menacing whisper of water. Then the coffin door opened, and Shannon's lungs filled with liquid.

"Wake up! Wake up!" a figure, suddenly above her, cried.

Shannon gulped the now-abundant air. "Mom, what happened?"

"I don't know," her mother replied. "I just got home from work and heard screaming."

Slowly the events preceding the dream came back to Shannon. "I had a nightmare," she said.

"No wonder." Her mother picked up the Poe book with the ghoulish cover. "Doesn't Mr. Reed ever assign anything cheerful?"

"Well," Shannon thought about it, "we read *Catcher in the Rye*."

"Oh great," her mother scoffed. "Suicidal ideation. Very cheerful."

"I'm all right, Mom. I think I'm just stressed out about final exams."

"Well," she brushed the hair out of her daughter's eyes, "did you eat dinner?"

"Not really," Shannon answered.

"Well, let me get you something. I'll be right back."

"Okay, Mom."

Alone now, Shannon picked up the cruinne and said, "Why are you here?" Instantly, a long string of vapor appeared at the base of the ball. Then blue circles blossomed on it like buds on a vine. Six of them were large while the rest were small, and when her mom returned with food, the vision disintegrated.

"Here, honey." A peanut butter and jelly sandwich was placed on Shannon's nightstand along with a glass of milk.

"Thanks," Shannon said.

"Are you sure you're all right?" her mom asked.

"Yeah." She forced a laugh. "Just trying to graduate."

"Well, if you're okay, then I'm going to bed." Her mother hid a yawn with her hand.

"I'm fine, Mom. Good night."

"Good night, honey."

Shannon looked into the cruinne again in hopes that the vaporous vine would reappear, but the glass stayed dark. She knew that the orb was responsible for her nightmare. However, she wasn't angry because now she understood the horror of drowning, and for the first time, Shannon felt genuine sympathy for the ghost in the glass.

Before going to bed, Shannon looked into the dark orb and said, "I'm sorry you're suffering, and I'm going to help you." After turning out the light, memories of the stressful day drifted through her mind. Just as she abandoned hope of a peaceful sleep, a strange light made her sit up. The radiant orb had bathed her bedroom in various shades of blue—cyan, indigo, sapphire, turquoise. Feeling like a child wrapped in her mother's arms, Shannon put her head on the pillow and slipped into a peaceful dream.

14

When Shannon texted Frankie the next morning about her plan to visit Aunt Mary after school, he told her she was nuts and absolutely refused to go until Saturday. However, when Shannon explained yesterday's conversation with Mrs. Walker and her nightmare, he softened, but with his work schedule, the best he could manage was Friday. However, Friday was too far away, and she decided to go by herself. Fortunately, it was her mother's day off, so Shannon was able to use her truck. Yet it never occurred to her that this thing called "visiting hours" existed until the colossal nurse at the front desk educated her.

"See that sign over there?" The battleaxe pointed to a banner above the door.

"Yes, I see it," Shannon replied.

"What does it say?"

Although the nurse was trying to belittle her, Shannon played along. "Visiting hours are from nine a.m. to two p.m. Monday through Friday and—"

"Very good." The woman cut her off. "Now what day is today?"

"Tuesday," Shannon replied.

"And what time is it?" the colossus continued.

"Okay, okay, I got it," Shannon snapped. "But it's super important that I speak to her today."

The nurse turned toward her computer and said, "Whatever it is can wait until tomorrow. Good day."

Shannon wanted to rip the fatty a fresh one but realized this would be fruitless, so she employed another strategy. "Okay, see you tomorrow." She started to walk away and then turned and said in a saccharine voice, "May I please use the restroom before I go?"

The nurse pointed a gigantic finger down the hall, and Shannon walked toward the bathroom, concocting the rest of her plan. Unfortunately, the front desk blocked passage to the patients, so there was no way around the gargantuan gatekeeper. However, in a stunning case of serendipity, a gaggle of candy stripers came down the hall, pushing a hospital screen. Without blinking, Shannon jumped behind the divider and followed them into a waiting elevator.

Aunt Mary wasn't there when Shannon arrived, and somehow the room looked smaller with nobody in it. She tried to imagine what it would be like waking up here every morning surrounded by monitors and tubes, waiting for someone to take the bedpan away. Suddenly, Shannon heard a piercing cry that made her heart sink, and peering into the hall, she saw a tragic scene. A nurse was trying to push a wheelchair-bound woman into a room, but the old lady was grabbing the doorjamb with both hands.

"Let go, Helen, please," the nurse pleaded.

"No!" the patient howled. "You can't make me!"

"Do I need to call the orderlies?" the caretaker threatened.

"Call whoever you want," she sobbed. "I'm not going!"

The nurse pressed a button on the wall, and very soon two men in green scrubs came running down the hall. Without saying a word, each grabbed one of the old lady's arms while the nurse seized her feet, and they carried her into the room like a sack of potatoes.

"No! No! No!" The woman's sob was the essence of despair—it was the cry of every frightened person in the world wrapped into one piteous sound. Then the door slammed shut, and Shannon could still hear her muted misery through the walls. After a few minutes, silence resumed, the door opened, and the orderlies left. Soon after that, the nurse came out and walked toward Aunt Mary's room. Knowing she had to avoid detection, Shannon hid behind a curtain until the footsteps faded away.

After surreptitiously visiting a few floors and looking into some rooms, Shannon almost abandoned her search until she heard the sound of a microphone announcing numbers and remembering Sadie, the dimwitted nurse, saying something about Bingo. Through the window of a door, Shannon saw an array of ancient people sitting around tables and looking down at cards with pencils in their hands. Some looked engaged while others stared off into fields of fragmented memories. In the center of it all sat Aunt Mary—her brow creased with joy, her eyes shining. Fortunately, there were only a couple of candy stripers monitoring the event, so Shannon slipped in without worry. Aunt Mary lit up like a Christmas tree when she saw Shannon approaching.

"Shannon, my dear!" she cried. "How lovely to see you."

"Hello, Miss Dolan," Shannon replied.

"Please call me Mary," the old lady said.

"Oh." Shannon blushed. "I couldn't—"

"Well, then call me Aunt Mary like Frankie does," Mary insisted.

"Okay."

"Speaking of Frankie," the venerable lady said. "Where is the big oaf?"

"Oh, he's working, so I came alone. I hope that's okay."

Aunt Mary took Shannon's hands and said with moist eyes, "My dear, it's a pleasure to see you, and I appreciate it more than you know."

When the microphone announced another set of numbers, a voice by the window screamed, "Bingo!" and Mary threw her pencil on the table. "Rats!" she said. "I was so damned close."

"Well, it looks like they're going to play another round," Shannon offered.

"Ah, screw it." She stood up. "I never win anyway. Come on."

They walked to a couch near a window overlooking downtown Syracuse. When they sat down, Shannon noticed Mary's rosary.

"Those are beautiful." Shannon pointed to the blue prayer beads.

"Oh, yes." Aunt Mary touched them. "They were a communion present from my mum."

After this, a silence ensued as the old woman's memories filled the room.

"Nice view," Shannon said.

"Yes, I'd rather be there," she pointed to the distant skyline, "but this will have to do, I suppose. Anyway, enough of that. How are you, my dear?"

"I'm good." Shannon paused. "I actually wanted to talk to you about something."

"Go ahead, my dear."

"Well," Shannon began, "the last time I was here, I started to tell you about the glass orb—"

"The *what?*" Aunt Mary tilted her head.

"Oh, I mean the cruinne." Shannon could tell she botched the pronunciation because the old lady scowled.

"It's cren-ya," Aunt Mary corrected her.

"Yes, that," Shannon said. "Anyway, Frankie gave it to me a couple of years ago—"

"That big fool! I told him it was dangerous."

"Anyway," Shannon continued, "the last time I was here, you said something about Fiona."

"That's right, my dear." She looked out the window. "Poor Fiona."

Shannon didn't want to intrude on Mary's reverie, but the sun was starting to set, and she felt like they were running out of time. "Who's Fiona?"

"She's my baby sister," Aunt Mary said with glistening eyes.

"Your sister?" Shannon asked. "Well, what happened to her?"

"She died," Mary replied.

"I'm sorry if this is painful," Shannon said. "We don't have to talk about it anymore."

"No, no, it's okay." Aunt Mary forced a smile. "It happened a long time ago."

"Well," Shannon began, "can you tell me how she died?"

"Of course, she died of yellow fever aboard the *Ulster*."

"The *Ulster?*" Shannon asked.

"The ship that brought us from Ireland to America. You

see, we were poor, so we had to ride in steerage, and the conditions were terrible. It was cramped, crowded, and damp. Our suitcases scattered everywhere. We slept four to a bunk—"

Shannon recognized the scene Aunt Mary was describing because she'd seen it in the orb many times. Now it was clear that Fiona had produced the visions.

"Was she buried at sea?" Shannon asked.

"Yes, yes, she was, poor child." Aunt Mary looked at the ceiling as if her sister's hasty funeral was unfolding up there. "So many were dying, and we promised we'd never leave each other, but one morning she was gone…" Her voice trailed off.

After a moment, Shannon asked, "Can I please ask you one more question?"

"Of course, my dear," the old lady replied.

"Did they put your sister in a coffin with a door that dropped her into the sea?"

"That's right, my dear. A trap coffin," Aunt Mary said. "How did you know?"

"Fiona showed me," Shannon answered.

"Oh, I see." The old woman folded her hands.

After a moment, Shannon asked, "What do you think she wants?"

"Well, my dear," Aunt Mary said, "I think she wants to go home."

After saying goodbye, Shannon went down the stairs and managed to avoid detection when she passed through the lobby because the big nurse was gone and some slovenly security guard at the desk was watching Netflix on his iPhone. While driving home through the deteriorating light, Shannon pondered everything she'd learned from Aunt Mary. Most of it made perfect sense except the spirit's fear of drowning.

However, Shannon thought of something that had never occurred to Aunt Mary—her sister wasn't dead when they dumped her into the sea.

When Shannon got home, she called Frankie and told him about her conversation with Aunt Mary. She left out the part about the spirit's hasty entombment because Fiona's death was already tragic and this last detail seemed gratuitous.

"Jesus!" he said. "Her sister died on a boat?"

"That's what Aunt Mary said," she replied.

"I wonder why nobody ever told me." His voice was sad because buried secrets always climbed out of their crypts and brought pain to those they were designed to protect.

"Sorry, Frankie," Shannon offered.

"It's okay," he said, "but it's just weird to find out I had another aunt. I kind of feel cheated."

"I know," Shannon added, "but Fiona needs your help now."

"What do you mean?" Frankie asked.

"Well, Aunt Mary said she wanted to come home, so maybe we can help her get there."

"Yeah maybe." His words were soaked in doubt.

"Do you have any idea where her *home* might be?" Shannon asked.

"No idea," Frankie said. "My house?"

"But she was already at your house, remember?"

"True." He remembered the orb in the attic. "Maybe she means my grandparents' house."

"Good point!" Shannon said. "Where was it?"

"Somewhere over on Tipp Hill," Frankie replied.

"Do you know which street?" Shannon asked.

"No, but I can find out," Frankie said with assurance.

Frankie learned that his grandparents had lived on Milton Avenue in the Tipperary Hill section of Syracuse, which was settled by the Irish laborers who built the Erie Canal back in the 1800s. Of notable fame was "The-Green-On-Top" Traffic Light, the only stoplight in the country where the green signal was on top and the red signal was on the bottom. According to legend, when traffic signals were installed back in the 1920s, some local hoods broke the light because the British "red" was on top of the Irish "green." The city replaced it, but the ruffians broke it again. After a few rounds of this, the city decided to keep the light inverted.

When Shannon and Frankie pulled up, they saw that the little yellow house where Aunt Mary grew up was now a marijuana dispensary called "High Times."

"Something tells me this isn't where Fiona wants to go," Shannon said.

"Not unless she's jonesing for a hit of weed." Frankie laughed.

"It's not funny." She smacked him on the arm. "She's not haunting you!"

"I know, I know," he said. "I'm sorry."

"I don't want apologies. I want ideas. Now where do you think her home is?"

"Not sure." He paused. "Ireland, maybe?"

Shannon thought about it. "No, she wouldn't have remembered Ireland. I think we need to ask your Aunt Mary."

"Not a problem," he said. "We can visit her Saturday."

Shannon lit up. "Hey! That's Holy Saturday!"

Frankie looked at her as if she'd just spoken Swahili. "What the heck is Holy Saturday?"

"It's the day before Easter, dumbass," she snapped.

"Yeah, but I still don't see why—"

"Because we can bring her an Easter basket, and I'm sure she'd love that," Shannon said.

"Oh, right, right." The significance finally dawning on him.

Shannon pointed to his head. "Remember that thing up there attached to your shoulders, Frankie?"

"Yeah," the boy answered.

"Well, then use it once in a while."

"Okay, okay." He laughed.

On Good Friday, Shannon went to the Cod Cove on James Street after school and bought fish and chips because this was their routine before her parents divorced. Furthermore, her family seemed closer after attending Palm Sunday mass together, and she wanted to preserve the positive vibes by wrapping herself in tradition. However, upon arriving home, she found a note from her mother saying she and Sarah had gone to Skaneateles, the crowning jewel of the Finger Lakes, and wouldn't be home for dinner. She felt a little stupid standing there with a bundle of cod in her hands. Then she realized that a few things still had to be done before tomorrow. Although Frankie promised to buy an Easter basket for Aunt Mary, Shannon was afraid the man-shopper would screw it up by purchasing a cheap one at CVS. So she popped the fish in the fridge, took an Uber to the mall, and bought a beautiful basket packed with seagrass, scented soap, chocolate eggs, hand lotion, a stuffed bunny, and a tiny book of psalms.

Upon returning home, her mom and Sarah were still gone, and for a moment Shannon felt the sting of rejection. Yet she quickly realized that her mom was just trying to spend time with Sarah before she went to California. Looking around at the quiet kitchen, something occurred to her—after eighteen years of breakfasts, lunches, dinners, and birthday cakes, an empty house would be a mother's worst fear because it announced the day when love moved out and loneliness moved in.

After bringing a plate of fried fish into the living room and watching TV, Shannon went upstairs to work on her Poe essay that was due next week. On the top step, she saw purple lights playing around at the base of her bedroom door. Upon entering, it seemed like the cruinne was crying because lavender beads were sliding down the glass, and a tense silence filled the air as if the world was holding its breath. With a visceral sense of propriety, Shannon put her phone on silent and quietly did her homework to maintain the somber mood as it continued to rain inside the orb.

15

Shannon hadn't noticed all the tulips blossoming in the neighboring yards until she was waiting for Frankie on her front steps. It was as if some wayward angel with a brush and a palette snuck down and painted the world while God was asleep. As she was admiring the colorful display, Frankie pulled up in his truck. When she got into the cab, he inquired about the present in her hand.

"I thought I was supposed to get her the Easter basket," Frankie said.

"Well," Shannon looked around the cab, "where is it?"

"I haven't gotten it yet," he replied.

"Ah, I see," she said. "And when were you planning to buy one?"

Pulling away from the curb, he replied, "On the way there."

"Oh, how thoughtful." Her words were laced with lethal sarcasm.

"What's wrong with—"

"Just drive, Frankie."

Upon seeing the teens, the portly nurse at the front desk picked up a phone. Shannon feared retribution for her illicit visit earlier in the week until a doctor wearing horn-rimmed glasses appeared.

"Are you Frankie?" the man asked.

"Yes, sir," the teen replied. "I'm here to see Mary Dolan."

"Why, yes, of course," he said kindly. "I'm Doctor Conan. Let's have a chat."

As Frankie and Shannon followed the bespectacled man toward a couch, they exchanged bewildered glances. But when the doctor explained what happened, their confusion turned to sadness. Apparently, Aunt Mary had suffered a stroke the day before, and they wouldn't know the full extent of her injury for several days. The doctor assured them that she was resting comfortably and promised to call when he had any updates. Then he walked up to the front desk and spoke with the gigantic nurse.

After sitting on the couch for a several minutes with a dazed expression, Frankie finally said, "Let's get the hell out of here."

"Hold on." Shannon walked up to the doctor. "Excuse me, can you please see that Miss Dolan gets this?"

"I'll take that." The nurse reached for the gift.

"I'm not talking to *you*," Shannon snapped. "I'm talking to *him*."

"Of course I can." Doctor Conan took the basket. "I'll put it in her room right now."

When the man left, Shannon felt heavy eyes on her, so she returned the nurse's glare with a ferocious scowl of her own, and the two locked eyes. Even though the water buffalo outweighed Shannon by two hundred pounds, Shannon refused to withdraw her stare, and they frowned at each other for a solid minute. Slowly, a malevolent smile cracked the caretaker's pasty face, and she looked away.

"What the hell was that?" Frankie asked when they got into his truck.

"What was what?" Shannon asked.

"You and that nurse were giving each other the evil eye," he said.

"Oh, we're just vying for territory," Shannon said.

"What?"

"Forget it," she said. "It's girl stuff."

Driving down Seneca Turnpike, they passed a lonely cemetery commemorating the fallen soldiers from the War of 1812. The solemnity of the place reminded Shannon that she still hadn't offered condolences to her friend.

"I'm sorry about your Aunt Mary, Frankie," she said.

"Me too," he replied. "I was just starting to get to know her again."

"Well," Shannon said. "She's not dead."

His tone grew bitter. "She might as well be."

"Frankie!" she cried. "That's not true!"

"Yes, it is!" he countered. "Have you ever seen someone whose had a stroke?"

"No—"

"Well, I have. My grandpa looked like someone bashed in the side of his face with a telephone pole. Couldn't talk, couldn't remember anybody. A total shitshow."

Shannon suddenly had a selfish thought—if Frankie's prognosis was accurate, Aunt Mary couldn't help her unravel the mystery of Fiona. Meaning she'd be stuck with the ghost the rest of her life. However, a grove of purple lilac trees along the road reminded her of the lavender tears inside the cruinne. This made her realize that Fiona had been crying because her sister was suffering. Suddenly, it occurred to Shannon that the ghost in the glass felt love and pain like everybody else and that she had to find a way to help her even if it took the rest of her life.

WHEN SHANNON WALKED into her kitchen, the counters were covered with brand new items, including a comforter, sheets, pillows, towels, cups, plates, silverware, and luggage.

"Hi, honey!" Her mother walked in.

"What's all this?" Shannon asked.

"It's for Sarah's dorm," her mother replied.

"Oh." The word caught in Shannon's throat. "She's really leaving, huh?"

"Yes, honey."

Shannon unexpectedly burst into tears. "Mom, I've been such a horrible bitch to her, and now she's leaving."

"Well," her mother embraced her, "she's not gone yet. We still have a few weeks."

"Yeah, but if you only knew—"

"You mean about Frankie?" her mother asked.

Shannon wiped her eyes. "Sarah told you?"

"She didn't have to."

"Yeah, but," Shannon looked around, "how did you know?"

"I have eyes, don't I?"

"Well…" Shannon paused. "How do I fix it?"

Her mother's voice became as soft as clouds. "Search your heart and you'll figure it out."

For the past two years, Mom had done her best to make Easter morning special by making frittatas, but it lacked the magic of the past, and Shannon resolved to fix that. So she went to the store and bought a slew of plastic eggs, Smarties, Skittles, Sweet Tarts, Tootsie Rolls, Hershey's Kisses, and jellybeans. She also bought three baskets and packed them with lip balm, soap, scented candles, seagrass, bubble bath, nail polish, and Godiva chocolates. Then she purchased a bag of flour and three small pails. Finally, she hid everything in her closet and waited. Sarah came home around ten and went straight to her room. Then her mother stumbled in after her hospital shift, ransacked the refrigerator, and went to bed. After she was certain they were both asleep, Shannon went to work. She stuffed the plastic eggs with candy and hid them downstairs. Finally, she dipped her fingers in the flour and made a magical trail of bunny footprints that led to their Easter baskets. When she turned off her light, a pale moon drifted across the sky and into her dreams.

A shriek tore Shannon from sleep. At first she thought that it had come from the cruinne, but the glass was silent. However, a second shout from below, followed by footsteps on the stairs, indicated that her handiwork had been discovered. When her mother burst into her room, trailed by her yawning sibling, she pretended to be confused.

"What's going on?" Shannon asked.

"The Easter Bunny came!" their mother answered.

"Seriously, Mom?"

"Seriously," their mother replied. "Let's go."

When Sarah saw the trail of bunny prints on the floor downstairs, her eyes lit up like they used to before their father left. And for the first time, Shannon realized how hard his departure had been for her sister.

"Well, what are you guys waiting for?" Their mother

handed out the three pails waiting by the stairs. "Let's see what the Easter Bunny brought!"

As if suddenly possessed by juvenile demons, the trio began frantically running around the house looking for eggs. Some were visible—a pink one on the mantle, a yellow one by the stove, a purple one in a picture frame. However, most required some searching, like the blue egg in Sarah's shoe, the green one in the pocket of their mother's robe, and the red one in the microwave. Each time an egg was found, the proud owner would scream, "Found one!" and then show it to the others. After a furious forty-five minutes of searching, they counted the eggs in their pails. Sarah had the most, which meant she got to lead the way down the bunny footprint trail that led to their Easter baskets.

Interestingly, as the family made breakfast together later, nobody asked who had decorated the house. It was as if her mother and sister, who had rejected the existence of the Easter Bunny long ago, needed to believe in him today. Therefore, the magic that Shannon hoped for had mostly been achieved because her mom and sister were happy. However, even though Shannon and Sarah had shared a few barbs and took turns stirring the pancake batter together, there was still a barrier between them, an invisible scar left behind by Shannon's bitterness. She wanted to apologize to her sister for being a horrible bitch, but contrition wouldn't change the fact that she cut Frankie out of Sarah's life. What made it worse was knowing that, of all the crimes one could commit, destroying love was the worst. Especially the kind of tenderness she saw beneath the streetlamp on Christmas Eve—the way Frankie and Sarah held each other in the halo of light with darkness crashing around them. That kind of love only came around once, and Shannon had ruined it.

16

———

Aunt Mary's prognosis was good but not great. Because she had suffered the stroke at night and staff didn't know about it until morning, the bleeding had disrupted her flow of oxygen, causing some brain damage. Apparently, her surgery went well, and she knew where she was, but her speech was labored and her left hand wasn't working. Fortunately, the stroke caused Frankie's mother, Debbie, to have a change of heart, and she went to Van Dyke for the first time in a year.

Frankie's description of their first visit had Shannon in stitches. Aunt Mary had an oxygen mask strapped to her face so her mouth was obscured, but her eyes were clear beacons of communication. The old lady looked at her niece with a bewildered expression as if she was a stranger. However, she gave Frankie a surreptitious wink, and he knew that his great aunt was messing with his mom. When Debbie, in hopes of prompting Mary's memory, began relaying family updates like Frankie's upcoming graduation, Aunt Mary pretended to fall asleep, and Frankie had to bite his tongue to keep himself from laughing. After a while, Debbie grew tired of the one-sided conversation. When she went looking for the doctor, Aunt Mary smiled at Frankie and told him everything would be all right with her big bright eyes.

SHANNON BARELY NOTICED April's passing, but the azaleas and buttercups growing in the gardens let her know May had arrived. Because graduation was only three weeks away and she had to ace her final exams in order to walk across the stage in June, she dove headfirst into her homework with tutoring after school and late nights at the library.

However, there were a few unresolved issues in her life that couldn't be resolved with studying. One in particular was directly related to commencement. Every time her teachers talked about caps and gowns or her classmates talked about parties, she thought of Bobo. If she hadn't pulled him into her cheating scheme, he'd be graduating with her. In fact, he would have been the first Billings to finish high school, breaking the cycle of failure that plagued the family for decades. Thus, when she thought of him on his dark porch among the faded furniture and broken toys the last time they spoke, her heart was swallowed by shame.

She tried to diffuse her guilt with rationalizations—Bobo was already on academic probation, so he would've dropped out anyway *or* he smoked pot at lunch and it was only a matter of time before they caught him. But these justifications fell apart like wet newspaper because Bobo may have been a lazy pothead, but he was a survivor, and he would've found a way to get that diploma if Shannon hadn't sealed his doom. Therefore, even though graduation kept her motivated, the thought of tassels and confetti had become tantamount to treason in her mind. Furthermore, after overhearing Miss Britten and Mr. Felice in the copy room, she knew Bobo's expulsion had been groundless because nothing had been stolen. Miss Parish had kicked him out simply because she thought the boy was a loser. Shannon was tempted to go to the school board and expose her principal's iniquities. However, doing so would mean incriminating herself since she'd have to explain why Bobo was in Cameron's room, which would lead to her own transgressions. She also realized the futility of her argument because she was trying to absolve Bobo of stealing by proving he cheated.

Adding to Shannon's list of sorrows, Sarah was going to the West Coast in three weeks, and their relationship was still torn. Consequently, Shannon had the nagging feeling that if the rift wasn't mended, the physical distance would pull them even further apart. She thought that, perhaps, telling Frankie and Sarah it was okay to date would fix things, but this was dumb since they hadn't needed her permission in the first place. Regardless, her logical twin wouldn't begin a relation-ship when she was leaving soon, even if it meant going to California with a broken heart. Furthermore, Shannon's instincts told her that attaining Sarah's forgiveness wouldn't be this easy—it would require some kind of selfless act that would make her dig deeper into her character than she ever had before.

Finally, now that Aunt Mary couldn't communicate clearly, Shannon felt there wasn't much hope in helping Fiona find her way home. She tried summoning the ghost, but the glass stayed as silent and purple as the lilac trees outside. So her quest to help the spirit, like her mission to mend fences with Sarah, had been an absolute failure. Thus, unlike the rest of the seniors experiencing a potpourri of emotions, including the bittersweetness of closure, Shannon felt as if her life was unraveling, and she didn't know how to pull it back together. However, on her way home from school one day, she found a little clarity. Driving past McDonald's, Shannon noticed Bobo on the curb taking a cigarette break, and the grimy red apron he was wearing drove nails of guilt into her heart.

"What's up, Bobo?" she said after pulling into the parking lot and walking over to him.

"Oh, hey, Shan." He flicked his cigarette butt into an oily black puddle.

"How's work?" Shannon asked.

"It's cool," Bobo replied. "I just finished my shift."

Shannon sat down on the curb next to him and began to cry. "Bobo, this is all my fault."

"Whaddya mean?" the boy asked.

"You'd still be in school getting ready to graduate if I hadn't fucked up your life," she responded.

"Nah," he said. "You actually did me a favor."

"Oh, right," she waved her hand at the parking lot littered with trash, "big favor."

"Listen, Shan, I fucking hated school, and I'm glad I'm gone," he said.

"So you'd rather be doing this?" She pointed to the golden arches puncturing the sky.

"Actually, yeah," the boy answered. "I'd rather be doing this."

"But, Bobo, this is a dead-end job, and you know it."

"Yeah but," he took out another cigarette and lit it, "this ain't my only gig."

"What do you mean?" Shannon asked.

His face lit up. "I've been working with my Uncle Ray at night, and it's super cool."

"Doing what?" Shannon inquired.

"Well," Bobo said, "he's an electrician. Got his own business."

"So, wait," she paused, "you're an electrician?"

"Oh hell, no!" He blew out a plume of smoke. "I carry stuff and clean the work areas, but he's slowly teaching me things."

"So then," Shannon watched a breeze carry a Big Mac wrapper across the parking lot, "you want to become an electrician?"

"Hell yeah, but—" He paused.

"But what?" Shannon asked.

"Well, I gotta go to trade school and get a license," Bobo replied.

"So do it!" she encouraged him.

"Well, I would but—"

Shannon guessed at the rest of his unfinished sentence. "But you need a high school diploma."

"Yeah." He looked down. "Or a GED."

"So get your GED," she urged.

"I can't pass that fucking test," he said.

"How do you know?" she asked.

"Cuz the math is super hard." He took a long drag and exhaled. "Fractions, percentages, variables. I can't do that crap."

"I'll help you," Shannon suggested.

"Look, Shan, this is awfully nice of you—"

"Listen, Bobo," she cut him off. "I fucked up your life, and I *need* to help you."

"Well," the rouge of shame swept across his face, "there's

kind of another issue."

"What is it?" she asked.

"It costs two hundred bucks, and I can't afford it."

"I'll pay for it," Shannon immediately offered.

Bobo shook his head. "I can't let ya do that."

"Why not?" she pressed.

"I just can't."

She started to offer again, but Bobo held up his hand and said sternly, "You're not paying for it."

"Okay, okay." Shannon considered her dilemma. Then a thought occurred to her, and she pulled out her phone.

"What are ya doing?" he asked.

"Hold on." She scrolled for a moment. "Holy shit!"

"What?" Bobo peered at her iPhone screen.

"Electricians make fifty bucks an hour!" The words flew out of her like candy from a burst pinata.

"Yeah, I know. That's why my uncle lives in Fayetteville," he said, referring to the affluent suburb.

She stood up. "Then you can pay me back when you get your license."

"Shan—"

"And I'm not taking *no* for an answer. Besides," she smiled, "when you're a rich snob, you can do all my electrical work for free."

"Okay, okay," he finally acquiesced. "But I'm paying you back."

"Bobo, if you don't pay me back, I'll come to your country club and find you," she teased.

The next GED test was May 31st, which, ironically, was one day before trade school started, and because scores were available within twenty-four hours, Bobo could conceivably begin classes the day after the exam. With only three weeks to prepare, Shannon created a rigorous study schedule that included sessions at her house four nights a week and a Saturday afternoon tutorial following his shift at Mickey D's.

When Bobo had said the test was hard, he wasn't kidding. It included an array of subjects, and the practice questions were surprisingly difficult. For example, in the Language Arts section of a practice test, one was supposed to read two excerpts from *The Great Gatsby* and then explain how Fitzgerald used colors to symbolize avarice. However, neither teen could see what "yellow cocktail music" or a "silver pepper of stars" had to do with greed. In fact, the only thing they remembered from reading the book back in eleventh grade was that a bootlegger banged some rich dude's wife and ended up dead in his swimming pool.

However, the math problems were the most daunting. Bobo could barely do addition, so helping x find y was out of the question. And though Shannon had become more proficient in algebra, she didn't have the skills to teach it, so she brought in the Meltzers for back up. At first, Mookie was reluctant to help. Although he and Bobo had been childhood buddies, life had pulled them apart, and he wanted to avoid the tension of estrangement. But when Shannon offered to cook him dinner every night, he accepted. Consequently, the group Shannon dubbed "The Core Four," named after the quartet of Yankees who won four World Series titles in five years, began.

This tetrad of teens wasn't as cool or entertaining as their baseball counterparts, but they were definitely interesting, and their study sessions were a spectacle to behold. Surrounding a big pile of books at the Delaney's kitchen table sat Mookie giving instructions, Echo repeating everything his brother just said, and Bobo holding his head in his hands.

Meanwhile, Shannon served an eclectic cuisine ranging from pesto pasta and garlic bread to apple pancakes with whipped cream on top. At first, Mookie's teaching style was perfunctory. He seemed to be watching the clock. However, when Shannon explained the truth behind Bobo's expulsion and the impact the GED would have on his life, a surge of enthusiasm swelled up inside the brainiac, and he became a passionate instructor. After each practice test, they went over the incorrect answers, and after a while, Bobo was able to help x find y.

The Language Arts section, however, was still giving Bobo nightmares until Shannon's mom paid a visit to the group one night. She told the boy to bullshit his way through it because chances were the people grading the test didn't know the answers, either. She was even kind enough to sit down and give him a lesson in the art of poppycock. "Start your sentences with adverbs like *clearly, furthermore*, and *moreover*," she told him, "because they make you look confident, and throw in phrases like *while it may seem* or *one might object* because they suggest an open mind. Finally," Shannon's mother added, "if you get stuck, just rephrase the question, throw in a quote, and you'll be fine." And after a few tries, he was able to deconstruct "The Road Not Taken" even though he had no idea what the hell Frost was talking about.

One Saturday, Bobo had to cover a shift for someone who quit and couldn't make it over for tutoring, so Shannon met him at McDonald's during his lunch break. As he was trying to analyze an excerpt from *Huckleberry Finn*, a novel they had both pretended to read sophomore year, she saw a bunch of little kids having a birthday party at one of the tables. This prompted her to ask him a question that had been bothering her.

"Bobo, this is going to sound dumb, but do you remember your tenth birthday?" she inquired.

"My *what*?" He looked up from the arcane text.

"Your tenth birthday," Shannon answered.

Bobo looked around, genuinely confused, so Shannon provided more clues. "Mookie Meltzer was there, Becky Blum, Snickers, and—"

"Sarah," he finished her sentence. "Yeah, I remember now."

"Well, it doesn't really matter," she continued, "but I was wondering why I wasn't invited."

Bobo turned the color of a gravestone. "My mom said I could only invite one of you."

When Shannon saw the pain that the memory brought him, she offered, "Oh, it's okay. I was just wondering."

"No, it's not okay." He looked out the window. "See, my dad had just gone to prison, and we were broke, but I couldn't choose between you guys, so my mom did. I'm sorry, Shan."

It occurred to Shannon that the only time she ever saw Mookie without Echo was the illusory birthday party in the orb, and she realized that the same invitation criteria had applied to the Meltzers as well.

"Bobo, it's not your fault. Besides, I went to a Syracuse Chiefs game with my dad, and Nick Bottom hit a walk-off run in the tenth."

"That's cool," Bobo said with relief because the exclusion of Shannon at his party had been a source of sorrow for him. Now he was glad she knew the truth.

ON A LOVELY SPRING evening as Shannon was studying in her bedroom, she heard an engine revving outside. For a moment, she thought it was Mookie and Echo horsing around in their mother's Subaru, but it didn't sound like the Outback's timid 2.5 liter. Because her dad had been a car guy, she had a good ear for motors, and the noise outside sounded like a V-8. Sure enough, when she looked out her window, she saw a white Ford Fairlane with a red stripe down the side in front of her house. While trying to decide whether it was a '62 or a '63, she got a call from Frankie.

"Aren't you coming down?" he asked.

"Is that you out there?" Shannon asked.

Frankie replied by beeping three times.

Shannon said, "Okay, I'll be right down."

When she went outside, Frankie rolled down the window. "Want to take a spin?"

"Whose car is this?" she asked while getting in.

"It's mine." He stepped on the clutch, shifted into first gear, and pulled away.

"But, Frankie, where did you get it?" Shannon inquired.

"My dad," he replied. "It's my graduation present."

"But we didn't graduate yet," she said.

"Yeah, but he's going to be in London during commencement, and he wanted me to have it now."

Shannon looked around at the deep-pleated seats, the wall-to-wall carpet, and the enormous steering wheel. "It's beautiful, Frankie, but where—"

"Everything's original," he interjected. "Even the aluminum gauge panels and the cigarette lighter."

"That's nice," she replied. "But where are the seat belts?"

"Not sure." He looked around.

After probing the space between the squab and the cushion, she found the faded strap and fit it into the buckle. "Aren't you going to wear yours?"

"Well, we're only going for a little spin—" He felt her reproachful eyes on him. "Fine," he said and buckled up.

When Frankie pulled onto James Street and headed toward downtown, Shannon listened to the engine. "What's under the hood?"

"It's the 260 V-8," he replied.

As they were driving past the Snowdon Building, once a luxury hotel turned crack house, Shannon saw two mangled cars in the middle of State Street. Suddenly, a terrifying thought occurred to her. "Oh my God!"

"What's the matter?" Frankie inquired.

"Are we in the car your uncle smashed?" she asked.

"The what?" he probed.

"Your uncle that died," Shannon said. "Didn't he smash a Fairlane into a tree?"

"Yeah." The boy laughed. "But that car was totaled."

"Yes, but," she looked around, and suddenly the crimson interior gave her the creeps, "didn't Aunt Mary say she saw you die in a Fairlane?"

"Yeah," he replied. "But this isn't the same car. My dad bought this from a guy in Poughkeepsie."

"Frankie, pull over." She pointed to the curb.

"I can't pull over here," he said.

"Pull over now!" she screamed, and he drove into a 7-Eleven parking lot.

"Shannon, what the hell is wrong with you?" Frankie asked.

"Your Aunt Mary saw you die in the cruinne while driving a Fairlane," she replied.

"So what?" he asked.

"*So what*?!" Shannon shouted. "She said the same thing about your uncle, and it turned out to be true."

"But my aunt said I was driving my Uncle Mike's Fairlane, and that thing got demolished. This is a different car," he reassured her.

After a moment, Shannon asked, "Was your uncle's car white with a red stripe?"

"White," he thought about it, "but no red stripe."

She saw that he wasn't taking her seriously. "Frankie, the point is, she saw you die in a Fairlane. It doesn't matter if there was a stripe or not."

"Well," he searched for rationalizations, "I mean, we'll never *really* know if she saw stuff in the glass or not."

"What?" she protested. "But I saw stuff, too!"

"Besides, even if that ball does show stuff—"

"Even if?" she asked indignantly.

"Let me finish," Frankie said. "I'm trying to say that it's not always accurate."

"What do you mean?" she inquired.

"Well," he took a deep breath, "you said it showed me and Sarah in the treehouse—"

"No," she corrected him. "It showed me a girl with yellow underwear whom I assumed was Sarah."

"But you thought it was Sarah," he offered.

"Yes," she reluctantly agreed.

"See?" he remarked with smug satisfaction. "That's all I'm trying to say. It's not a hundred percent reliable."

Shannon could tell that Frankie would keep fencing with her all night, so she tried a different approach. "Okay, I see where you're coming from, and maybe the cruinne isn't totally accurate. But your Aunt Mary *did* see your uncle crash into a tree, and your uncle *did* crash into a tree."

"Yeah, but—"

"Listen, Frankie, how about this?" she offered. "Don't drive this car until we get all this stuff with Fiona settled."

"What?!" he erupted. "Don't drive my car because of your imagination?"

His words cut into her skin because she thought he believed her. "My imagination?"

"Yeah, I mean," his tone grew derisive, "all this stuff about the cruinne being magical—"

"But you saw it for yourself!" she reminded him. "Remember how the ball was blue?"

"Well," Frankie reasoned, "I think it was reflecting the daylight."

"But it was dark outside!"

"Actually," he said condescendingly, "it was dusk."

"Fine." Shannon opened the door and got out.

"Where are you going?" he asked.

"Home!" she shouted.

"Come on, I'll drive you," Frankie said. "This neighborhood is full of creeps."

"No shit!" Shannon slammed the door. "I just realized that."

As she walked up James Street past all the old mansions that had fallen into ruin, her mood slowly shifted from resentment to bitter understanding—Frankie *had* believed her last week. However, ghosts and crystal balls weren't socially acceptable tenets, so he had abandoned his convictions and slipped back into the warm bath of conformity.

17

When final exams arrived, there was a palpable sense of anxiety among the seniors at Baldwin High School. Yet it was less about the tests and more about the finality of it all. Twelve years of grudges and gossip with all the same people was coming to an end. Soon these faces that had become the landscape of their lives would be gone, scattered to the wind like autumn leaves. Some would be off to college, some would start working, while others would end up in prison. However, more tragic were those that wouldn't go anywhere, those who would simply become more bloated and faded like dead fruit refusing to fall from the tree. Sadly, Shannon could already guess the destinations of her peers—Piper Martin and Annie Belmont, the sycophants in her English class, would find sanctuaries in higher ed. Then both girls would labor under the delusion of happiness in some suburb with neighbors as boring as them. Neil Huff, Tommy Santos, and Roger Miller would work up the corporate ladder and find disillusionment in the clouds. Porky Peterson, too heavy for any kind of ladder, would take over his family's pastry shop when his father passed away. Because of his disregard for authority and total lack of compunction, Spider Rizzo was headed for jail. Though Shannon had never liked the burnout, she felt badly that his pitiful fate had already been cast in stone.

Yet, while the destiny of her classmates seemed clear, she couldn't see ten minutes down her own road because Sarah was going to California in three days, and their relationship was still badly frayed. In an attempt to mend their bond, she offered to help her sibling pack. But Sarah said it was done, and when Shannon invited her to lunch, Sarah said she needed to pack. Meaning her twin didn't care enough to cloak her rejections with any kind of subtlety. Finally, upon seeing an airline ticket on the kitchen table, Shannon prayed for anything to disrupt the gravity pulling her twin away, and her appeals were answered in the most circuitous way.

One day prior to Sarah's departure, Shannon woke up to the sound of rain coming down like nails, and thunder hammering in the distance. While checking her phone, she learned that multiple power lines were down. Furthermore, a broken tree had crushed a garbage truck, a telephone pole was split in half, fallen wires touched off a brush fire in Fayetteville, and a section of the highway near Onondaga Lake was closed due to flooding. Additionally, many buildings were without power, including Baldwin High School, so school was canceled, and today's final exams would be postponed until tomorrow. She happily rolled over, closed her eyes, and let the monotonous melody of rain take her back to sleep.

At eleven o'clock, Shannon finally got out of bed. On her way downstairs, she saw that Sarah's door was closed, so she tiptoed to the kitchen. Her mom was at work because, regardless of rain, typhoon, blizzard, or hurricane, hospitals stayed open. So Shannon made coffee and planned out her afternoon.

Although today's school closure meant two finals tomorrow instead of one, she was glad to have more time to study for her government exam because it was going to be a beast. Section one was a hundred multiple choice questions based on all the crap they'd learned since September, including a billion different dates, acts, amendments, bills, statutes, tariffs, and taxes, while section two was composed of ten short-answer questions where students had to respond to scenarios, analyze quantitative data, or identify trends and patterns based on visual representations. Reluctantly, Shannon pulled out her review packets, spread flashcards across the kitchen table, and took the dreaded plunge into boredom.

Two hours later, a crack of thunder startled her. When she looked out at the rain that showed no signs of stopping, she realized that Sarah hadn't come down yet. In fact, there hadn't been any sounds of stirring upstairs. Suddenly, Shannon had the irrational fear that Sarah had already left for California. She rushed upstairs and burst into her sister's room, which was empty except for a half-packed suitcase and boxes of stuff for her dorm stacked against the wall. Then Shannon began to wonder where her sister was on this stormy day. After texting *where r u?* to her sibling, Shannon went back to the table and began studying again. Around three, with her mind melting from the overload of tedious information, she took a break and realized Sarah hadn't texted back. The feeling that something was wrong began to blossom again, but she dismissed her anxiety.

Bobo texted that he couldn't come over to study because his Uncle Ray, the electrician, was busy trying to help his clients restore their power and needed his nephew's help. Shannon was secretly relieved because after swallowing a slew of boring facts all day, she just wanted to chill. And after watching three episodes of *Gilmore Girls*, she decided to take a nap.

Upon entering her bedroom, she was surprised to see that the cruinne, which had maintained its lavender hue since Aunt Mary's stroke, was an oval reflection of the storm outside. But, upon further inspection, there were a several differences between the glass and the gloomy day—outside the sky was charcoal, whereas the ball was violet, and it wasn't raining inside the cruinne. Another disparity were the red lights slowly forming at the base of the orb. Adding to their mystery was the amorphous white shape that suddenly appeared beneath them. It almost looked like a submerged fishing net with rubies caught in the knots. However, as she was pondering the enigmatic vision, the rumble of a V-8 engine disturbed her meditation. When Shannon looked outside, she saw Frankie's Fairlane idling in front of her house with two plumes of exhaust drifting up into the sky like ghosts. Suddenly, the passenger door opened, and Sarah got out and slammed the door. Then Frankie peeled away, and his car was swallowed by the sodden dusk.

Sarah was standing in the vestibule with her face in her hands and raindrops clinging to her long blond hair when Shannon came downstairs. After realizing her twin was there, Sarah looked up and said, "He wanted to see me before I left, okay? But it's over. I'll never speak to him again."

Shannon, still reeling from the turmoil of the last two minutes, asked, "Frankie?"

"Yes, Frankie!" Sarah screamed as she brushed past her twin.

"Sarah, wait." She followed her sister into the bathroom. "It doesn't have to be over between you two."

"Oh, right," her twin said while drying her hair with a towel.

"I'm serious," Shannon said. "I want you guys to be happy."

"*What?*" Sarah snapped. "The girl who said she *hates* me wants me to be *happy*?"

"I never said I hated you."

"Yes, you did!" Sarah threw the towel on the floor. "Christmas Eve when you saw us together, you said, *I hate you*." She spaced out the words to revive her sister's memory, and the enunciation worked. Shannon not only remembered saying the horrible words, she also recalled her sister's shattered expression when she said them.

"Sarah, I am so sorry."

"Give me a break." Her sibling walked into the kitchen.

"Listen," Shannon trailed after her, "I acted like a total bitch, and I apologize. I never hated you, and I *do* want you and Frankie to be together and to be happy."

"Easy to say now that I'm leaving and it's impossible."

"Sarah, I don't blame you for being mad, and I can see why you don't believe me, but will you please give me the chance to explain?" Shannon pleaded.

Her sister filled the kettle with water and put it on the stove. "Fine. Go ahead."

"For starters, me and Frankie are friends, that's all."

"Could've fooled me," Sarah scoffed.

"Listen, I was mad at you because," Shannon said, recognizing her true feelings for the first time, "I felt like Frankie was mine, something you didn't have, and then you took that, too."

"Sounds kind of creepy." Sarah put a teabag into a cup. "You say *mine* like he was a possession or something."

"But to me he was! My one thing not engulfed by your shadow."

"My shadow?" Sarah poured the boiling water into her cup. "What the heck is that?"

"Oh my God! You really don't know, do you?"

"What don't I know?"

Tears filled Shannon's eyes, "How hard it is to be your sister."

A softness crept into Sarah's voice. "What do you mean?"

"You're the prettiest, smartest, most popular girl at Baldwin High School, and you're great at everything. You get the best grades, you win all the awards—"

"But—"

"Listen, Sarah," her voice cracked, "when people see me, they think of you and everything I'm not."

"That's not true." Sarah's shaky tone belied the conviction behind her words.

"Yes, it is, and the cruelest part of the joke is that we're twins and we're supposed to be alike, but we're not alike at all."

Sarah sat down and looked into her tea, "I didn't realize you felt like that."

"Did I tell you what Mr. Reed said on the first day of school this year?" Shannon asked.

"No—"

"When I walked in, he said, *Oh, bummer. I thought you were Sarah.*"

"What?!"

"Yes! He saw a Delaney on his roster and thought you were in his class."

"Well, he's just an asshole," Sarah remarked.

"Yes, he *is* an asshole, but that's been happening to me every day of my life."

"Shan—"

"But you know something?" Shannon asked. "I was almost glad he said it."

"Why?" Sarah asked with pain etched into her voice.

"Because it's worse when people don't say it—their faces fall and their silent disappointment makes me want to crawl in a hole and die." She burst into sobs, and if it weren't for Sarah's arms suddenly wrapping around her, the heaviness of her heartache might have dragged her to the floor.

"You know something?" Sarah whispered into her ear after a minute. "All these years I've been jealous of you."

"What?" Shannon wiped her eyes and looked at her sister with a dubious expression. "Why the hell would you be jealous of me?"

"Well, first of all," Sarah pulled a tissue out of her pocket and wiped her sister's face, "do you remember Mom got us those painting kits with the wooden easels and palettes for Christmas when we were kids?"

"How could I forget?" Shannon replied. "You got paint all over my room and I got in trouble."

"Oh, that's right." Sarah smiled. "But do you remember we each made a painting for Mom?"

"Yeah," Shannon searched her memory, "you made a Christmas tree."

"That's right, and you made a Nativity scene."

"Okay, so..."

"Shannon, yours was beautiful, remember? You had Baby Jesus holding a star in his cupped hands and the angels in the sky were the same color as Mary's eyes?"

"Oh, yeah, I forgot about that."

"Well, I didn't because it was awesome," Sarah said.

"Well, your Christmas tree was nice," Shannon offered.

"My Christmas tree was crap!" Her sibling laughed. "It looked like a pile of vomit."

"It wasn't that bad—"

"But my point is that art came so naturally to you. You knew about color, texture, and dimension without ever being taught, and I was so jealous, and then there was—" Sarah stopped herself.

"Then there was what?" Shannon probed.

"Then there was Dad," her sibling said.

"What about him?"

"Oh, come on," Sarah said incredulously. "You were his favorite."

"No—"

"Shannon, *please*." She stressed the word to show the futility of her sister's argument. "You guys went everywhere together."

"We went to games together, but you hated baseball."

"Whoever said I hated baseball?" Sarah asked.

"Well," Shannon thought about it, "I assumed you didn't like it because you never wanted to go."

"I always wanted to go," Sarah replied, "but I was never invited."

"Yeah, but that time we went to Yankee Stadium, you were miserable."

"I was miserable because Dad talked to you the whole time, not because I hated baseball."

"I'm sorry," Shannon said, "I didn't realize that."

After reflecting, Sarah offered, "It's not your fault."

The emotional catharsis spawned a moment of silence,

but it wasn't one of the awkward pauses that had been a signature of their strained relationship the past two years. Rather, it was the comfortable stillness of two souls at ease with one another. Additionally, the world itself was quieter because it had finally stopped raining.

"Hey," Shannon pointed out the window, "looks like we're not going to have to build that ark after all."

"Thank goodness," her sister said. "I'm not in the mood for a forty-day cruise."

After a minute, Shannon said, "Sarah, can you forgive me for being a jealous, vengeful bitch?"

"If you can forgive me for being completely oblivious to your feelings," her sister replied. After shaking hands, they hugged each other. For the first time in two years, the chasm between them, caused by a mixture of misunderstandings and secret pains, was gone. In fact, they were so swept away by the rapture of their reunion, they hadn't heard the clamor of their mom's truck pulling in the driveway or the bell wreath on the front door jingle.

"What did I miss?" Mom asked when she walked into the kitchen.

Sarah replied, "Just a little spring cleaning."

"Well, it's about time." The woman wrapped her arms around both daughters. After savoring the beautiful moment, she added, "Too bad it wasn't a little spring cooking. I'm starved."

"Let's order pizza!" Shannon shouted.

"Yeah!" Sarah cried. "And let's make popcorn and watch *The Sound of Music!*"

"But, honey," their mother looked at Sarah, "you're leaving tomorrow. Don't you have to pack?"

"Nope. My flight doesn't leave until late afternoon, and Shannon can help me if I need it. Right, Sis?"

"Right," her twin agreed.

"Well," their mom looked out at the violet sky, "I'm not sure what delivery guy is going to drive in this."

"But it's not raining anymore," Sarah offered.

"Yes, but many roads are closed, and a section of highway near the mall is flooded."

When her mother said the word *flooded*, images Shannon had seen inside the cruinne earlier today poured into her mind—the violet sky, the hazy red lights, the amorphous white shape. Suddenly, it all made sense. "Holy shit!" she screamed. "Sarah, where is Frankie?!"

Her astonished twin asked, "What?"

"Frankie." She shook her sister. "Where was he going?"

"Shannon," their mother stepped between them, "what's the matter?"

"I don't have time to explain everything right now, but Frankie is in trouble, and I need to know where he is!"

Sarah, trusting the urgency in her sister's tone, said, "He bought me something, but I told him to return it."

"Where?!" Shannon shouted.

"The mall," her twin replied.

"Come on!" The three of them ran out the front door and piled into the pickup truck.

The ride on Interstate 81 was fairly smooth. However, turning onto Harborside Drive, they were met with a sea of rubberneckers looking out their windows at something up ahead. The horn of a firetruck trying to maneuver through the traffic blared when they reached the crushed guardrail and saw the red taillights of Frankie's Fairlane submerged in Onondaga Lake. Before the truck came to a stop, Shannon was running down the embankment, and the last thing she heard before diving into the water was her mother screaming, "Stop!"

She was nearly blinded by the fetid mixture of sediment, animal shit, and debris. However, a bright moon slowly emerged from the clouds, and she could see Frankie slumped against the steering wheel with black water pooling around his chest. Shannon pulled on the door, but it wouldn't budge. Running out of air, she swam to the surface, took a few breaths, and headed back down into the murky depths. The polluted water was now just below his chin. While yanking on the door, something sharp cut her foot. Reaching down to grab her torn flesh, she found a jagged rock and hit the passenger window with it several times until the glass shattered. But the water now gushing into the car was causing it to sink deeper. So Shannon grabbed Frankie's arm, and because he wasn't wearing his seatbelt, he started to slip right out. But his foot got wedged between the steering wheel and the dashboard, and the car began pulling him down. With her strength waning and her head reeling from lack of oxygen, she looked at the boy's defunct face illuminated by the moon above and started to say goodbye. Then an angel with long blond hair swam by, and the car released its grip on Frankie just as it sank to the bottom of the lake.

18

T he long trail of light that pierced her curtain of sleep looked like a comet racing across the sky. But when Shannon opened her eyes, the shooting star was merely a bank of fluorescent lights surrounded by faded ceiling tiles in an unfamiliar room. Fortunately, her mother and sister materialized beside her bed.

Her mother kissed her cheek. "How's my baby?"

"I think I'm good," Shannon said while grasping for clarity. "Where am I?"

"Saint Joe's," her mother replied.

Suddenly, Shannon's scattered thoughts formed a mosaic of understanding, and she started to sit up. "Oh my God! Where's Frankie?"

"He's fine." Her mother gently pushed her back into the bed. "He's got a concussion, but he's going to be all right."

Then she looked at Sarah, who was wearing hospital scrubs darkened by a knot of wet hair, and a realization slowly blossomed in her mind. "Was that you in the water?"

"Yes," her twin replied with a mist of recent tears wrapped around her words.

"I thought you were an angel," Shannon remarked with a trace of disappointment.

"Nope. Just me." Then Sarah took her sister's hand. "Thank you for saving him."

With their fingers woven together, Shannon said, "We did it together, like always."

"Yeah, but," a stifled sob rattled her sister's words, "the paramedics said that if you hadn't smashed that window, he—"

"Okay, okay," Their mom interrupted. "There will be time for all that later. Now Shannon needs to rest."

"Can I go home with you guys?" Shannon asked.

"Not tonight," her mother replied. "You swallowed a bunch of polluted water, and they're checking your bloodstream for toxins."

"So when can I leave?" she inquired.

"Hopefully, tomorrow if everything looks good, but now you need to get some sleep."

"Okay, Mom, but can you do me one favor before you go?" Shannon asked.

"Sure, honey."

"Can you please turn off that hideous light?" She pointed to the fluorescent monstrosity above them, and they all laughed.

After her family left, Shannon examined her mood—she was happy because Sarah had come to her aid but slightly crestfallen because it hadn't been divine intervention. However, the moon that illuminated the gloomy water hours ago, which was now outside her window, made her remember something that her grandmother used to say—*whether you recognize them or not, angels are all around you.*

SHANNON WENT from being a social pariah to a hero after the papers published the story of her courageous rescue. Consequently, when she returned to school, people who used to hate her acted like her best friends. However, she liked the phonies more when they were her enemies because now she knew their convictions were simply bacteria formed in the cesspool of public opinion. Even Mr. Cameron, the insufferable snob, was so desperate to get on her good side that he offered to let her take the final she missed at home. However, she didn't want any favors from him and opted, instead, to take it on "Make Up Day." Which was where she found herself the day before graduation.

Because there were only a handful of students finishing up exams, the school seemed different. It wasn't the intimidating arena ruled by cliques and rumors. Rather, it was an aging building filled with echoes and trapped memories. As she sat at a table in the gymnasium with her government exam in front of her, Shannon clearly recalled her freshman orientation in this same room four years ago. A pervasive sense of promise had filled the air as she received her schedule and then followed the others to the library to get their books. She remembered being excited about the lockers in the hall because they only had cubbies in middle school, and now she wouldn't have to carry books around all day. Yet her hopes quickly shattered when her father left, Frankie drifted away, and Sarah's light devoured her.

Back then, Shannon had felt as if an angry mob had

nailed her to a cross for no reason. But now she knew that pain was a part of life and that everybody was crucified sooner or later. Furthermore, she learned that pain and joy, like winter and spring, were cycles, and that her barren branches would blossom again with time. In fact, it was a conversation Shannon had with Bobo the night before that made her appreciate the patterns in life.

Sarah, who decided to stay another week and walk at graduation, knocked on Shannon's bedroom door and said there was someone downstairs who wanted to see her. Worried it was another bootlicker pretending to be her buddy, she asked her sister to say she wasn't home. Yet Sarah refused to play along with her sister's charade, and she was forced to go downstairs.

When Shannon opened the front door, Bobo was standing on the stoop holding something behind his back. "Come inside," she urged her friend.

"Nope, ain't got time." He motioned to the truck idling by the curb. "I gotta go to work with my uncle."

"Well, how's it going?" she asked.

"I wanted to show ya something." He pulled out the GED diploma he'd been hiding.

"Bobo!" She threw her arms around him. "I'm so proud of you."

"Shan," a tear slipped down his cheek, "I'm the first person in my family to ever graduate, and I wanted to say thank you."

"You're welcome," Shannon said.

"And," he pulled an envelope out of his pocket, "this is for you."

She looked inside at the two crisp hundred-dollar bills. "What's this for?"

"It's the money you lent me for the test."

"But, Bobo, you don't have to give me this." She started to hand it back to him.

"Oh, yes, I do." He turned around and walked down the steps. Watching him, she realized he had a totally different gait. He was no longer shuffling along like a tired shadow at dusk. In fact, with his hair combed and his shirt tucked in, he was a totally different person because his winter of despair had become a glorious spring.

In the midst of her reflections, the passing bell, which would ring all summer for nobody, chimed, and Shannon realized she was only halfway through her grueling exam. She pushed her memories aside and got to work. Although her studying had been disrupted by Frankie's near-death experience, she was surprised by how much she remembered. In fact, Shannon even knew the difference between administrative adjudication and appellate jurisdiction. Moreover, she was somehow able to discuss the inherent flaws in the Articles of Confederation. Upon finishing her last question, she handed her exam to the peon who'd been assigned the task of monitoring misfits on Make Up Day and left the gym. When Shannon passed Mrs. Walker's office, she noticed that the counselor's door was open and decided to stop in.

"Well, well, well, if it isn't our little celebrity." Mrs. Walker gave her a hug when Shannon walked in.

"I just wanted to stop by and say thank you for everything," Shannon said.

"Sounds like we all should be thanking you," her counselor replied. "Not every day you have a hero in your midst. How's Frankie?"

"He's still in concussion protocol, but he's good."

"Excellent." Mrs. Walker pointed to a chair. "Take a load off."

While sitting down, Shannon noticed that the orchid by the window was wrapped in yarn. "Is something wrong with your plant?"

"No, no," Mrs. Walker replied. "Just taking the old girl home with me for the summer."

"Oh, okay."

"So did you pass all your finals?" her counselor asked.

"Well, I just finished Cameron's, so we'll see," Shannon replied.

"I'm sure you did just fine. And how's your duppy?" Mrs. Walker asked.

"Fiona?" Shannon thought about it. "If it wasn't for her, Frankie would be dead."

"What do you mean?"

"She showed me his accident before it happened, but I know that sounds crazy."

Mrs. Walker leaned back in her chair. "Girl, Jamaicans believe in ghosts that leave their skin at night and feast on babies' blood. Don't talk to me about crazy."

"Oh, okay." Shannon laughed and then looked out the window. "But now—"

"But now, what?" her counselor asked.

"Well, Frankie's aunt said Fiona wanted to go home, but I can't figure out where that is."

"So ask his aunt," Mrs. Walker responded.

"I would, but she had a stroke and—"

"Oh." Mrs. Walker sighed. "I'm sorry to hear that."

"And," Shannon continued, "we went to the place where her parents used to live, but it's a weed dispensary now."

"You're not thinking this thing through," her counselor said sternly.

"What do you mean?" Shannon asked.

"You said Fiona's a little girl, right?"

"Right," Shannon answered.

"Well, home to a little girl isn't a house, is it?"

"No." She thought about it. "Home to a little girl is her mom."

"Bingo!" Mrs. Walker said. "Now you're using your pretty head."

"But…" Shannon paused. "How do I get her back to her mom?"

"Oh, I have a feeling she'll let you know now that she's finished her business."

"Finished her business?" Shannon asked.

"Saving Frankie, that's why she was here, don't you think?" her counselor asked.

"Oh, right," Shannon agreed.

"It's not a good feeling to have loose ends, is it?" Although Mrs. Walker's question was innocuous, a subtle change in tone made it seem incriminating. However, before Shannon had time to process the inflection, Mrs. Walker flipped back to her usual effervescence. "Well, I've got a lot of work to do, and you've got to get ready for your big day tomorrow."

When they stood up, Mrs. Walker gave her another hug. "I'm proud of you, girl."

"Thank you, Mrs. Walker."

"I'll see you tomorrow. Oh, and remember, the tassel goes to the left side."

"The what?" Shannon asked.

"The little doohickey on your cap." Her counselor moved

an imaginary string with her hand. "It goes from right to left when you graduate. Drives me nuts when kids mess it up."

"Okay, Mrs. Walker." Shannon laughed. "I won't forget."

On her way down the hall, Shannon began to wonder if Mrs. Walker's question about loose ends had been a loaded one, or if she was experiencing a sudden bout of paranoia. However, upon hearing Miss Parish's serpentine voice coming out of her office, she realized what the loose ends were. The main doors at the end of the hall led to liberation. All Shannon had to do was keep walking and nobody would ever know she had cheated on her midterms. But she didn't want that stain on the fabric of her soul and opted for confession. Upon entering the principal's office, she saw Mrs. Mahoney staring at her computer with her usual puzzled expression.

"Oh, hello, dearie." The archaic secretary looked up from her screen. "What can I do for you?"

"I just wanted to say goodbye," Shannon replied.

"Are you leaving us?"

"Yes, Mrs. Mahoney. I'm graduating tomorrow."

"Oh, heavens to Betsy!" she cried with a faraway look in her eyes. "It seems like only yesterday you were a freshman!"

"I know," Shannon said. "I was just thinking about that this morning."

"Don't know what I'm gonna do in the copy room without you." Then she whispered, "I hate those machines."

"Who's out there, Margaret?!" an arid voice hissed from a partially open door.

"It's Shannon Delaney," Mrs. Mahoney replied. "She's just stopped by to say goodbye."

"Well, send her in!"

When Shannon went into the Dragon's Lair, Miss Parish was wearing one of her summer catastrophes, a lime-green pantsuit with lime-green heels, and the smile under her nose looked out of place like a pair of lips on a hearse.

"Shannon! How are you?"

Shannon was stunned because this was the first time Miss Parish had addressed her by her first name. "I'm good," she replied.

"Please sit down," the principal suggested. "Did you see your article?" She handed her a newspaper with *Baldwin Senior Saves the Day* sprawled across the top.

"Yes, I think so," Shannon said.

"Did you read what I said about you?" the dragon asked.

"I'm not sure."

"Go ahead." Miss Parish pointed at the paper. "Second paragraph."

Shannon began perusing the article until Miss Parish said, "Aloud, please."

Shannon found the sentence and read, *"Shannon exemplifies the high standards at Baldwin High School. She is courteous, diligent, gracious, humble, and trustworthy."* When she said the word "trustworthy," a light went on inside her. It was like finding money on the street when you're broke.

"That's very kind of you, Miss Parish. Thank you."

"Of course, my dear." The principal stood up. "And if there's anything I can ever do for you, don't hesitate to ask."

"Actually," Shannon said, "there *is* something you can do for me."

Because Miss Parish wasn't expecting Shannon to accept her offer, a slight annoyance colored her words. "What is it?"

"Do you remember Bobo?"

"Who?" The woman sat back down.

"Bobo." Shannon corrected herself, "I mean Robert. Robert Billings."

Now the principal's affected sweetness disappeared. "Yes, I remember him. What about him?"

"Well, he passed his GED," Shannon said.

"Okay—" Miss Parish paused as imaginary ellipsis points hung in the air.

"And," Shannon continued, "I was wondering if you would let him walk at graduation."

"What?!" the principal shouted. "That is totally out of the question! Robert was expelled!"

"Yes, but," Shannon said, "he was expelled for no reason."

The principal slammed down a scaly fist. "How dare you?!"

"How dare I what?" Shannon asked. "Tell the truth?"

"That boy broke into a classroom and stole a laptop!" Miss Parish yelled.

"That's a lie."

Miss Parish looked around with the confused expression of someone who just woke up from anesthesia. Then she said, "What did you say?"

"I said that's a lie," Shannon replied. "You expelled him because you don't like him or his family."

"Why, that's outlandish!" the dragon erupted.

"Oh, I agree," Shannon concurred. "Expelling someone for no reason *is* outlandish."

"Get out of my office!"

Shannon stood her ground. "I'm not leaving until you explain why you expelled him."

"I don't need to explain anything to you, Delaney!"

"Okay, fine." Shannon stood up. "Have fun explaining it to the school board."

"What?" the principal asked.

"If you don't tell me why you expelled him, I'm going to

the school board, and something tells me they'll believe a girl who is *courteous, diligent, gracious, humble,* and *trustworthy.*"

Miss Parish, now completely befuddled, said, "Okay, please sit down."

After Shannon acquiesced, the principal said, "Robert stole the keys off Mr. McCrory's maintenance cart and broke into a classroom."

"Isn't it possible that Mr. McCrory forgot to lock the door?" Shannon asked.

"No, it isn't," the principal snapped.

"Miss Parish," Shannon chuckled, "Mr. McCrory hung mistletoe for a Halloween dance and crashed the Zamboni into a bake sale. Don't tell me he couldn't forget to lock a door."

"Well," Miss Parish looked away, "Robert was in the building after school let out, which is trespassing—"

"I'm in the building right now after school let out. Am I trespassing?"

"*And,*" Miss Parish stressed the word in a vain attempt to pick up steam, "he wouldn't tell us why he was in there."

"Oh, I can tell you why he was in there," Shannon said dispassionately.

"*You* can?"

"Of course," Shannon replied. "He was trying to erase the answers I wrote on my desk."

"What answers?" the principal asked.

"The answers that I used to cheat on the government midterm."

"What?!"

"Yeah," Shannon continued. "I came across Cameron's midterm in the copy room, and I wrote down the answers on my desk. Oh," she laughed, "I also cheated on a precalculus test."

"Why, of all the—" Miss Parish fumed. "You insolent little—"

"Anyway, Bobo was supposed to erase the answers for the government midterm, but he got stoned at lunch and forgot." She chuckled.

The dragon exploded. "I'll have you expelled for cheating!"

"And I'll have you fired for lying!" Shannon shot back. "You kicked Bobo out for theft, and you know damn well nothing was stolen. Cameron's MacBook was with IT the whole time. Oh, and by the way," Shannon continued, "good luck expelling the student you just raved about in the papers."

Miss Parish's face fell like a cake taken out of the oven too soon. "Delaney, what do you want?"

"I already told you. I want Bobo to walk at graduation."

"That's impossible," she whispered.

"No, it's not," Shannon said. "Just give him a diploma cover and nobody will know the difference."

"But the superintendent—" the principal stammered.

"Miss Parish," Shannon interrupted, "there are four hundred students graduating. The superintendent isn't going to notice one kid."

Finally, the principal looked up with defeated eyes and nodded her assent. Going through the office, Shannon waved goodbye to Mrs. Mahoney and walked out the doors of Baldwin High School for the last time.

19

Parents in the stands began clapping when the seniors walked onto the football field in their caps and gowns while the marching band butchered "Pomp and Circumstance." Shannon saw her mother in the first row beaming with pride. Then she noticed the empty space where her father should have been. Apparently, Carol the home-wrecker had a miscarriage, so Paul Delaney couldn't make it to the graduation. Shannon marveled at the irony because her dad was prioritizing a dead child over his two living daughters. But now it was clear that Shannon and Sarah had become miscarriages in his mind when he left town with his mistress two years ago.

The foldup chairs in front of the makeshift stage on the fifty-yard line didn't seem far away during rehearsal. However, as she approached the momentous milestone, her legs now felt wobbly and weak. Fortunately, because they shared the same last name, Sarah and Shannon were able to sit together once the stressful walk was over. Like everyone else, they turned to watch the rest of the students making their pilgrimage toward adulthood.

Both girls cringed when Chet came down the aisle wearing an orange football helmet instead of a mortarboard. Apparently, he had abandoned his plans of playing for Cal after Sarah dumped him and decided to go to Syracuse. Although his family was rich, the university gave him a full-ride scholarship. The school even promised to let him wear 47, his high school number, which rankled some folks. Not only because Joe Morris, the school's all-time leading rusher, wore it, but because freshmen were supposed to prove themselves before making such lofty demands. However, the coaches didn't want to lose him to Boston College or another rival, so they granted his request.

Adding to Chet's good fortune, it was recently announced in the local newspaper that he was engaged to Ashley Baldwin, an airhead from Sedgwick Farms, the most affluent neighborhood in Syracuse. The Delaney twins were happy for him because he could continue to live his benighted life of pomposity and privilege.

Tears of admiration blossomed in Shannon's eyes when Bobo and Maryanne Newman passed by because, unlike Chet, both had overcome tremendous obstacles to get here, and she truly admired their resiliency. And the sisters gave Frankie a thumbs-up when he strolled by with *Physical Graffiti*, his favorite Led Zeppelin album, glued to the top of his mortarboard.

Miss Parish read a hackneyed speech she stole off the internet about following dreams and changing the world, after which people applauded loudly. Not because of her impactful message, but because it was over. Following the principal's banal performance, Mookie Meltzer, the valedictorian, gave an impassioned appeal about empathy and the importance of helping others. This made Shannon smile because she knew that tutoring Bobo had inspired his words.

After the speeches were through, Dr. Byrnes, the superintendent, a bloated sexagenarian with a pile of dyed red hair, began calling the names of the candidates who filed onto the stage, received their diplomas, and returned to their seats amidst soft applause. Because Sarah had downplayed her role in Frankie's rescue, the volume of the clapping only went up a notch when her name was called. However, when Shannon's name was read, an uproarious ovation shook the stage.

After a solid minute of raucous cheering, Dr. Byrnes patted the air with her hands. When the ovation faded, the superintendent presented Shannon with the Clara Barton Award for Courage in honor of the courageous Civil War nurse who started the Red Cross. Upon receiving the prize, as well as her diploma, Shannon walked across the stage. On her way down the stairs, she locked eyes with Miss Parish, and though the interaction only lasted a second, something akin to mutual respect was exchanged. After returning to their seats, Shannon and Sarah screamed wildly when Bobo and Maryanne walked across the stage, and they did the same for Frankie, who blew a kiss to both of them.

Although both girls had been invited to numerous graduation parties, they decided to order pizza and watch *The Sound of Music* with their mother one last time before Sarah went to California the next day. During the part where Mother Superior sings "Climb Every Mountain," Sarah paused the movie and said to her sister, "Can I ask you something?"

"Sure," Shannon replied, chasing a wayward olive that had fallen off her pizza.

"How did you know that Frankie had crashed into the lake?"

"Yeah," their mom piped in. "How did you know that?"

"I'll tell you," Shannon said. "But you're going to think I'm crazy."

"We already *know* you're crazy," Sarah joked. "So you might as well tell us."

Shannon started by telling them all about Fiona and the visions inside the cruinne—the Fairlane submerged in Onondaga Lake, Sarah and Frankie beneath the streetlamp. Furthermore, after explaining Bobo's birthday, both finally understood why Shannon had been upset about the party ten years later. When telling them about the Pink Moon, she left out the part about Ali Clark because she had promised her she wouldn't tell, but Sarah interrupted.

"Is that why you burst into Frankie's treehouse?"

"How did you find out about that?!" Shannon asked.

"Frankie told me," Sarah replied.

"Wait," their mother said. "What happened?"

After giving a detailed account of the night at Frankie's treehouse, her mother said, "Holy shit! You took their picture?!"

"Yeah," Shannon said abashedly, "I was angry."

After Shannon said the word *I*, something occurred to her —there were many times when she had blamed Fiona for her transgressions as if the ghost had taken possession of her spirit. But now she knew that every hurtful word and every selfish act had come from the bowels of her own soul.

"I understand that," her mom interrupted her reflection, "but why do you think Fiona showed you that vision?"

"Because she was mad at me."

"What for?" Sarah asked.

"Probably for not giving her enough attention," Shannon replied. When she saw the bemused expressions on her listeners' faces, she continued. "See, Fiona died when she was little, so even though her spirit is old, she's still a little kid, which is why she can be moody and vindictive." Then she added, "Like me."

After pondering her own shortcomings, Shannon told them Aunt Mary's story about Fiona succumbing to yellow fever, the recurring visions of the coffin, and her theory of the premature burial.

"She was still alive when they dumped her into the ocean?" Her mother pressed her hands to her mouth as if the tragedy had just occurred.

"That's the only thing that would explain her fear of drowning. See," Shannon continued, "even though some of the visions are confusing, they all make sense if you think about them. Like the red lights in the water. Confusing at first, but now we know it was Frankie's car."

"So," Sarah said, "she was here to save Frankie?"

"I think so," Shannon replied.

"Then I wonder why she—" Sarah paused.

"Why she showed me you and him beneath the streetlamp?"

"Yeah."

"Like I said before," Shannon continued, "she was jealous, and if she could drive a wedge between us, it might bring me closer to her."

When their mom reached for another slice of pizza, she accidentally pressed the "play" button on the remote, and Mother Superior began singing again.

"Turn it off!" both girls cried at the same time.

"Okay, okay, hold on." Their mother pressed the "power" button, and the nun's face vanished.

"It's not even Peggy Wood singing," Shannon said.

"Probably why they just showed her silhouette," added Sarah.

"Okay, but wait a minute," her mother interjected. "You said Fiona was still here, right?"

"Right," Shannon answered.

"Well, I wonder why," her mother said. "I mean, you saved Frankie—"

"Yeah, I know," Shannon asserted. "See, there's still one thing I can't figure out."

"What is it?" Sarah asked.

"She wants to go home, but I can't figure out how to get her there."

After the three of them considered the conundrum for a minute, Shannon added, "Mrs. Walker said that Fiona wants to be back with her mom and that she'll show me how to get her there."

"Well," their mother said, "I trust Mrs. Walker."

"Me too," Sarah agreed.

Then something incredible occurred to Shannon. She had been talking to them for two hours about a haunted orb that showed prophetic visions and they hadn't showed any signs of doubt. "So wait," she said, "you guys *believe* me?"

"Of course we do," her mother and sister said together.

"But why?" Shannon asked. "I barely believe it myself, and it all happened to me."

"Well," Sarah said, "I wondered how the heck you knew me and Frankie were outside at two in the morning on

Christmas Eve. Then when Frankie told me you burst in on him with a camera, I knew something was up."

"And," her mother added, "you've been doing some very strange things lately."

"Like what?" Shannon asked.

"Well," her parent answered, "there've been several times I've heard you talking to someone in your room. Then you had that incident in Mr. Cameron's class, and I was very worried."

"You must've thought I'd lost my mind," Shannon said.

"Well" her mother continued, "we talked about you going back to Dr. Murdock, the psychologist, again. Remember?"

"Yes," Shannon answered.

Her mother added, "But somehow I knew in my bones that this wasn't a mental health issue." Two tears leaked out of her left eye. "I knew that there was something else, something I couldn't put my finger on. Now this all makes sense."

"Sorry I put you guys through this," Shannon said.

They both joined her on the couch and put their arms around her.

"That's okay," Sarah said. "We still love you even though you brought a freaking ghost into the house."

After laughing, they turned the movie back on and sang every song until the Von Trapps crossed the Alps at the end.

SYRACUSE in the summer was normally a horrid mixture of heat and stifling humidity. However, June 3rd was one of those rare occurrences that made living in Central New York worthwhile. A thunderstorm that passed through in the night left cool breezes playing in the flowers beneath a cornflower-blue sky, and temperatures stayed in the seventies. It was a perfect day except for one thing—Sarah was leaving. Although Sarah had said she was packed, their mom found a bunch of her clothes in the hamper. She also found her daughter's driver's license in a drawer. So they took everything out of her suitcase and started again. However, Shannon knew that these hasty preparations were a ruse to keep them busy so nobody had to think about Sarah's departure.

When it was time to go to the airport, the ruse fell apart, and driving down Interstate 81 felt like going to a funeral. Passing the polluted lake that was almost Frankie's grave, and going by the mall, Shannon remembered Sarah saying something about him returning a present the night of the accident. Shannon wondered what the gift was but couldn't ask her sister now.

After Sarah checked her luggage, the family went to Starbucks and chatted about trifles, since speaking their hearts would mean too much pain. Finally, a voice on the loudspeaker said the flight to San Francisco would be boarding soon. Reluctantly, they all walked over to security and stood in line. When Sarah put her backpack on the conveyor belt, Mom and Shannon each gave her a hug. Then she walked through the metal detectors and vanished into the crowd.

Driving home from the airport, Shannon got a text from Frankie and cringed because she thought it was going to be about Sarah. However, her heart, which had been breaking all day, broke again when she read the words, *Aunt Mary died. Call me.*

"Oh crap!" Shannon said.

"What's the matter?" her mom asked.

"Frankie's Aunt Mary died."

"Oh no!" her mom exclaimed. "Do you know how it happened?"

"No." Shannon showed her the brief text.

"The poor dear."

When Shannon called Frankie, he told her that his aunt died of a heart attack in her sleep and didn't feel any pain. He also said it was probably for the best because the last time he saw her, she had seemed very sad. Apparently, Aunt Mary had thought that her ability to speak would return after physical therapy. However, despite the massive efforts, her mouth remained as inert as a dead fish. And for a woman who loved to talk, this was torture. Frankie said that when he went to Van Dyke last Saturday with his mom, his normally spunky aunt had just stared at the wall the whole time. Though the nurses said she was tired, Frankie knew she was waiting for death.

When Shannon walked into her bedroom, she had expected to see the lavender rain that had been inside the cruinne since Aunt Mary's stroke. But instead of an atmospheric dirge, the ball was casting a bouquet of colorful lights around the room. Shannon sat down on her bed, looked into the ball, and said, "Where is your home?" As soon as the words were uttered, the colors in the glass diminished one by one until all that was left was green, which slowly became a maple tree on a grassy hill. As Shannon was perusing the vision, her mother walked into her room, but rather than disappearing, the chimera continued to blossom.

"Oh my God!" her mother pointed at the cruinne.

"Have a seat." Shannon patted the bed. "Fiona is showing us where she wants to go."

After her mother sat down beside her, sunlight hit the

illusory tree, and three shadows shaped like crosses appeared on the hill.

"What do you think it means?" her mom asked.

"I don't know," Shannon replied. "But I'm sure we'll find out."

BECAUSE AUNT MARY had been in Van Dyke for ten years, the friends she once had had either forgotten about her or died. Therefore, her funeral was very small. Because Shannon was used to the vibrant congregation on Christmas and Easter, the scattering of mourners in the first few pews at Saint Vincent's made her sad. However, nothing was more depressing than the effigy in the open casket—the heavy makeup the mortician used turned Aunt Mary into a clown, and the beautiful lady Shannon had known was gone. In fact, if it weren't for the blue rosary beads threaded through her waxen fingers, Shannon wouldn't have recognized her.

Following the funeral procession down James Street, Shannon was surrounded by nostalgic visions. She saw herself and Frankie riding their bikes past the Bishop's House, which was said to be haunted by a clergyman who hanged himself. Then she saw them throwing snowballs at cars, and one of the icy spheres that melted in her mind became a flickering candle in Frankie's treehouse. Suddenly, as if a breeze passed through her memories, the trembling light dissolved and reality returned with a vengeance as they passed through the gates of Woodlawn Cemetery where everyone on the north side of Syracuse was buried. Going down a sinuous road behind the hearse, Shannon saw a sea of names etched into gravestones, and a terrifying thought occurred to her: maybe there was no heaven. Maybe the idea of an afterlife had been a scam created by ancient magistrates to get people to behave. Maybe Saint Peter at the Pearly Gates was merely propaganda. Maybe, she thought, it all ended here beneath a rock with your name on it. However, when the procession came to a stop and Shannon saw three Celtic crosses beneath a maple tree, her doubts vanished, and she knew where Fiona wanted to go.

Her mother, also recognizing the scene, exclaimed, "Oh my God! Shannon, it's the hill in the cruinne!"

"I know," Shannon said calmly.

"Well," her mother stammered, "what do we do now?"

Shannon answered, "We go to a funeral."

As Father Curtain sprinkled holy water on the coffin and spoke about ashes and dust, Shannon looked up at the beautiful blue sky, which reminded her of the beads on Aunt Mary's rosary. Suddenly, she remembered the blue circles that appeared in the cruinne a few weeks ago, and now it all made sense. Fiona wanted to be in heaven with her mom, but she was waiting for her sister.

When Shannon approached the coffin to pay her last respects, she looked at the moss-covered graves of Frankie's grandparents. *Thomas Dolan, Doris Dolan.* She thought of these people who left behind everything they had ever known in Ireland, crossed an ocean, lost a daughter, all for a better life in America. She tried to imagine their courage that no longer existed today in a world where doors opened automatically and toilets wiped your ass for you. Then Shannon looked at the name on the newest monument. *Mary Dolan.* Peering into the freshly dug grave filled with afternoon shadows, Shannon said a prayer for her departed friend.

After the service, mourners were invited to Frankie's house

for a funeral reception. In most cultures, food was considered the key ingredient when comforting grieving people. For example, at an Italian wake, there were boundless trays of baked ziti, lasagna, meatballs, and veal along with a mountain of baked goods, including cannoli and enough biscotti to choke a donkey. However, in an Irish house like the Frankie's, booze was the appetizer, entrée, and dessert. Quarts of whiskey, vodka, brandy, gin, and wine lined the sideboard, and by the end of the day, only the bottles would be standing.

At one point during the drunken revelry, Frankie gestured for Shannon to follow him onto the back porch. When they were alone, he handed her a small velvet box.

"What's this?" She looked at the diminutive package.

"Well," he blushed, "I was wondering if you could send it to Sarah."

"But what is it?" Shannon asked.

"See for yourself," he said.

When Shannon opened the box, there was a small silver pendant with Saint Christopher engraved on it.

"This is beautiful, Frankie. Why don't you send it to her yourself?"

He avoided Shannon's question. "See, I tried to give it to her the day of that big rainstorm, but she told me to return it."

"That's why you went to the mall?" she guessed.

"Yeah, and needless to say, I didn't get there." He alluded to the accident by grabbing an imaginary steering wheel with his hands. "Anyway," he continued, "I tried to return it a couple days later, but they wouldn't take it because I didn't have the receipt."

"Well, did you tell them you were in a car crash?" Shannon asked.

"Nah," he replied. "I didn't want to go into all that."

Then something occurred to her. "Frankie, you had this with you the night of the accident?"

"Yeah," he answered. "It was in my pocket."

"But Frankie, look," she rubbed her finger across the velvet box, "there's nothing wrong with it."

"I know," he replied. "Kind of freaky, right?"

"Very freaky," she said, "and did you know that Christopher was the patron saint of travelers?"

"Yeah, dummy," he quipped. "I bought it for her trip to California."

"No, no, you're missing the point," Shannon said. "Christopher protected you the night of the car crash."

Frankie gave her an incredulous look, but she plowed through his skepticism. "The paramedics said you should have died because you weren't wearing a seatbelt, and all you got was a concussion."

Just as Frankie was about to refute Shannon's reasoning, one of his drunken uncles staggered onto the porch. "Oh, excuse me," the red-faced man said. "I thought this was the bathroom."

"That's okay, Uncle Pat," Frankie said. "It's the last door on the right."

"Got it. The last door on the right," the man said as he stumbled back into the house.

"So will you send it to her?" he asked.

"I'll make sure she gets it," Shannon replied.

As the daylight began to wane, the guests turned to coffee in hopes of shaking off their inebriation. Then, when an impatient dusk stood outside the windows, they all began saying their goodbyes. As usual, Father Curtain drank too much, so Shannon's mom had to drive him home. Fortunately, Frankie was able to help load the pickled priest into her truck. Realizing they'd probably also need help getting the friar into the rectory, Shannon asked him if he'd come with them, and he instantly acquiesced. However, she had ulterior motives for her request because she knew Fiona's soul was ready to take flight, and she needed Frankie's help.

Once they were on the road, Shannon said, "Mom, let's stop at our house first."

"What?" The woman pointed to the unconscious priest in the backseat. "Don't you think we should get him home?"

"He'll be fine for a few minutes," Shannon replied. "I have to show Frankie something first."

Guessing her daughter's thoughts, her mom said, "How do you know it will still be there?"

"Because I know it will."

"Can somebody please tell me what's going on?" Frankie asked.

"You'll find out in a minute," Shannon answered.

After parking in the driveway, they rolled down the windows so Father Curtain wouldn't die of asphyxiation. Then the trio went into the house and marched straight up the stairs. Sure enough, when they entered Shannon's room, the vision of the burial site was still glowing in the glass.

"Holy shit!" Frankie pointed at the cruinne. "It's Woodlawn Cemetery!"

"I know it is," Shannon said softly.

"But," he peered into the glass, "what does it mean?"

Shannon explained everything that had happened since they last spoke—the vision of his Fairlane in Onondaga Lake, the lavender rain after Aunt Mary died, and now the gravestones in the glass.

Frankie thought about it. "That's where she wants to go?"

"Yes," Shannon answered. "She wants to be back with her family."

"But we can't just bury the ball there," he objected.

In the midst of Frankie's protest, they were all surprised by a shrill voice behind them saying, "Jesus, Mary, and Joseph!" Turning around, they saw Father Curtain in the doorway pointing at the cruinne. Obviously, he had woken up and stumbled into the house in search of his lost afternoon.

"What in the name of the devil is that?" The priest shook a gnarled finger at the ball.

"It's Fiona, Aunt Mary's sister," Shannon replied without hesitation.

He looked at her as though she had three heads, and his crimson skin turned scarlet.

"It's okay, Father." Her mom walked over to him. "Please, come sit down." She led the man to the chair by the desk. Then she instructed her daughter to go downstairs and get him a glass of water. Upon returning from the kitchen, Shannon explained the visions inside the cruinne, the burial at sea, and Fiona's desire to be with her family. By the time her fantastic tale was finished, the light of a full moon had painted the trees outside her window white.

"You know," the priest said in a soft voice, "in the town of Killarney where I'm from, we had the ghost of a boy who got trapped inside a grandfather clock."

"How did that happen?" Shannon asked.

"Well, it's not nice to talk badly about the dead," the padre continued, "but Davy Dwyer was the dumbest child that God ever put on this good earth, and he couldn't find his way out of a paper bag."

Shannon's mom laughed. "So what happened?"

"Well," Father Curtain began, "we had an epidemic of the typhus, and all the Dwyers perished, but while the rest of the souls climbed the stairs to heaven, Davy took a wrong turn and got trapped in the clock."

"But Father Curtain," Frankie interjected, "I thought souls only got trapped in mirrors."

"Oh, no, my boy," the priest said. "That's a common misconception. It has nothing to do with the reflection; it's the glass. You see," the man continued, "because glass is transparent, souls can't see it. So some get trapped like poor Davy."

"Did they ever get the boy out?" Shannon's mom asked.

"Not that I know of," the priest replied. "But a daft dairy farmer named Mike Flanagan bought the clock, and he wouldn't know if there was an elephant in there."

"Is that what happened to Fiona?" Frankie asked.

"Most likely," Father Curtain responded.

"So, then, will she be stuck there forever?" Shannon asked sadly.

"No, no, my dear. Jesus calls all the souls to him, and eventually," he made the sign of the cross, "they all get there."

"So what do we do?" Shannon's mother asked.

"Well," the man replied, "Fiona needs a proper Christian funeral."

Frankie turned as white as a sheet and said in a tremulous voice, "So we're gonna bury her?" He pointed out the window. "Now?"

"Don't be absurd," the priest rejoined. "We're not going to bury anything."

"But," Frankie stammered, "how will she get out of there?" He pointed to the cruinne.

"Oh, something tells me she'll find her way once the rituals have been completed," the friar answered.

They drove to Saint Vincent's Church so Father Curtain could pick up his vestments. Then they headed to Woodlawn Cemetery, and not even Salvadore Dali could have imagined the surreal scene about to unfold. Because the gates were locked, they were faced with an eight-foot fence. Mom, Shannon, and Frankie were spry enough to scale the barrier, but there was no way the old priest with arthritis and a bad case of gout could make the climb. For a moment, it seemed as if Fiona's journey would have to be postponed. However, Shannon disappeared for a moment and came back from her mother's truck with a pair of bolt cutters.

"Shannon!" Frankie exclaimed. "You can't cut the fence!"

"Why not?" she asked.

"Because it's public property!" Frankie was hoping that the adults would echo his sentiments, but they remained as silent as the graves. "Besides," he continued without much steam, "we can always come back tomorrow."

"Frankie, look at us!" Shannon pointed at Father Curtain with a bottle of Holy Water, Mom holding the glowing cruinne, and herself with the bolt cutters. "Do you really think we can do this during the day?" Before waiting for him to respond, she said, "We have to do it *now*."

After walking to a remote spot away from the streetlights, they took turns cutting a whole in the fence. Once the aperture was sufficient, the quartet climbed through and followed the winding road with the help of the full moon and a sky full of stars. After a macabre journey past tombstones and mausoleums, they found the maple tree with three Celtic crosses beneath it.

"Okay, my dear," Father Curtain said to her mom, "hand me the cruinne." Once she complied, he carefully placed the glass ball beside Aunt Mary's grave. Then he instructed the mourners to stand with him in a small circle. After sprinkling Holy Water on the orb, the priest said, "O God, by whose mercy the faithfully departed may find rest, bless this grave, and send your holy angel to watch over it. Deliver Fiona from every bond of sin, that she may rejoice in you with your saints forever. We ask this through Christ our Lord. Amen."

For a few moments, the cruinne went dark, and only milky streaks of the moon above could be seen in the glass. Then a tiny blue light no bigger than a rosary bead formed at the base of the ball. Soon other lights blossomed that slowly became the swaying lanterns in the bowels of the ship that brought the Dolans to America. Slowly, the steerage compartment became the dark confines of Fiona's coffin and muted sobs could be heard through the glass. Then the scene was suddenly torn away like a page ripped out of a book, and the cruinne began filling with bright blue water. For several moments, the astonished mourners watched as the liquid crept up the sides of the orb. Once the fluid reached the crest, it began to churn. They watched the water agitated by unseen winds smash against sphere until long thin cracks appeared in the glass. When the cruinne could no longer withstand the storm, it shattered, and a fountain of sapphire stars flew into the night sky. Father Curtain made the sign of the cross as the celestial bodies flew around the cemetery like a flock of birds, then soared into the firmament.

As the last embers of Fiona's light mixed with the Milky Way, Shannon blew a kiss at the night sky, bid farewell to her friend, and began to cry because she was saying goodbye to more than just a ghost. It was now clear that Fiona had been a reflection of herself—her own heart had been a glass ball packed with grudges, and now it was time to let go of the petulance that had wallpapered her youth.

After giving her mother and Frankie a big hug, Shannon saw Father Curtain on his knees beside the broken cruinne. "Don't cut yourself, Father."

"Oh, I won't." The priest sniffed his fingers. "Well, I'll be damned."

"What is it?" Frankie inquired.

"Seawater," the man replied.

"What?" Shannon's mother demanded.

"See for yourself." The priest motioned toward the damp ground.

Sure enough, when they sniffed the liquid, it smelled like salt. "What do you think it means, Father?" Frankie asked.

"I haven't a clue," the friar replied as he carefully picked up the pieces of broken glass and placed them in a pile by the maple tree.

As Shannon listened to the others marveling at the mystery of the seawater, she thought of Fiona's premature burial and was glad nobody else realized that the liquid had come from a dead girl's lungs.

After dropping off Father Curtain at the rectory, the trio drove in silence because the intensity of Fiona's funeral had stolen their energy. When they pulled up in front of Frankie's house, he gave Shannon a small hug, got out of the truck, and went inside without saying a word.

Driving away, Shannon caught sight of the treehouse and images of childhood afternoons poured into her mind—jaunts with Frankie through the Misty Mountains, outwitting Orcs on the ashen plains of Mordor, and destroying the ring on Mount Doom. When they turned onto the next street, the wooden structure vanished, but the memories remained because memories didn't disappear like objects in a rearview mirror. Rather, they brightened with time like stars in one's soul.

20

June tumbled into July, and before Shannon could blink, August had arrived with sunflowers and apologetic evening light. She'd been working as a hostess at Ryans, an Irish dive on Park Street pretending to be a fancy restaurant, and she was getting ready for her classes to start. Unlike most of the other frazzled freshman entering community college, Shannon actually had a major in mind. However, her concentration hadn't been decided with careful thought; rather, it had come to her by a chance encounter.

Salem Hyde Elementary School was having a teacher luncheon catered by Ryans, but the delivery guy was out sick and the duty fell onto Shannon's shoulders. After loading up the back of the van with trays of stew and soda bread, she headed to her old stomping grounds. Upon entering the school with the serving cart, she was shocked that the once seemingly enormous place was actually very small. The desks, drinking fountains, and dilapidated bleachers seemed like décor inside a dollhouse. Only Miss Mack, the lunch lady with the hairnet and skin yellowed by cigarette smoke, was unaltered by the passage of time.

After helping "Miss Macaroni" (a nickname given to Miss Mack by some urchin years ago), Shannon took a stroll down memory lane before driving back to work. She visited the art room where her ceramic Santa blew up all the other pieces in the kiln. Then she went to the classroom where Snickers Sanchez shit his pants.

On her way out, she passed the display cabinet and was shocked to find the Gandalf painting she made in sixth grade still casting spells behind the glass. Her rendering showed the wizard walking down a cobblestone path in Middle Earth with a russet sun sinking behind him. His cloak was covered in trinity knots, and the same interconnected arcs covered his staff, which had a stream of yellow light pouring out of it. Stuck to the top of the painting was a blue ribbon signifying first place in the Merrill Bailey Art Award, a contest show-casing the talents of elementary students all over Central New York. She remembered having her picture taken but couldn't recall any family celebration because Tilly, her grandmother, had passed away that winter, and embers of Shannon's achievement had been swept away by the funeral. However, as she looked at the wizard staring back at her, her love of painting and her fondness for this school coalesced into a potent epiphany, and she knew she wanted to be an art teacher.

After work that day, Shannon drove to the local commu-nity college and registered for classes. To meet the criteria of her new major, she had to submit an art portfolio, so she went home and scoured the house for fragments of her former passion. Not surprisingly, her mom had kept most of her work, including the nativity scene Sarah was so fond of and a depiction of Bilbo Baggins drawn in charcoal. However, Shannon realized that she needed something more recent and set out to find a worthy subject.

The next morning she brought her sketch pad outside and drew a clothesline strewn with linen next door. While it was a worthy effort, the drawing lacked inspiration, and she didn't want to showcase her talents with some drab picture. After a long, fruitless search, Shannon found the motivation she was looking for inside.

Walking into her bedroom, she noticed a pale ring on her nightstand left behind by the cruinne. Sitting down on her bed with a wistful sense of nostalgia, she drew her finger around the faded circle and pictured the orb ablaze with visions. Instantly, as if a lasso had been thrown around her soul, Shannon was running downstairs to get her sketchpad. When she returned, she got to work. Although there were many visions to choose from, her favorite memory was the cruinne holding onto the cerulean sky long after the light had dimmed. So she brought the memory back to life with acrylics, and within three hours, a bright blue orb glowed on the canvas.

After finishing, she wanted to show somebody her accomplishment, but her mom was at work. So she face-timed Sarah. After three rings, her sister's pretty face filled the iPhone's screen. "What's up, Sis?"

"Not much," Shannon replied, "but I wanted to show you something." She turned her phone toward the painting.

"Wow," Sarah exhaled, "that's incredible."

"Do you think it's good enough for my portfolio?" Shannon asked.

"Your what?"

"Oh, right." Realizing she hadn't told her sister about her

plans hatched only yesterday, she said, "I've decided I want to major in art so I can become a teacher."

"That's awesome!" Sarah exclaimed. "I always told you how good you were at art."

"I know." Shannon turned the phone toward herself. "Hopefully, you're right."

"Trust me, I'm right."

Although Sarah was truly happy for her, Shannon detected a trace of sadness in her normally effervescent sister's voice, so she asked, "How's it going out there?"

"Good," her twin replied. "The fall semester starts next week, so I'm just trying to get ready."

"Have you made any friends?"

"Yeah, a few. My roommate is super nice, and so are a few girls in my dorm."

"Oh, cool," Shannon said. "Any hot surfer boys out there?"

"Well," Sarah's voice turned gray, "I haven't seen any yet. But hey," she added, "I'm late for an orientation meeting, so I have to go."

"Sounds good, Sis."

"Congratulations on your painting and your cool plans!" Sarah said.

"Thanks, I'll see you later."

After hanging up, Shannon looked at her painting. But rather than a cerulean orb, she saw Frankie and Sarah standing in a halo of light beneath a streetlamp outside, and she knew there was still something she needed to do.

～

BECAUSE THE FAIRLANE sat at the bottom of Onondaga Lake for two days, the engine, transmission, and fuel system were destroyed by water. Furthermore, the upholstery and carpets were ruined, and the insurance company declared it a total loss. However, Frankie, being a stubborn mule, had it towed to his garage, and for a week straight, he dried out the vehicle using industrial exhaust fans. After that, he scoured the internet for engine mounts, adapters, alternators, generators, headers, exhaust manifolds, and everything else needed to restore the 260 V-8 engine. Lastly, he ripped out the upholstery and spent the rest of the summer replacing it with the original seats and rugs.

When Shannon walked up Frankie's driveway, she saw him standing beside the Fairlane with a big smile on his face. Although she was happy for him, she shuddered to see the car that had almost been his coffin.

"Shannon!" he cried while holding something shiny in the air. "You're just in time!"

"What the heck is that?" She pointed to the object in his hand.

"It's a cigarette lighter!" the boy shouted.

"But, Frankie, you don't smoke."

"No shit, Sherlock, but it's the last thing that was missing from the Fairlane," he pointed to the car, "and it just came today!"

"That's nice." She feigned interest. "So are you gonna put it in there or what?"

"Yup." He opened the door, hopped in, and pushed the lighter into the socket. "There! Now it's complete!"

"So will this thing run now, Frankie?"

"Hell yeah," he answered. "It's as good as new."

"Could it make it to California?" Shannon inquired.

"It could make it to Paris if there wasn't an ocean in the way." He wiped a speck a dust off the dashboard with his T-shirt.

"Then why are you still here?"

"Why am I what?" he asked with a bemused expression on his face.

Shannon repeated the question. "Why are you still here?"

Frankie said, "Where else should I be?"

"You should be driving to San Francisco, dumbass."

"Well," he started to catch her drift, "why would I do that?"

"Because there's a girl out there who loves you!"

"But Shan—"

"And that girl happens to be my sister, so you better get going," she demanded.

"Well, I'm supposed to start classes tomorrow, and—"

"Listen, Frankie, that night I saw you guys beneath the streetlamp, it was like your souls were stitched together, and I don't know much, but love like that only comes around once, and if you don't grab it now, you're going to regret it the rest of your life."

Frankie stared at the steering wheel for a minute, and then he turned the key and the engine started with a roar. "Fuck it! You're totally right! Shannon, I gotta go."

He started to pull away, but Shannon called his name and ran down the driveway.

"What?" he said when she caught up to the car.

"Don't forget to give Sarah this," she said, handing him the velvet box with the Saint Christopher medal inside.

"Thank you," he said. "For everything."

"You're welcome," Shannon replied. "Now get going!"

Without saying another word, he took off down the road,

and Shannon heard the roar of the V8 engine slowly fade away.

ALTHOUGH THE WEATHER in Central New York was depressing nine months out of the year, autumn was a bastion of relief and stunning beauty. Hillsides were ablaze with crimson leaves, chrysanthemums popped out of the ground, and powdery clouds tumbled around like underpants in the dryer. Adding to the glory, Thanksgiving and Christmas were right around the corner, football had begun, and playoff baseball was in full swing. Furthermore, as far back as Shannon could remember, her mother had always been a Halloween fanatic.

Something about this pagan celebration took possession of the woman, and their house looked like the set of a bad horror movie. The front lawn was covered with tombstones. Spiderwebs dripped from the branches. Paper skeletons danced in the breeze. Pumpkins flickered on the front steps. Witches flew past the windows, and a gigantic Frankenstein crawled out of the chimney. Furthermore, while most people were content to hand out candy to trick-or-treaters, Shannon's mom went crazy baking snacks. Consequently, the neighborhood ghouls came in droves for graveyard brownies, pumpkin patch cookies, and zombie brain cupcakes.

Additionally, her mother always dressed up for Halloween. This year she went as Sully from *Monsters, Inc.*, and she insisted that Shannon go as Mike Wazowski. Making matters worse, Mom FaceTimed Sarah, so her twin (along with Frankie, who was now attending Berkeley Community College with hopes of transferring to Cal next year) got to see

Shannon wearing a neon-green costume with one eyeball. Unable to contain his witty commentary, Frankie said it was better than some of her past costumes.

While Sarah had always been content to wear a store-bought ensemble, Shannon had always insisted on making her own, and some of her efforts were legendary. Like the time she went as Nearly Headless Nick from *Harry Potter*, but the paper mâché mask glued to the Elizabethan collar turned to mush in the rain. Or the following Halloween when she made Smaug, the dragon from *The Hobbit*, out of cardboard. Shannon stapled green garbage bags to it to protect it from the elements. Fortunately, the costume turned out to be waterproof, but nobody knew what the hell it was. Some thought Shannon was Dory from *Finding Nemo*, while others thought she was a garbage truck. However, when a little goblin called her a gigantic booger, she took the costume off and tore it to pieces.

After the lovebirds hung up, mother and daughter passed out treats until they ran out. Then they turned off the porch light, discarded their costumes, and cleaned all the pans and bowls dirtied by the baking tsunami that blew through their kitchen. Although many laughs had been shared at her expense, Shannon was happy because she hadn't seen Sarah this joyful in years. Even through her mother's old iPhone 5 screen, she could see the rouge of joy in her sister's cheeks and the misty light of love in her eyes.

Passing the hallway mirror on her way upstairs, Shannon was pleasantly surprised because the grouchy face that lived in the glass had been replaced by a pretty smile. And perhaps for the first time, she actually saw herself, not the person diminished by unreasonable comparisons to Sarah, but *Shannon*. After peeling away from her reflection, Shannon went to her room and turned off the light. But before hopping into bed, she looked outside at the jack-o'-lanterns flickering on her neighbor's steps.

She remembered learning that Halloween had come from an ancient Celtic festival called Samhain where pagans celebrated the harvest at the end of summer and wore costumes to ward off ghosts. Mr. Cameron, her high school government teacher, had said during one of his rants that science terminated the supernatural world. However, Shannon knew he was wrong because spirits were everywhere, waiting for someone to tell their stories and set them free.

www.ingramcontent.com/pod-product-compliance
Lightning Source LLC
Chambersburg PA
CBHW071223210726
48293CB00002B/549